LANE'S END

Julie Round

OLDSTICK BOOKS

© Julie Round 2011
Lane's End

ISBN: 978-0-9557242-0-6

Published by:
Oldstick Books
18 Wiston Close
Worthing
BN14 7PU

The right of Julie Round to be identified as the author of
this work has been asserted by her in accordance with the
Copyright, Designs and Patents Act 1988.

A CIP catalogue record of this book
can be obtained from the British Library.

To Mary, with love.

1

The visitor had said his mother was dead, that she had died and gone to heaven. Heaven was up in the sky, wasn't it? Was she in the sky? All Bernard could see through the window were shifting, rolling grey clouds.

He didn't really understand death. In fact there was a lot about living he did not understand. Only his mother had known how to help him and for 30 years she had taught, guided and protected him. It was because of her patience that he could manage the routine of daily life. He might not be able to read but he could make a cup of tea and count beyond ten. She it was who encouraged him to put pocket money left over in a jar on the mantelpiece 'for a rainy day.'

Now the lady was talking too fast, just like they did on the television. He caught the words fall, ambulance and hospital.

He had been at Treetops Day Centre where he spent every Saturday and Wednesday morning. When he came home his mother had gone and the lady from the Social Services was waiting for him.

"Do you understand what I am saying, Bernard?"

He nodded. He wished she would stop talking and let him think.

"Is there anyone who could come and stay here with you?"

Bernard tried to imagine someone else other than his mother living in their house. Who had he seen there – the vicar, the man who read the meter, the plumber, the milkman, the lady who delivered the church magazine? He couldn't see any of them taking his mother's place. Who would read him stories, buy his clothes and take him to town on the bus?

"I don't know," he mumbled.

"How old are you, Bernard?"

"I don't know," he said again, feeling foolish, because he knew, somehow, that he should remember.

"Do you have any relatives?"

Bernard shook his head.

"Who sends you Christmas cards?"

This was easier. It was only January and mother had put all the cards in a drawer in the sideboard.

Bernard got up and shuffled across the room. He took out the six cards and handed them to the lady.

"Is it raining?" he said.

"Yes, actually," she replied, not looking up. "Sunshine and showers today. Bernard, do you know these people?" and she read out the names.

"No, only the vicar, 'cos he's a reverend." He knew his mother would be proud that he had remembered.

"Well, I really ought to be going. Would you like me to arrange Meals on Wheels for you?"

Bernard giggled – the image was too funny for words.

"Does it cost much?" he asked.

"I'll leave you a pamphlet – the telephone number is on the bottom. I'll let the vicar know you are on your own and he'll help you with the other arrangements."

She stood up briskly and headed for the door.

"Mum isn't coming back, is she?"

"No – she died in the hospital. I'm sorry Bernard – but

don't you fret – everything will be taken care of." She hesitated. "We'll need to see where your mother kept her private papers. In the drawer?"

"Yes, where I got the cards."

"I'll leave them for now. It would be best if there's two of us when we look at them. Don't worry about the house – I'm sure we can sort something out. If you are sure you'll be all right I'll be back on Monday," and she bustled out of the front door.

Bernard rushed to the bathroom and shut the door. This had been the place where he could sit and think but now the silence in the house seemed heavy and his head was throbbing. He had to decide what to do. There was no one here to tell him.

When he returned to the living room he felt cold so he turned on the electric fire and looked again at the pot on the mantelpiece. He knew it was full of money and he knew that when it got too heavy his mother would take out some of the coins and replace them with notes.

He sat down and picked up the last book his mother had been reading to him. He stared at the picture on the cover. There was a man with a green coat who had a stick with a bag on the end resting on his shoulder. He had a pointed hat and was walking along a road. In the sky was a vivid rainbow and where the rainbow touched the purple hills in the distance was a shiny golden pot with coins tumbling out of it.

He remembered then. Gold was even more valuable than notes. If he could find gold he would be rich and if he was rich he could have servants. Servants could do all the things his mother had done. They would not do it for love

– but they would do it for money. His head ached with the reasoning but he felt better.

He had begun to take charge of his own life. He knew what he had to do. He wasn't ready to be on his own. He must find the gold at the end of the rainbow.

Bernard had always been fascinated by anything that shone. He loved his mother's silver necklace and diamond and gold rings. He was entranced by the glittering earrings she wore at Christmas and the lights and baubles on the tree.

His favourite stories had large colourful illustrations and were of myths and legends. As she read his mother would bring to life the magic of Aladdin and the menace of Treasure Island.

While the reality of everyday life was blurred and muddled the images left in his mind by his favourite tales were clear and bright.

His love of colour had practical implications, too. She hugged him with pleasure when he proved to her that he could remember that red meant stop, yellow meant be careful and green meant go.

At his visits to the day centre his favourite task was cutting up material and making collages, which they hung on the walls.

He wrestled with a phrase that had been troubling him. "Don't worry about the house," the social worker had said. Until then it had not entered his head but now he made the connection.

He remembered the girl at the day centre who always seemed to be angry about something. She had screamed with rage when he used a scrap of material that she wanted. "You mummy's boy," she had shouted, "If you didn't have her to look after you you'd have to share a house like the rest of us do."

He twisted his fingers together and pulled them apart. His hands were sticky. He lifted one to his face and began to chew his nails.

If he couldn't stay in his house what would he do?

He did not want to be locked up.

He did not want to be ordered about.

His mother would not have wanted that.

She wanted him to enjoy life.

He looked again at the 'rainy day' pot. He must go, but where? Pulling at his hair he went to the back door and opened it, stepping out into the garden searching for a sign.

He could see the hills from his garden. The rain was easing now. Part of the sky was blue and part still grey and threatening. Yet beyond the bushes at the end of the garden and above the outline of the hills there arched a multi-coloured trail – a rainbow – the most magical sight Bernard had ever seen. The picture in the book had been exciting enough but he had never realised how big the real thing could be. This was the sign he had been waiting for.

He would take a bag of those things he could not do without and follow the line of the rainbow until he found the gold. With gold he could pay to live where he liked. He might even go on a boat to see another country.

His mother had talked once about going on a cruise. She brought home brochures and described the rooms and the pools and the entertainment. She showed him pictures of all the exotic places the ship visited and even bought herself a sequin top for the dinner with the captain.

He couldn't remember all she told him but he had caught her sense of anticipation.

The dream did not last long, however, and when he asked if they could look at the 'holiday books' she sighed and said they would have to wait until they had more money.

He did not have a sack to tie to a stick so he began to pack a suitcase.

He tried to remember the last time they had gone away from home. When he was a little boy they had travelled by train to a caravan. His father had been with them then and there had been a lot of shouting and tears. After that there had only been his mother and himself.

He thought he had better pack everything his mother would give him clean at the weekend. He put aside pyjamas, clean underwear, a towel and a sweater. Then he went to the bathroom for his toothbrush and wash bag. He added a spare pair of shoes in case those he was wearing got wet. Then the frustration of not having someone to reassure him made him choke. He felt angry and uncertain.

It was all too difficult. Should he take the kettle? Did he need to pack food? Should he include a mirror, scissors, his mother's brooch, books, photos, papers?

In the end he settled for an apple and a photograph of his mother. If he took her picture it would feel as if she was with him. He put the money from the pot in his cash belt, put on his boots and a mackintosh and left the house.

At first he could not see the rainbow and he stumbled along the lane, his eyes raking the sky, his hands shaking so much that he nearly dropped the case. Then he rounded a bend and saw the hills in the distance with the eerie arc of light, incomplete but still touching the land.

There was a loud blast from a car horn as he hesitated on the edge of the pavement. Mud from a puddle splashed his trousers but he felt nothing. His quest was all consuming – to find the treasure and be someone his mother would be proud of.

He was missing her company. Without her his world was blurred.

If she had been with him she would have been making him aware of every detail of his surroundings, pointing out the difference between the brick houses and the ones painted white, showing him landmarks like the church spire, making him remember the bus stops and stopping to look in the gardens.

He reached the last shop of the parade and looked up at the sky. The rainbow was still there but was partly obscured by rooftops. He hurried uphill, to the car park by the woods.

After trudging through the little copse he came out onto the wide slope of the hillside. If he could get up higher he would be able to see where the rainbow ended.

He was breathing heavily and the light was fading but as he reached the crest of the hill the sun still shone and one end of the rainbow was still visible. It dropped down between two hills and he could just make out a tiny building. A flash of light reflected off a distant window, like a beacon, and then the rainbow vanished.

At least, he thought, he would not have to go back to the town. He could hear the hum of traffic, which meant he might have to cross a road, but the direction was clear.

He was thirsty and leant on a gate to eat his apple. The wind was cold and he wished he'd remembered his woolly hat.

If only he could find someone to help him - someone to tell him he was doing the right thing. But there was no one so he pocketed the core of his apple and set off.

He had been right about the road. It was a busy dual carriageway with no provision for pedestrians except a grassy bank. He walked along it for some minutes until he saw a muddy track on the opposite side. Then he waited until his side of the road was clear and ran to the central reservation.

Now he was marooned – two lanes of traffic going one way behind him and two going the other in front. It seemed as if just as he saw a gap and thought about crossing another vehicle would scream past. He took one step into the road and a motorbike swerved around him. He jumped back, shaking and sweating. He had to get across. Why didn't they stop?

A taxi overtook a white van. They all had their lights on, now, and it was becoming harder to judge their speed.

Then there was a hush – the only vehicle a black car in the distance. Bernard stepped into the road and ran to the other side. He did not feel safe until he was several yards up the track. If this led to the house between two hills he would have found the end of the rainbow.

A little stream ran down the hill next to the path and Bernard realised again how thirsty and hungry he was. When he heard a dog bark it was a welcome sound, as he had felt more and more alone as the day wore on.

A man with a stick and a sheepdog were walking up the track.

"Good day," said the man, "You looking for the public footpath?"

"I don't think so," said Bernard. "I'm looking for the house in the hills."

"There's only one house up this way – that's mine. Who do you want to see?"

"I don't know," replied Bernard, hugging his case tight to his chest. "I don't have anywhere to stay."

"Well, my wife and I put up visitors in the summer. We don't usually let the room in winter, but I suppose we could. Are you a walker?"

"Yes. " Surely the man could see he did not have a car or a bike?

"I expect we could accommodate you for one night. Let's get up there before it gets dark – there's no lights along here."

Bernard could not believe his luck. Not only was the man leading him to the end of the rainbow but he was offering him a bed as well. If he was no trouble perhaps they would let him stay, at least until he found the gold.

They reached a stone wall with a wooden gate and Bernard had a flash of inspiration. The gold could not be out in the open, as it was in the illustration. It must be hidden; either in the house or buried in the ground. The rainbow had gone. He was going to need another sign to find the treasure.

The lady of the house was small and round, with a scarlet apron. She made Bernard think of the robin on one of the Christmas cards.

She showed him into a small, blue bedroom. There were flowers on the bedcover. Bernard would have preferred

something plain. However he had little time to explore before she was calling him for tea.

"There's enough for three," she smiled. "I expect a big fellow like you has a good appetite?"

Bernard didn't know how to reply so he just pulled out a chair and began to sit down. He didn't reach the seat. Instead he jumped up with a start and rushed towards the door.

"Hands," he mumbled, stumbling into the kitchen and up to the sink.

"Oh. I'm so sorry I didn't show you round. I was so busy cooking," apologised his flustered hostess. "Here" and she handed him a towel and then continued to pile stew onto large dinner plates. The smell made Bernard's mouth water.

The meal was delicious. They finished with jam sponge and custard and by the time he was offered tea or coffee his stomach was full and his eyelids were drooping.

"There's no TV in your room," said the lady, who had told him her name but he had forgotten, "Would you like a book or some magazines?"

Bernard blushed. He always watched TV with the sound off and only looked at the pictures in books.

"Too tired," he said, and then, as an afterthought, "Thank you."

He was rewarded with a beaming smile. It was strange the effect those two words could have.

"It is twenty five pounds a night with the evening meal. Is that OK?"

"Now?" asked Bernard.

"No. When you know how long you are staying would be fine."

She showed him the bathroom just across the landing from his room and leaving him holding a soft clean towel bobbed off down the stairs.

He opened the door of his room. He hadn't noticed before but now it smelt funny.

There were bowls of dead leaves on the windowsill. He opened the window and emptied them out. A cold wind made him close it again quickly and he looked round for his case.

Once in his pyjamas he felt nervous about leaving the room but he peered out and seeing no one around moved swiftly to enter the bathroom. As he reached for the light cord there was a furious roar.

He stood in the centre of the room quaking with fear. Then, leaving his toothbrush on the sink he relieved himself and fled back to the safety of his room.

He could still hear the dreadful hum as he climbed into the bed and curled into a ball. It was only when it ceased that he stopped shaking and dropped into an exhausted sleep.

2

Rose Davis had inherited Lane's End Cottage when her parents died. As the only child she had helped them with the orchard and the chickens and, having spent most of her youth as a solitary carer, was grateful when Tim Smith came courting.

She'd known Tim for many years. He had a few sheep and a couple of ponies and liked to run his dog in local sheep dog competitions. He rented the ponies out for children to ride. He'd often helped her father with the fruit and vegetables he sold at market but he lived in his brother's pub so he had no property of his own.

She knew the cottage and land were as much of an attraction as herself but she also knew that without him she would have to sell up and move somewhere she could manage alone.

He was strong, rugged and quite good looking, if rather taciturn. She loved to make him laugh and enjoyed the obvious satisfaction he got from her home-cooked meals.

He didn't seem to care that she was a little tubby and he even complimented her once on her dark brown curls.

"Don't ever get your hair cut," he'd say, burying his face in her locks. Whether it had anything to do with the beer shampoo she used, or not, she didn't know.

Rose got little companionship from her husband. He made her feel useful rather than loved, but once they started to rent out the two spare bedrooms she felt content. The Downland Way was a favourite route for walkers and their cottage was the only bed and breakfast for miles around.

Rose had just settled into her winter routine of cleaning and baking when the newcomer had arrived. He seemed rather a lost soul, she thought, not a regular tourist, and she was surprised her husband had welcomed him.

It was only when Bernard had gone to bed that she discovered Tim's motivation.

"That's a stroke of luck. Just when I needed another pair of hands a big strong lad like that shows up."

"Are you going to offer him a job?"

"Not if I can help it. Did you see what a dozy fellow he was? I bet I can get him to help round here for bed and board."

Rose said nothing. She had learned the hard way that to argue with her husband was not a good idea.

"We don't know if he wants to stay."

"I think he is hiding from something. He's definitely an odd one, that's for sure."

Bernard was concentrating on his porridge the next morning when Tim began to question him.

"You on holiday, then?"

"No." Why did the man want him to talk now?

"How long you fixing on staying?"

"Until I find something."

"What you expecting to find?"

"I'm not sure."

"Then how'll you know when you find it?"

Bernard shrugged. He didn't feel like trying to explain himself. He wanted to enjoy his breakfast.

Tim continued, "How would you like to help out while you are here?"

"What could I do?"

"You could help dig over the vegetable patch, for a start."

Bernard's face lit up. Digging was something he would definitely like to do.

"Really? You would let me do that?"

"Of course."

"Can I start today?"

Tim grinned. "Sure thing. Straight after breakfast I'll show you where we keep the tools."

Bernard looked at the plate of bacon and eggs that Rose had placed in front of him.

"Is it Sunday?"

"Yes, it is."

"Good," responded Bernard, "Fried breakfast on Sunday."

"I'm sorry I didn't catch your name," said Rose.

Bernard looked perplexed. "I didn't throw…"

Three people laughed; Rose with amazement, Tim scornfully and Bernard out of a sense of embarrassment. Then Tim stopped and asked, "Well – what do we call you?"

"Bernie," said Bernard, using the name his mother had used when they were alone.

While her husband was showing Bernie what to do Rose went up to the room she had given their visitor. She made the bed, putting the pyjamas under the pillow and then looked for the suitcase. It was under the bed, not locked, and she pulled it out and surveyed the contents.

There was very little of interest, only a silver framed

photograph of a middle-aged woman and a chunky sweater. Bernie obviously had not packed for a long trip.

Perhaps her husband was right and he was some kind of fugitive. What could he be running away from? She would cycle down to the village tomorrow and ask around.

She put the suitcase back where she had found it and turned back to the window.

All the pot pourri had gone. What had the silly man done with it? He only had to tell her if he didn't like the scent. She made a mental note to ask him after lunch.

He looked very content, turning over the soil with a spade. He'd soon ruin that one shirt. She'd have to see if some of her father's old ones would fit him. He was a good foot taller than her husband. He has a nice, open face, she thought, but his hands looked too soft to be a manual worker.

Still wondering, she returned to the kitchen. Tim expected a full roast dinner at two o'clock.

Bernard worked steadily through the morning – watching the soil pile up in neat rows as he turned it over. He wasn't surprised that Tim didn't stay to help. He was happy to work alone. He was digging for treasure and he didn't want anyone else finding it first.

By lunchtime the job was complete. Bernard had reached the edge of the orchard and found nothing but a few pieces of brick, some rotting potatoes, some stalks and a rusty fork. His back ached and his head felt fuzzy.

His brain was trying to tell him something but there were no words.

He stared at the area he had just dug. Why had Tim wanted it dug over?

He'd wanted to plant something. What had it looked like before he dug it?

He looked at the little pile of stones and stalks that Tim had shown him how to put on one side.

Vegetables! Vegetables had been growing there, which meant the ground had been dug before. If the gold had been there Tim would have found it.

Bernard was exhausted but relieved. It was obvious the treasure was still hidden.

He would have to look elsewhere.

Tim arrived back from the pub and they all sat down to eat. After the meal Bernard helped Rose with the washing up while the man of the house sat in the lounge with the paper.

"He'll probably fall asleep," said Rose. "I usually leave him alone for the afternoon.

"Would you like a bath?"

"Bath on Tuesday and Friday," replied Bernard. There had been no strange noise in the bathroom that morning but it still made him nervous. He had not tried the light.

"Oh, fine. Do you think you will still be here on Tuesday?"

Bernard frowned. He had forgotten he was a guest in the house.

"I don't know," he mumbled, "Going out," and rushed upstairs. He needed to be on his own to work out what to do next.

If the rainbow ended at the cottage the treasure must be nearby, but undiscovered.

He would walk round the house and see if he could spot a hiding place.

The track ended at the cottage gate but there was a stile between the wall and the woods, with a narrow footpath beyond.

He sat on the stile and looked back at the side of the cottage he had never seen before.

There was something very strange about it. The path from the gate went round the house on this side, which had only a strip of lawn sloping uphill towards the trees.

He stared at the roof and the chimneys, his eyes following the brickwork down from the upstairs windows to the ground floor.

He almost laughed out loud when he realised what was peculiar. The cottage had two identical front doors. This side of the house was the front and it was not one cottage but two.

Now Bernard wanted to go back to the cottage and see inside. He had never noticed the extra door and if he did not explore he would never know if the treasure was hidden there.

He turned back. He would ask the robin – lady for some material and make her a present. He could do that inside the house and wait for his chance.

When Bernard appeared at the kitchen door Rose had just found some shirts, washed them and hung them on the radiators to dry.

"Please, Mrs - Do you have any bits of cloth you don't want?"

"Oh, Bernie. Call me Rose. What do you want them for?"

"I make pictures. I need scissors too."

"OK. I'll look upstairs. Would you like a cup of tea?"

Bernard tried unsuccessfully to follow her thinking. He remained silent but Rose filled the kettle and then bobbed upstairs. She returned with an armful of clothes, mainly ladieswear.

Bernard was overwhelmed. He wasn't used to handling complete garments and was even more surprised when she tore off a sleeve, saying cheerfully, "Don't worry about ripping them up. I was meaning to have a clear out."

He sat at the kitchen table and began to tear and cut the cloth.

When she handed him a cardboard box he dropped the fragments into it - silky slices, soft, brushed nylon squares, patches of floral skirt and assorted shapes of velvet and cotton.

He painstakingly cut off the buttons and discarded the strips of material with buttonholes and zips.

He struggled with a woollen jumper until Rose showed him how to unravel it and wind it into a ball.

They were engrossed in the task when a shout from the lounge broke their concentration. "It's past five o'clock. Aren't we getting any tea today?"

Rose jumped up, looking flustered. "Coming dear," she called, re-filling the kettle and piling scones and jam onto a tray.

"Best take all that upstairs, love," she whispered and went through to the other room.

Bernard looked out of the window of the dining area. He could see trees. This was one half of the front of the house.

He went through the door to the bottom of the stairs. Turning away from them he noticed a curtain on the outside wall. Lifting it he found one of the two wooden outside doors. The cottages were still divided here, with the stairs on this side being the ones used. It was on the other side that they no longer existed. That was the mysterious side and he would need to wait until he was alone to explore further.

Bernard heard shouting from downstairs and hurried into his room. He would stay there until it was peaceful again. Anger disturbed and confused him. This wasn't like living with his mother. He took out her picture. What would she want him to do?

Keep on trying. He would. He couldn't give up now.

At breakfast next day Tim asked cheerfully, "How do you feel about horses, Bernie?"

"White ones?" asked Bernard, remembering an illustration in one of his books.

"No, afraid not. One's a chestnut and the other's a bay – but as long as you aren't scared of them you can help me today."

"What do I have to do?" He left the spoon in his porridge and looked up warily.

"You don't have to ride them or anything," Tim joked. "It's just that the stables are dropping to bits and I need someone to help mend them. How are you with a hammer?"

Bernard wasn't used to being asked so many questions. He didn't really know how to answer the last one so he just shrugged and continued eating.

"I think Tim wants to know if you have ever used a hammer to knock nails into wood," Rose explained politely.

Now he understood. "Oh, yes. I like doing that."

"O.K. then. Outside in twenty minutes." Tim stood abruptly and left the room.

"I see you found the shirt I left for you," said Rose.

"Yes, thank you – and is that jacket for me to wear?"

"Of course. We don't use them any more and it will be cold down on the field. I'll give you some gloves and when Tim goes off to the pub come back and get a warm drink. I'm going to the village but if I'm not back there will be some sandwiches on the table. The door key is in the outhouse, in a flower pot."

Bernard was not sure where the outhouse was but he didn't have time to figure it out now. He had sensed the urgency in his host's command and wanted to be ready before he became angry.

Tim and the dog were waiting. Bernard followed them down the lane to a wide gate and then down the side of a field to a corner with a collection of ramshackle wooden buildings surrounding a stone-flagged yard. Piles of wood and corrugated iron were stacked up against a section of high brick wall beyond which was a muddy road.

Tim let himself into the newest looking building and took down a number of tools. Handing them to Bernard he picked out a box of nails and screws and muttered, "Come on then."

Bernard heard a whinny from one of the stalls.

"That's Rusty – the greedy one, but it's Prince I'm worried about. He's kicked a hole in his stall and there's a fierce draught blowing through. I'll get him out and show you."

Bernard watched as Tim opened the stall door and brought out the pony. He hadn't seen a horse close up before. Its coat looked more like a woolly carpet than the smooth silkiness he had expected- but it shook its head and the black mane rippled in the weak sunlight.

"There's a post in the field I tie them to," explained Tim. "You go inside and you'll see what I'm on about."

Bernard entered the stall. There was almost no light and the place smelled strange, like grass and vegetables and manure, yet with a curious warmth. He could see the slats of wood that had been dislodged by the horse and bent down to collect a couple of rusty nails from amongst the straw.

"You'd better sweep that up," said Tim from the doorway. "I'll get some fresh wood and go round the back."

Bernard found Tim easy to work with. He said little but when he did his instructions were clear and simple. Once the hole was filled they renewed the straw and Tim fed and watered the animals.

"Tomorrow I'll show you what Jenny can do," said Tim, gesturing towards the dog as they trudged back across the field."I have to do my stint at the bar now. You want to come, or will you go back?"

"I think I'll go back."

"Fine. I'll see you later," and man and dog continued down the lane.

Bernard felt a flicker of excitement. If he was the only person in the cottage he might be able to search for the gold.

He stood in the freshly dug garden and stared at the house. There were only two other buildings on the land. In the corner of the garden furthest from the house was a garage and behind it what had once been a greenhouse but now looked neglected. The door was hanging off its hinges and most of the flowerpots inside were cracked like the remaining glass panes. Bernard looked back at the house. Where else had he seen flowerpots?

Then he remembered. Tim had got the garden spade out of the other side of the porch. He tried the handle and to his relief the door opened. Inside equipment and boxes were neatly stacked and a row of clean flowerpots stood on a high shelf. The first pot was empty but when he reached into the second he found the key.

The warmth of the kitchen soothed him as he removed his jacket and placed it on the back of a chair. The sandwiches were cheese and pickle and they made him thirsty. He was too impatient to make tea so he had a glass of water and moved into the lounge.

He'd spent so little time in here that he hadn't really studied it. The TV was in the corner near the window. The fireplace, like that in the other room, was on the far wall. To his right he saw what he was hoping for, another door. This should lead to the front of the house.

Bernard looked out of the window. There was no one in sight. He approached the door. It was very plain, with a keyhole beneath a silver handle.

He pulled the handle down and pushed at the door. Nothing happened. He tried again, with more force. Then, in desperation, he pulled at the door. It would not budge.

It was locked. If anything were hidden behind it he would not find it.

He slumped on the settee with a growing feeling of uselessness. Disappointment washed over him like a wave and he felt his eyes pricking with tears.

When he felt like this his mother would go to the chocolate store and give them each a piece. Then she would list all the things that made them happy.

"I'm lucky to have found this place," he recited. "I am lucky I am warm and fed."

"I am happy that the sun is shining," and with that he had a sudden urge to be back outside again.

He had time, now, to spend how he liked and with no one to read him stories he would have to create his own adventures. He would start at the stile and look for the next sign.

He laughed out loud with pleasure when he reached the gate. Looking over at the stile he could see a fat yellow arrow etched into the wood. There could be no clearer indication of where he should go next. He set off up the path and into the trees.

As he walked the path seemed to get narrower and the wood thicker. He was constantly tangled up in brambles and ducking to avoid low branches.

The path curved round to the left and flattened out. He was trying to fend off tall stinging nettles when he realised he was walking beside a barbed wire fence. Every so often there was a sign on the fence but as Bernard could not read he had no idea what it said.

Suddenly the path fell away before him. Looking down, he saw steps cut into the hillside. They were green and slippery but he descended without mishap and found a metal gate at the bottom, set into a dark holly hedge. The path on the other side of the gate was almost a tunnel but it soon came out onto a tarmac road. Bernard stopped. Should he go left or right?

He chose right and followed the road with the hill on one side and a field on the other until it opened up in front of him into a massive white bowl. The ground at his feet was littered with white crumbs and the sides of the bowl were cliffs of white rock topped by straggly vegetation. To his left were some grey sheds but in front of him, cut into the cliff, were three gaping holes. He had found caves!

The only place where treasure was more likely to be than in the ground was in caves and the yellow arrow had led him here. He was certain it was where he was meant to be.

When Rose returned the first thing she noticed was the key still in the lock in the door. Bernie had obviously been back as the sandwiches had gone but when she called upstairs there was no reply. She replaced the key in its hiding place, unpacked the groceries and made herself a cup of tea and sat at the table with the paper. She didn't usually buy the daily local paper but she was anxious to see if any mention was made of their lodger. It wasn't until page five that she found reference to a missing man. The cremation of Mrs Anne Longman had been arranged for the following Friday but the son of the deceased, James Bernard Longman, had disappeared. Anyone knowing his whereabouts was asked to inform the local police or the vicar of St Luke's Church.

Rose felt certain this was ' Bernie' and went upstairs to see if she could find more clues. She had become quite fond of their visitor.

Since their only daughter had left home at the earliest opportunity she had not allowed herself to become attached to anyone. She felt angry at herself for allowing her husband's constant criticism to drive their only child away. Lots of men would have been happy to have a daughter but not Tim. He had wanted a son, someone to show off to, someone to help run the business, a younger version of himself. His selfish attitude drove a wedge between them, soured their time as a family and caused Katie to take up a position in a residential home, where her caring nature was appreciated, rather than trying for more education. She came to visit them at Christmas but it was never a relaxed day and the two women spent most of their time together in the kitchen.

Rose almost hated her husband for the way he treated their daughter.

"Don't know why you chose to do such a miserable job," he'd said the previous month. "If you'd had any gumption you could have been a proper nurse or set your sights a bit higher and brought in some real money."

Now as she stood in the little bedroom trying to imagine what made a young man run away from his mother's funeral her eyes fell on the silver framed photograph on the table by the bed. Surely that meant he was coming back? Perhaps he could not bear the thought of her dying? Perhaps he, too, needed to get away from his father?

Rose remembered her own father, warm, loving and industrious – until he lost his wife to cancer and followed her a few months later.

She shook herself out of her reverie and went downstairs to boil the potatoes for a cottage pie. Cooking was still a pleasure, and Tim was always in a better mood after a meal.

While Rose was cooking tea Bernard was entering one of the caves. It was dusk and before long he could barely see where he was going. Then his leg struck something hard. He bent down and his hands touched wood, planks of wood, making some kind of container with a crackly material over the top, which he guessed was plastic sheeting. He concentrated and ran his hands over the pile in front of him. It was shoulder high and had square corners and the contents felt like smaller boxes. He felt round to the rear of the block and found another – and another. Then he gave a yelp of pain as he stabbed his foot on what felt like a crate. Crouching down he found the rim and probing tentatively inside he realised he could feel bottles. Puzzled, he stumbled further into the cave until he no longer had any sense of direction. It was cold and dark and there was no gold.

He no longer felt lucky. Instead, he was beginning to feel frightened. He could hear his own breathing but nothing else – until a light flashed across the wall and a distant engine hummed and stopped. There was the sound of a door slamming and then voices.

Someone shone a torch onto the roof of the cave and Bernard realised he had travelled some distance and was completely out of sight of the entrance. Should he call out and say he was here or would he be punished as if he was a thief?

There was the sound of unloading and muttered grumbles as men brought more boxes into the cave. "You want anything while we are here, George?"

"Yeah, six bottles of red and twenty packs of fags. What happened to the gate they had across this entrance to keep out nosy parkers?"

"It fell down. No one comes up here. They're frightened off by the notices."

"Don't be too sure. Kids today think DANGER and PRIVATE are an invitation not a warning."

The light shone on a crate a few feet away and Bernard could hear people shifting crates and making bottles rattle.

"I'll bring some wire down tomorrow. Come on, Jenny."

Bernard froze. Jenny was Tim's dog. It was Tim who was storing stuff here – but why? He considered moving towards the light but he was too late. The vehicle drove away and he was once more in complete darkness. The decision had been made for him.

His relief was short-lived, however, as he heard Jenny barking. He waited, tense, as the sound came nearer. There was a whistle from outside the cave and he heard Tim's voice, "What's up, Jenny - you found something?"

Jenny stopped barking but he could hear her tail thumping against a hard surface. A torch played on the box in front of him.

"Who's there?" called Tim. The dog gave a short bark.

"Come out, or I'll set the dog on you."

Bernard was used to doing what he was told. "All right. I'm coming," he stuttered.

Jenny barked again, a friendly, excited bark and Bernard stroked her as he clambered out from between the pallets.

"Bernie! What are you doing here?"

"I'm sorry. I just went for a walk." Bernard was shivering. Had he done anything wrong?

"Never mind, mate. Come into the hut and get warm. Now you are here you can do me a favour."

Bernard relaxed and followed Tim into one of the portacabins. It was sparsely furnished with two chairs, a table, a cupboard and an oil fire, which Tim lit with difficulty as he was relying on light from his torch.

"Sorry there's no electric. There used to be a generator when the quarry was in use - but they took it when they left."

Bernard did not respond. He still felt guilty at being discovered hiding somewhere he should not have been.

"You still looking for something?" probed Tim.

"Yes, but I don't think it was in that cave."

"Of course not. That's my stuff. It belongs to the pub. I'm just keeping it cool for them. What were you going to do next?"

"Look in the other caves."

"Good idea – but best wait until daylight, eh? Meanwhile I've got a little job for you. Could you be a security guard for one night?"

Bernard did not answer. He hoped Tim would explain.

"It's not as hard as it sounds. It just means sitting here for the night, watching out to see that no one comes and steals anything from the cave."

"Just for one night?"

"Yes. Until I can get some wire for the entrance. It would be appreciated."

"I mustn't go to sleep?"

"Well – if you do nod off it shouldn't matter. No one could rob us without making a noise. I'll be back in the morning. There's cans, grub and blankets in the cupboard."

Bernard found it impossible to say no. He nodded assent.

"Great. I'll bring you a flask tomorrow."

"Wait. Where's the toilet?"

"Next door. You can get to it through there. See you a.m."

Tim, dog and torch disappeared down the road and Bernard was left with only the light from the oil fire.

He opened the cupboard and felt inside for the blanket. He found a bar of chocolate and a can with a ring pull. The liquid inside was unfamiliar and not very sweet but he drank most of it and settled into the surprisingly comfortable chair.

Gradually his eyes grew accustomed to the dim light and he felt confident enough to venture into the next cabin. The smell of stale urine made him scurry back to his post. The sides of the chalk pit looked like white curtains in the moonlight. Tomorrow he would see inside the other caves. Perhaps one of them contained the treasure he was seeking.

Rose was waiting for Tim when he returned home late.

"There you are. Is Bernie with you?"

"No. Why should he be?"

"He went out this afternoon and hasn't come back."

"I don't think he knows what day it is, let alone what time we have tea."

"Well, it's getting baked up in the oven. I'll serve ours and put some aside for him. I've got some news."

"After I've eaten, woman. Don't rabbit on while food is on the table."

Rose found it hard to digest her meal. She was bursting to tell Tim what she had discovered.

"Right. What is it?" he asked at last.

"It's Bernie. I've found out who he is. He's James Bernard Longman and he comes from town. His mother has just died and everyone is looking for him."

"What do you mean, everyone?"

"The police, the vicar, the newspapers – oh, Tim, we've got to tell them."

"Hold on a minute. What if he doesn't want to be found?"

"He'll miss his mother's funeral."

"Well, she won't know will she?"

Rose knew his opinion of religion. "At least we must show him the paper."

"Not very easy – seeing as he isn't here."

"He'll come back. He's left all his stuff. Unless he is lost? Tim, he's not very bright – perhaps he can't find his way back?"

"Not much we can do this time of night. If he doesn't come back I'll take Jenny to look for him in the morning. Don't go reporting that you've seen him until we can talk to him. He's a grown man and not your responsibility."

Rose had to agree, but she couldn't help worrying.

3

Bernard woke to the unfamiliar smell of the oil fire. He was stiff from sitting in the chair all night and his hands and feet were cold but the sun was shining on the far edge of the chalk cliff.

Why did he feel happy? Then he remembered. Today he was going to check out the other two caves. If they found gold he and Tim would have to share it, but he didn't mind. He was beginning to think of the Smiths as his family and Lane's End cottage as his home.

Tim arrived with a flask of tea and a bacon sandwich.

"I've brought a big torch," he said, "When you're ready."

Bernard folded up the blanket he had been covered with in the night and returned it to the cupboard. Tim was fidgeting impatiently.

As they left the hut the sky turned grey as clouds hid the sun. Bernard shivered.

"There's a wind getting up," commented his companion and led the way into the cave.

The further they went the narrower the tunnel became. To Bernard's disappointment there was nothing there, only a damp, slippery feel to the walls and a few bits of rusty machinery on the floor. The tunnel ended abruptly, with no sign of another entrance, a crock of gold, a chest of treasure or even a handful of precious stones.

They turned to retrace their steps but had only gone a few yards when Bernard felt a heavy object land on the back of his head. He gave a gasp and fell forwards as the light went out.

When Bernard awoke it was with a severe headache and the sense that he was blind. Then he realised his head and face were covered in rough sacking. He tried to remove it but his arms were pinned down to his sides. He was seated on a hard surface that felt as if it was moving. Fear made his limbs seem frozen and when he tried to move his feet he found they were, indeed, stuck – or bound together.

He gave a whimper. The material over his face was musty and damp. He had to get out of that before he did anything else.

He found that if he hunched one shoulder, lifting it up under his ear, and made his hand into bird's head, like people do when they make shadows to amuse children, he could wriggle his arm out of the restraints. Once he had one arm free it was no effort to release the other and pull the sack over his head.

He took deep breaths and rubbed his eyes to try to focus on his surroundings. It was difficult to concentrate with the pain in his skull but he was aware of wheels going over bumps. He must be in some kind of truck.

All around him were wooden boxes and cardboard packing cases. He had his back up against what must be the driver's cab and he could only see cracks of light round the sides of the rear door. There were no windows.

Why was he in a lorry? Where was he going? What should he do now? He needed to undo the ropes round his feet and he needed to go to the lavatory.

If he could bang on the back of the cab perhaps the driver would help him? Some instinct told him not to trust his abductor until he was in a stronger position to protect himself. He bent his knees and reached down to feel the knots round his ankles. Shutting his eyes he felt for the ends and pushed them gently towards the centre. Bit by bit the loops loosened and he untangled the knots.

He was sweating and his fingers were sore by the time his feet were free but he rubbed his legs to restore the circulation and was about to stand when the lorry braked and he was thrown against a pile of crates. To his surprise they shifted under his weight and slid down the van. They were empty!

He had no time to consider the implications before the rear door was flung open and a bearded man stood, his back to the light, peering in at the load.

"Hallo there!" he called.

Bernard did not reply. He had never seen this man before. Why did he sound so cheerful if he was the one who had tied him up?

"You OK in there?" The man had climbed into the rear of the lorry and was edging forward round the collapsed boxes.

"Can I get out?" asked Bernard, feeling the urgency of his request.

"Oh, good- you've got undone. I didn't dare help you until we were well away."

"I need…" stammered Bernard, stumbling forward.

"OK, OK – behind the hedge – but don't run off. We need to talk."

It was raining heavily and even if Bernard had known where he was he didn't feel like running away.

The driver closed the van door and gestured for Bernard to get in the cab. Handing him a chocolate bar he said, "Here, have this – just until we reach a caff."

Bernard was feeling rather sick but he took a bite and put the rest in his pocket.

"Why am I here?" he asked.

"That's down to your mate, Tim. He said you'd found his stash of goods and needed to be silenced."

"Silenced?"

"Got rid of – made to disappear – bumped off."

"You mean killed?"

"Got it in one, but don't panic – I'm not going to."

"You were told to kill me?" Bernard was astounded at the idea.

"Yes – to stop you talking to the customs. He said I was to wait until we were on the ferry and then tip you over the side. He said you could ruin his whole operation and he didn't think anyone would miss you. I'm sorry, mate."

Bernard put his head in his hands. Had the boxes in the cave been full of treasure after all? "What did he think I had seen?"

"The cigarettes and booze. He found you in the cave, didn't he?"

"That didn't belong to him?"

"Well, in a way it did. He'd paid for it – but not enough – not the duty."

Bernard was completely bewildered and seeing his reaction the driver laughed.

"You wouldn't have split on him, would you?"

"I don't know what you mean."

"Never mind. What we have to decide is what to do with you. We are nearly at the harbour. Will it be OK if I let you off there? Don't tell anyone you've seen me and don't go back to Lane's End."

Bernard nodded – he would do what anyone suggested. If only his head would stop throbbing and his eyes stop aching.

"Here," The driver gave him a five pound note and pulled up next to a bus shelter.

"Good Luck," he called and drove off into the gathering gloom.

Bernard felt ill. He staggered along the quayside until the railings ended at a set of steps, which led down to the waterside. He was attracted to the reflections in the river. It was almost dark and street lights were making flickering patterns in the water.

He was thirsty. He was nauseous. He was falling over…

He was warm. He was comfortable. His eyes had stopped aching. He opened them and knew immediately he was dreaming.

He was in a tiny palace. The walls were covered with tapestries. The ceiling was only a few feet above his head with a red and gold lamp hanging so near he could reach out and touch it. He was lying on a narrow bed covered with a richly embroidered blanket and the whole place smelled of wood and seaweed and spices and fruit. He had a sense that he was floating and, unwilling to wake up, drifted off into a deep sleep.

Bernard woke to the scent of warm soup and the jangling sound of a beaded curtain being pushed aside. A low voice whispered, "Are you awake, young man?"

Opening his eyes he saw the concerned face of an elderly lady. She was unlike anyone he had seen before. Her dark grey hair was long and loose and she had a purple and red bandana round her head.

Her neck was adorned with beaded necklaces and gold chains and her hands were covered with many different coloured rings. Her face was brown and lined but her eyes were green and sharp.

"Can you eat something?" she asked, her voice like the purr of a big cat.

"Yes, please," stammered Bernard – sitting up, and then realising that under the blanket his trousers had gone.

"You fell in the mud." She answered his unasked question. "Your jacket and trousers will be clean soon," and held out a spoon to him.

Bernard had never tasted such delicious soup and heavily buttered toast.

"Cocoa to follow, I think," she said and he accepted gratefully.

"Where am I?" he said eventually.

"On my houseboat. My name is Eliza. You are quite safe here. Has someone hit you on the head?"

Something made Bernard pause before he answered. What had the driver told him? How much of what had happened to him should he keep secret?

"I don't remember."

"Do you remember your name?"

Bernard was about to say *James Bernard Longman* as he had at infant school, but James was his father's name. He couldn't bring himself to use it now. He was nothing like his father. His father was unreliable. He couldn't imagine anyone trusting his father.

Two years of ordinary school had left the whole family in tatters, Bernard confused and guilty, his mother tearful and defiant and his father angry and disappointed. Bernard just could not keep up with the other children. He could not bear to be in a room with noisy chatter. He could not make sense of the symbols he was shown and was left alone to draw and fit puzzles together.

Once his father had left them Bernard was transferred to a special unit but he was so unhappy he was allowed to return home. From then on his education was in the hands of his mother.

What had made him think of his mother now? Was it the gentle look in Eliza's eyes or the way she seemed in complete control of the situation? He felt for the money belt. She had left it round his waist. "Bernard," he muttered sleepily.

"Well, Ned, you rest now," replied his rescuer. He did not have the energy to correct her.

When Bernard next woke the houseboat was rocking gently and a light was shining through the tiny window. He could hear seagulls calling outside and his trousers were hanging over the back of a chair. He dressed and went to look for somewhere to wash, bending as he did so to avoid bumping his head on the ceiling.

Outside, Eliza was sitting at a small table. Spread out in front of her was a large piece of paper on which was an intricate design. It reminded Bernard of the pictures in the book with Jason and the Argonauts, the kind of pattern that ancient people used. Then he noticed four buckets near her feet. Each bucket contained a different coloured pile of stones. There was a bright blue, a brilliant yellow, a quiet brown and a pure white.

Bernard was entranced. "What are these for?" he asked.

"The tiles? Oh – they are for my mosaics. I have to design one for the Ship Inn and I'm just deciding on colours. Would you like to see my pattern book?"

"Yes, please."

Eliza went inside and came out with a hefty album. When she opened it at the first page Bernard realised what she had been telling him. The first pattern was a circular shape with spokes, like a wheel but filled in with different coloured squares. He watched, fascinated, as she turned the pages. Each picture was more complicated than the last. Shapes gave way to birds, animals, trees and faces and, finally, a ship.

"That's the one I'm working on now," said Eliza, "but my fingers are so painful it is very slow work. If you are interested we'll go there after lunch and I'll show you how it is done."

The mosaic on the side wall of the pub was enclosed in a double circle of brown and white tiles, already in place. Bernard stood in front of it and opened his arms wide. He could just reach the edges with his fingertips.

"You can see it is a big job," sighed Eliza. "Would you like a drink?"

Bernard followed her into the pub. He knew about such places, of course, but he had never been inside one. There were dark beams in the low ceiling and he had to duck his head to avoid them.

"Sit down," commanded Eliza, "What would you like?"

Bernard felt himself getting uncomfortably warm in this strange environment.

"Water, please."

"Still or fizzy?"

"I don't mind."

Eliza brought a tall glass of water and another of black liquid with a creamy topping to their table. "The mortar is out the back and this is the finished design," she said, unrolling a large sheet of paper.

The three masted sailing ship sat resplendent on a sea of blue, its white sails surrounded by a golden sky. "If you could help me complete this I would pay you, of course."

"You want me to put the stones on the wall?"

"Yes."

"In a line."

"That's right. To fit the design."

"I could do that."

He was rewarded with a crooked smile.

Once she had shown Bernard how to place and secure the tiles he followed her design with painstaking precision. When he changed colours he would turn to her for confirmation and was content to see her nod in agreement.

It took two more days to complete the mosaic and they celebrated with a meal at the pub. Eliza had introduced Bernard to stout but it was not to his liking so he settled for lemonade.

"Ned Longman, you are an artist," she declared. Bernard didn't really mind her getting his name wrong. He felt like a different person. He had a home, a friend and a job. Eliza let him come and go as he liked and even taught him to cook simple dishes.

They had a request for a plaque on the harbour wall and a surround for a sculpture in the museum garden.

Eliza was worried. "We'll have to see the design of the statue and then you will have to work on the ground. I'd have a job getting down low. You'll need some overalls."

The sculpture was to symbolise 'growth' and the sculptor had decided to portray this as a mountain of coral – although the stone he used was to be encrusted with what looked like purple glass. It spiralled to a point and Eliza's task was to design a circle to surround it. She decided on sea creatures – fish, crabs, starfish and sea horses.

Bernard accompanied her to the local library where she found the pictures she needed and, once back home, watched as she drew the shapes ready to take the tiles.

Slowly he picked up a pencil and began to copy a fish. Then he went to the box of tiles and selected two colours, a muddy grey and a dark red.

It wasn't very different from the collages he used to do at the Day Centre and he was so absorbed that he did not notice Eliza watching him intently. She was doing a starfish, with a pale orange as an indicator in the corner and when she saw the colours Bernard had chosen she smiled.

"I think you are right, Ned," she said, "but we'll use two different reds this time and edge it all with purple and cream. We have also got to put lettering round it as it's to celebrate the museum's centenary."

Bernard shuddered. People had tried to make him read before and he could recognise a few letters – capital B, T and S, but when he saw the symbols together he would panic and forget everything he had been told. "You do those," he said hopefully.

"We'll go and check the site next week, as long as it is a fine day," responded Eliza. "If you go on like this, Ned, you'll soon be famous."

Bernard wasn't at all sure that he wanted to be famous, although he was happy that she was pleased with his work. He also enjoyed being recognised in the street. The local people would smile and greet him as he wandered through the shopping centre or along the waterfront.

"That's Ned, the artist," he heard one woman say to her young son.

One sunny Friday, when Bernard was working in the museum garden on his own, a group of elderly people were ushered through the double doors.

"Do you mind if we come out here for a while?" asked the curator. "We'll try not to disturb you."

Bernard frowned and pulled his box closer to him. He would have to stop doing the sea horse and fill in some spaces instead.

A young woman was helping a frail lady with a stick towards one of the benches.

"Keep your gloves on, Mabel," she said, "It may look warm but it isn't when the sun goes in."

She turned and noticed Bernard kneeling on the ground.

"Hallo. What are you doing?"

"Mosaic," said Bernard abruptly.

"Is this for the centenary? Can I see?"

"It's not finished."

"I'm sorry. I don't suppose you are used to people milling around while you are working," she said, blushing.

With her short hair and slight figure she looked like a delicate pixie, thought Bernard as he stared up at her.

He felt awkward. He could not continue while these people were here. Hurriedly he picked up his tools and containers and fled through the gate to the street. Almost running, he bundled everything back onto the houseboat and sat on his bed hugging himself. All his new found confidence seemed to be deserting him. How could he ever have imagined that he could lead an independent life? The moment he was left alone and his routine disrupted he fell apart.

Drenched with misery he awaited Eliza's return. What would she say when he told her he'd only done a fraction of the work planned?

He was asleep when Eliza came home but was woken by the enticing smell of home-cooked vegetable soup. It was served just as he loved it, with warm crusty bread and lashings of butter.

"What happened, Ned?" she asked tenderly when he was on his second helping.

"I ran away."

"Why was that?"

"People came. I couldn't work."

"Were they noisy?"

"Not really."

"Did they get in the way?"

Bernard felt his face getting hot. That was enough of questions.

"No – but there was a girl."

"Ah." Eliza took his empty dish and replaced it with a fruit yoghurt. The conversation was ended.

Yet in Bernard's mind there remained a picture of a small, slim girl with short, black curly hair, eyes that were almost violet and a mouth that was designed for laughter. He tried to remember what she was wearing and failed but thinking of her did ease the guilt he felt at leaving his post.

"I'm sorry," he said at last.

"It doesn't matter. A dose of rain would have made you do the same thing. We'll go down earlier tomorrow," and she patted his arm.

The next few days saw both of them crouched over the design. They had under a fortnight to the opening. Eliza was doing the lettering as agreed and Bernard was filling in the spaces and the sea creatures.

"I must have a break," breathed Eliza, sitting up, holding her back. "I'll not be long."

Bernard nodded, but did not look up. He was working on a crab he was especially proud of, the orangey tiles of the shell standing out from the calm creamy background.

"Hallo again."

He jumped at the sound of her voice.

"I've come to apologise."

He rose to his feet, flustered. It was the girl, alone this time, and she was wearing a pale green, belted coat. He forced himself to look at her face and, sure enough, there was a rueful smile.

Bernard smiled back. "I wasn't ready," he heard himself say.

"Don't run away again, will you?"

He blushed and looked at his feet.

"I'm sorry, again. I'm such an idiot. Please tell me about your design."

As if by mutual consent they crossed the path and sat on the bench facing the mosaic.

"I just help," began Bernard. "Eliza makes up the pattern and I put on the tiles."

"It's a lot of work. Who chooses the colours?"

"Both of us. See that fish. I did that."

"You're very good, Mr… what do they call you?"

Bernard hesitated. He still wasn't used to being addressed as Ned – yet that is what people called him.

"Ned."

"Well, Ned – I am pleased to meet you. I'm Katie," and she held out a hand.

He half turned towards her and took her hand in his. It felt ridiculously small and delicate and he feared he might crush it but she gave his fingers a squeeze and the effect was extraordinary.

Suddenly he wanted to know more about this new acquaintance. It was as if someone had introduced him to a fruit that he had never tasted before and it was so delicious he wanted more.

"Will you come back again?" he stuttered.

"I only have one day off a week but this is such a peaceful garden I'd love to – if I don't put you off."

"Just you. Not the others."

Katie giggled. "I'm not sure they'd like to be called that. They are the residents of the place where I work. We take them out somewhere different every week. We've been to a windmill, had a canal trip and next month we are going to a winery. If it wasn't for them I'd hardly get anywhere interesting."

Bernard let her words wash over him. He could not stop staring at her. Her face looked so alive and her voice was clear and warm.

"Anyway, thanks for listening. I'll see you next week, then. Bye Ned," and jumping up from the seat she disappeared into the museum.

Never before had Bernard felt this mix of pain and pleasure, combined with a sense of curiosity and a feeling that he must not let this person go. She had said she would come back and he hoped she was telling the truth.

He returned to the task in hand but the joy it had given him had gone. How could he wait a whole week until he saw her again?

Katie was up early. Some days she had two shifts, morning and evening and sometimes she was required to stay awake at night. She felt sorry for the girls who had to travel to work, some with families. She might only have one room but her meals were provided and laundry included.

She had thought she was settled. The home was warm and comfortable and well equipped. The twenty-five residents were all elderly ladies with a variety of physical ailments but they were mostly good-humoured and content. Relatives who visited expressed their satisfaction at the way their loved ones were treated.

Katie had been encouraged to take exams and gain certificates, which she had shown to her mother on her rare visits home. Thinking of her mother now brought back memories of the man she wished was not her father – the man who had wanted a son and had never forgiven Rose or herself for disappointing him. No matter how hard they tried to please him they could not make him feel a love that wasn't there.

She could still see the day Rose took her down to the stables. She must have been four, and her mother had been pleading with Tim to spend some time with his daughter. She had some new trousers, thick corduroy, which she hated, and strong boots that felt heavy on her tiny feet.

It was a cold day and Rose had insisted she wore a hat with ear flaps. Tim had sneered at the idea of a helmet. "Waste of money," he'd said and for once he was right.

When she saw the horse and it snorted she gave a terrified scream and ran across the yard. The pony reared in fright and knocked Tim to the ground. Rose ran to her daughter and hugged her trembling body as she sobbed, leaving Tim to look after himself.

Everything Katie did from then on was wrong. If she did well in a spelling test she was a *cocky little blighter.* If she made a card or a gift it was *a piece of tat.* When the only prize she ever got was for handwriting and the only exams she passed were in English and Biology he sneered, "No looks and no brains." Nothing she could do would please him and soon her main ambition was to leave home as soon as possible.

"I hoped you'd go to college," mused Rose one evening when Katie was finishing her homework on the kitchen table. "You would make a great nurse."

"It's too expensive – but don't worry. I have spoken to the careers officer and there may be some openings in a similar field." She did not tell her mother she was leaving home until she had been appointed.

Now she stretched out under the sheets, trying to ease her aching back.

Helping elderly ladies up and down steps, fetching and carrying trays of tea and biscuits and attending to their every need all contributed to the dull ache she felt at the lower end of her spine. She had promised herself she would do more yoga but that was not the exercise she was thinking of now.

The tingling warmth that reached her toes and fingertips came from a new source. After all she had said about men she had finally met one who seemed so different that she had found herself immediately attracted. *Men,* she had declared to anyone willing to listen, *were natural bullies – insensitive, selfish, loud and after only one thing.*

She had found refuge in "Windrush Residential Home for Ladies." It was a happy place and Katie had been content for three years. Now she realised how little of herself had been really alive.

This feeling of anticipation, the urge to laugh out loud, to focus on another human being – was this love? How could it be? She had only met him twice but everything about him felt right. He was tall, handsome, with brown eyes and a soft voice. He had seemed gentle, patient, considerate. He listened instead of blurting out his own opinions. He paid attention to detail and was obviously artistic. She felt comfortable near to him. Instead of being afraid to get close to a man she at last felt as if she would like his arms around her. "Don't get your hopes up, girl," she told herself, "He may have forgotten you already," and she curled up under the covers and tried to summon sleep.

Next morning she was sweeping the patio when the gardener arrived.

"Any big sacks handy, love?" he asked, "I'm just going to trim a couple of trees."

Katie fetched some of the strong garden rubbish sacks and followed him to the far end of the site. A low wall surrounded a sunken, square rose garden. A tall hedge of conifers kept the sun off the flowerbeds and consequently few of the residents ever ventured that far. Katie went to sit on the wall and noticed parts of the surface had crumbled away.

"Are you going to lower the hedge?" she asked.

"Yes. Then we can get some new flowers – I thought fuchsias and lavenders. The path is in pretty good condition and the steps just need a handrail. It could be a lovely spot."

"The wall needs fixing. I know someone who could do that – what do you think?"

"You'd have to run it by the manager but I'd appreciate the help."

Katie felt a burst of excitement. Had she started something that could lead to real happiness?

4

Bernard was feeling like a little boy again. He had been quite content, working on the mosaic, accepting the few pounds that Eliza gave him and becoming familiar with the Ship Inn and the local tea rooms. He had not expected someone who always seemed to wear long black skirts and floral tunics to care about clothes.

Yet here he was – in a gentleman's outfitters, trying on shirts and trousers for an occasion he would do anything to avoid.

"You just don't look right in formal clothes," muttered Eliza, scanning the rails until she spotted a SALE notice.

"Here," she called triumphantly to the assistant who had been hovering uncertainly.

"This is more like it." In one hand she had a brushed cotton casual shirt in red and green tartan and in the other a dark green body warmer.

"I have just the trousers to go with those," chirruped the assistant, "classic cords."

By the time they had added another shirt, underwear and socks Bernard was exhausted and followed meekly as Eliza led the way to the café for tea and scones.

"The outfit was a present," she explained, "but you can pay me for the rest later. I mustn't stop you learning the value of things."

Bernard thought of the money he still had hidden in his belt. If it was enough for the clothes should he give it to Eliza? He hadn't asked for the new clothes, although he realised now that he needed them. He'd been making do with cheap packs of socks and shorts from the supermarket.

"Now we are ready for the opening," Eliza was saying, "There will probably be a photographer – are you OK with that?"

Bernard thought a photograph of the sculpture and the mosaic would be excellent and hoped he could have a copy to show Katie. In fact, now they were out shopping he would like to buy her a present, something shiny – a piece of jewellery.

"Ned – Are you listening?"

"Yes, thank you. I like the clothes."

"Good. As long as you agree."

Bernard didn't know what he'd agreed to but he nodded and smiled.

"Going shopping," he said, and pulled back his chair.

Eliza was looking at him intently. She wanted him to do something, something he had done before, what was it?

Smiling, she pushed a piece of paper across the table towards him. Now he knew. It was his turn to pay the bill. She was carrying on from where his mother had left off; he realised, and suddenly felt his loss more deeply than ever before.

Perhaps it was because his mother was still in his mind, or maybe it was the talk of the photographer but when he found himself inside the jewellery shop he had no hesitation in asking for a locket. Given a tray of nine to choose from he began to worry about the cost but his eye was drawn to a silver one with a spider-web pattern engraved on it. "How much is that one, please?"

"With a chain, gift boxed, £120."

It was more than he had ever spent but he had enough money in his belt. Carefully he withdrew five twenty pound notes.

The assistant watched and nodded as Bernard offered another – then, as if realising the situation was unfamiliar, counted them out in front of him. Bernard grinned with relief. He had nowhere to keep his cash and so little to spend it on that his belt had been growing bulky.

He pocketed the gift and returned home. The mosaic was almost complete. The centenary was in a week's time and after that he would have no need to visit the museum.

It was raining hard when Bernard reached the houseboat. Eliza had unpacked the shopping and the smell of cooking filled the cabin. "It's shepherd's pie, tonight," she said. "Come and get warm. Did you find what you were looking for?"

Bernard blushed. He didn't want to explain to Eliza. "Yes – Must wash my hands," and he stuffed his coat into a cupboard.

That night Bernard was woken by a snarl of thunder. The little boat rocked and the timbers creaked. There was a flash of lightening and Bernard shuddered. He wanted to hide but there was nowhere to go. He felt his way towards Eliza and crouched down beside the old lady. She pulled a blanket over his head and held him tight while they waited for the drumming of the rain to cease.

"There's no need to fear rain," soothed Eliza. "We need it as much as we need the sun."

"I know. It's just so loud."

"Sometimes it's pleasant to be out in the rain."

"I once saw the sun and the rain together," and he told her of his search for the gold at the end of the rainbow.

"No one has ever found it," explained Eliza, "because no one ever sees where the rainbow actually touches the earth, but it doesn't matter. It is the search that is important. As long as we keep on looking for the better things in life we will find all sorts of good things on the way."

Bernard smiled. "Like I found you, here" he said.

He had never felt so comfortable with all aspects of his life. Being with Eliza, both at home and when he was working was calming and satisfying at the same time. He was constantly reminded that he had a skill, that it was valuable and that his company was appreciated. She did not babble on about things that did not interest him. He heard her murmur, "That was good for both of us."

Next morning Bernard hurried towards the museum. Evidence of the storm was everywhere, roof tiles on the pavement, tree branches across the street and deep puddles on the promenade. When he reached the museum the building looked intact but the curator was inside looking concerned.

"The glass in the rear door has been shattered," he told Bernard. "Be careful if you're going into the garden."

A cleaner was sweeping up debris as he stepped through the doorway and surveyed the scene of devastation before him.

Thank goodness the sculpture is not yet in place, he thought. The mosaic was undamaged but the shrubs and plants in the garden were torn and battered. He found a large box and began to clear up, trying not to step on the emerging bulbs while lifting the broken branches. The garden was a special place to him, now, and he wanted it to be as near perfect as he could make it.

Rose stood at the kitchen door wearing her coat. "Tim, if you are going out could you give me a lift into town?"

Tim turned at the gate. "OK. I'll be in the van. Where you going?"

"I'm going to the newspaper office to put in a new advert for the cottage."

"Don't spend a lot of money."

"They've got a special deal on at the moment."

"Right. Get a move on. I said I'd pick up the spuds today, not tomorrow."

Just clearing away Bernie's things had reminded her of how little she knew about him and going to the newspaper office would give her the opportunity of tracing his family and perhaps reuniting him with his few belongings.

She handed in the advertisement;

Lane's End Cottage, Chalk Pit Lane,
B and B £20 per night. 1 twin. 1 single.
Homely, comfortable and near Downlands Way.

She added the telephone number and then asked about James Bernard Longman. The girl found the original article and a description of his mother's accident.

Mrs Longman had been knocked down by a motorist. Although she had been on a zebra crossing the sun was low and the driver insisted he had not seen her until it was too late.

Rose felt a tide of sympathy for Bernie and resolved to discover what had happened once he had run away. She would start at the church.

Her heart was thumping as she rang the bell on the vicarage door. A tall, slim man with grey hair opened it.

"Can I help you?" he asked.

"I'm looking for the Reverend Baines."

"I am he. Would you like to come in?"

"Thank you." Rose was flustered. She knew she was blushing and wiped her feet nervously on the mat.

"Come into the study." The vicar's voice was deep and soothing as he held out a chair for his visitor.

"It's about Bernie," she plunged, "James Bernard Longman."

"Have you found him?"

"Yes – no – I mean, we did know where he was, he stayed with us, my name's Rose Smith, but he left and I don't know where he's gone."

"I see." The vicar waited but she did not continue. "What made you come to me?"

"I read in the paper that you took the service for the cremation of his mother. He left a photo. I just wondered what had happened to him."

"I'm afraid I can't help on that score. I'm in a similar situation. As an executor of Mrs Longman's will I have been allowed to hold on to some of their personal belongings in case Bernard returns but the house reverted to the housing association, as he was not there to pay the rent. I also have his mother's ashes, as there was no family member at the funeral. I can give you the name of the solicitor but I doubt whether Bernard would get in touch with him even if he did come back. How long did he stay with you?"

"Only a couple of days. I just hope he's all right."

"No news is good news, Mrs Smith. We must add him to our prayers."

Rose blushed again. It was a long time since she had prayed about anything.

"What about his father?"

"I didn't meet him. My predecessor said he left when Bernard was a boy but he's had no contact for over 20 years. I think James blamed himself for Bernard's condition – said he'd been contaminated by something."

"And his mother?"

"Anne? She was a romantic, devoted to her son, of course, but not the ideal person to prepare him for life. She took Bernard out of his special school because he was upset by the disturbed children there and tried to teach him herself. He became her life.

"She had no other interests except books. Bernard did spend two days a week at the Treetops Centre. You could ask there."

"Thank you. I might do that." But she had used up enough time already. She had to check on the market and catch the bus home. Tim would get the seed potatoes and the fertilizer from the nursery but she could note egg prices and find out whether there was a call for more home made apple pies.

They only had one booking for March so far and until they had more visitors she would like to spend her time baking. Of course the trees needed attention but that needed more muscle than she had. Dare she mention it to her husband? Tim had seemed so irritable of late, shutting himself away in his office in between mealtimes. She often went to bed without him and sometimes heard voices outside as if he was using the other front door.

Even the postman did not go round the front of the house, he left letters in a box at the back, but somebody did, someone who only came at night and somebody Tim did not want her to see.

She'd only just got indoors when the phone rang. It was Katie.

"Is it OK to talk?" she asked.

"Yes. He's not back yet. What's wrong?"

"Nothing. Nothing at all. It's good news. I have met a gorgeous man."

Rose's heart sank. Had her daughter fallen for the charms of some smooth operator?

"Oh yes. What's his name?"

"Ned. He's a sort of artist."

This was worse. If she did have to fall why couldn't it be for someone with a steady job? "How did you meet him?"

"He was doing a mosaic in the museum garden. Oh, mum - He's sweet and gentle and strong and wonderful."

"Well, don't go overboard. Take it slowly and don't bring him to see your father until you are sure."

"I won't – but you could meet us one day, couldn't you? We could have a coffee at the Harbour Tea Rooms."

"I'll see what I can do. It's nice to hear you sounding so happy. I must go now, bye love."

"Bye, mum."

Rose was concerned. She had never known her daughter take an interest in boys.

In fact she went out of her way to avoid them. She never asked to go into town to night clubs – she'd got a job that meant she often worked in the evenings– and now she was swooning over some artist fellow. She felt uneasy. Too much was changing in her life. There were too many unanswered questions.

She'd get on with cooking the fish she had bought for

supper. Perhaps tonight she and Tim could sit and watch television together like a normal married couple.

Bernard was walking slowly back from the museum when Katie almost collided with him.

"I've been looking for you," she said, "I have some good news."

"What?"

"Now you have finished the mosaic in the museum garden you'll be looking for the next job, won't you?"

"Eliza does all that."

"But I have found you a job. Something you'll be good at. It isn't as artistic as the mosaic – but it really needs doing."

"Where?"

"At my home. Well – not my home exactly – the care home where I work. There's an old wall. It is crumbling away. It has yellow brickwork and a tiled top. Come and see it and I'll show you."

Bernard laughed at her enthusiasm and let himself be led down the drive and out to the rear of the building. The garden was large and surrounded by trees.

Katie took him past the seating area and across the lawn until they reached the sunken rose garden. The low wall that surrounded it was obviously in a poor state of repair.

"We can find the bricks and tiles if you can fix the wall," said Katie. "What do you think?" It wasn't as appealing as the mosaic but it was broken and Bernard knew he could repair it.

"I'll talk to Eliza."

"She'll let you do it, I know she will." Katie sounded so excited that he wanted to hug her but he held back. He thought of the gift he had bought and felt pleased that he had something to give her. Perhaps after the ceremony, when he was dressed in his new clothes, he would feel brave enough to show her what he had bought. Now he just felt overwhelmed. A gentle touch on her arm was all he dared attempt.

"Got to get back," he mumbled.

"Of course. I'm sorry. I just had to tell you. I'll see you both at the unveiling."

"Mmm," he nodded. It was getting dark and he needed to get back to his refuge.

When Bernard arrived at the river he was surprised to hear shouts and giggles. At first he thought it was just children playing but when he neared the houseboat he saw it was a group of teenage girls.

The boat was sprayed with graffiti. The gangplank had been smashed and thrown into the water and they were untying the two mooring ropes.

"Hey, hey, the wicked witch is dead!" two of them were singing.

Bernard's heart thumped. What had they done to Eliza? Was it too late to save her? Anger flooded his head and body. His fists clenched and his eyes bulged. He let out a fierce roar and rushed towards the girls who scattered at his approach. He didn't bother to chase them. All that concerned him was Eliza. Luckily the boat was anchored and although one end had swung out into the river he could still leap onto the other. He pushed at the cabin door but it was locked.

"Eliza!" he called, "Are you OK?"

"Ned – I'm all right. Have they gone?"

"Yes. You can open the door."

"Tie us up first." The boat was rocking wildly but the ropes were long enough for him to carry them across and fasten them. He scanned the harbour side for the teenagers but there was no sign. Then he entered the cabin.

Eliza was pale but the grin on her face showed her determination.

"I'll put the kettle on," she said.

"What happened?"

"It's my fault. A silly lot of girls followed me from the shops, calling me names. Two of them were smoking and I made the mistake of telling them how foolish they were. One must have had some spray paint because once I was back here they all jumped on the boat and sprayed all the sides and the windows. Then I heard them smash up the gangplank. I don't know if they had been drinking but something must have made them behave like that. I usually get on so well with the local children," and her eyes began to water.

"I'll make the tea. You sit still."

"Lots of sugar, please, Ned. It was a bit of a shock."

"Right. Don't worry. I'll get a new gangplank tomorrow and clean off all the paint."

"Thank you, love. You're a treasure."

Bernard didn't feel like a treasure. Now the incident was over he found his hands shaking as he made the tea. What if they had really harmed Eliza? How could he manage if he was left alone again? Should he try to find out who they were? Would they come back again? His head buzzed with unanswered questions. He would wait until tomorrow and then perhaps things would seem clearer. For now, he was glad to have been in time to stop further damage.

Next day Eliza stayed in her bed while Bernard put everything to rights. He tried to get her to eat some lunch but she kept saying "later" until she drifted off to sleep.

In the evening she told Bernard he might have to go to the centenary celebration at the museum on his own.

"I can't," he said, "It was your idea."

"We only did the surround. The star of the show is Piers Moon who designed the coral spire. He's called it *Aspiration,*" and she gave a weak laugh.

"I don't want to go by myself."

"Isn't that nice girl from the care home going?"

"Yes, but I don't like crowds and fuss. Please don't make me go." He didn't add that he did not want to leave Eliza on her own.

"Well – I could write a piece for the newspaper that they could use with the photographs. If you go to their office and give in what I have written we can both stay home and Piers can have the glory."

There was a knock at the door. "Hallo," called a friendly voice.

"It's Katie," said Bernard.

"Your girlfriend?"

Bernard blushed.

"Well go and let her in."

"I just came to find out what you'd decided?" asked Katie once she was inside.

Bernard had forgotten all about the job at the care home. "It's difficult," he stuttered.

"Oh Eliza – please let him do it. It would be really easy."

"Do what?"

Katie explained to Eliza, who said she couldn't see why Bernard was hesitating, and then went on to tell them about the residents and how she spent her days. The time flew past until she looked at her watch and squealed, "I should have been on duty half an hour ago."

"I'll walk you back," said Bernard.

"Lock me in," called Eliza. "Go on, I'll be fine."

Bernard fingered the box in his pocket but Katie was walking so quickly he only had time to tell her about the vandals before she gave him a peck on the cheek and was gone. Tomorrow he would deliver the note to the newspaper office and maybe try and find out who Eliza's doctor was. Eliza was adamant that she did not need to see anyone but if she continued to refuse food he would have to get help. Perhaps Katie could advise him.

After working at the care home for a week Bernard found it was not as easy as he had anticipated. The work was fine but he could not get used to the constant interruptions. When Katie brought him a drink or sat on a cushion and watched him he was happy but when one of the residents came out to talk to him he was embarrassed. One lady coughed all the time and Bernard could not understand what she was saying.

Two others came together and kept asking him questions about his family. It seemed to Bernard that his evasive answers only made them more curious.

He came to look forward to seeing Katie hurrying down the path to keep him company. She would sit next to him and tell him about her day, unaware that, to him, just watching her and listening to her voice was enough, and a great many of her stories were not so much forgotten as never remembered. He liked to hear her laugh and tried to show an interest when she came back from one of the outings and described their trip, showing him a piece of pottery or a postcard. Most of all he liked the fact that she sat close to him and seemed utterly relaxed in his presence.

The gift for Katie was burning a hole in his pocket but he needed to get her to himself somewhere where they would not be interrupted. Circumstances made that very unlikely but, just as he had completed the wall, she ran down the path, crying.

"Oh, Ned – it's terrible. They are going to close the home. What will the old people do? They love it so much."

Bernard did not understand. "They are going to lock them in?"

"No – send them somewhere else, and then probably sell the house to be knocked down and made into flats. I'm so angry. How can they do this?"

Bernard did not reply. He just opened his arms and let her rest on his chest. Her shoulders shook and he felt the warmth of her through his clothes. It made him ache to have her sad. What could he do to help?

She pulled slowly away from him, reaching in her pocket for a tissue. "I'm glad you're here," she said.

"Katie – I've got you a present. Look." He held out the box and waited nervously while she opened it and looked inside.

"Ned – it's beautiful. I don't know what to say," and she burst into tears again.

Bernard was distraught. How had his gift made her so unhappy?

"I'm sorry," he muttered, his arms waving uselessly by his side. "Please don't cry."

"Oh Ned. It's just that I'm not used to… I think I love you, you big oaf," and she hugged him fervently.

Bernard felt a flood of relief. No one had told him he was loved since his mother died. Yet he was still bemused by the tears and unsure what to do next. Then he remembered what he had been intending to ask her.

"Do you know where the doctor lives?"

Katie's sniffs turned to laughter. "What on earth made you ask that?"

"It's Eliza. I think she's very ill."

Katie became serious, "and she hasn't seen a doctor?"

"No. She says I mustn't tell him. What can I do?"

"I'll come and see her. Don't worry. We'll get her better. That's something I can help with."

Rose had returned from market where she had been selling jams and chutneys. Her back ached and she hoped Tim would be satisfied with pie and salad. As she unwrapped a fresh stick of celery and went to throw away the newspaper her eye was caught by a strange photograph.

A bespectacled man with a ponytail was grinning manically at the camera. He was standing next to an upside-down cone that looked like a twisted mountain. Rose read the caption. *Piers Moon with his sculpture, Aspiration.*

Beside the picture was a description of the centenary celebration of the harbour museum with a list of the dignitaries present and the final paragraph ended, *The colourful mosaic surround of sea creatures was designed by Eliza Freemantle and completed by Ned Longman.*

Ned Longman! It must be a relative of Bernie's. Perhaps that was where Bernie had gone? Rose was no longer tired. She was on the trail - and by the time her husband came home she was humming contentedly to herself.

He came in and went straight upstairs. She found him dragging thick sweaters and waterproof clothing out of the wardrobe.

"We are going out on the boat on Saturday. I won't be back until Monday night," he said.

She was used to these trips and treasured the time to herself but waited until after tea, when he had shut himself in his office to ring her daughter.

"Katie, your father is going fishing at the weekend with his friends. Would you like to bring your young man round?"

"Oh, mum. I'd love to. I'm sure you'll like him – but he's very shy. Let's make it morning coffee, shall we, not a meal."

"Fine. Would 11o'clock Saturday be OK or are you working?"

"Saturday would suit both of us. I'll ring you if we can't make it."

Katie resolved not to tell her mother the home was closing. She would start looking for another post as soon as possible. Meanwhile she had a difficult time calming down the residents and their families. Although alternative accommodation would be found for all of them a few would find the change very stressful and she was afraid Mrs Granger might not survive.

"I've interviewed the son," her manager said, "and told him not to show his mother how upset he is – but I'm sure she can tell he is angry. We need to introduce them to Evergreens as soon as possible. Can you arrange a visit for her and Miss Poulter. It's the only place with a resident nurse."

As she went upstairs to her room Katie passed Miss Poulter's open door. The old lady was slumped in her chair, her eyes closed, her hands hidden under her favourite tartan blanket.

"Miss Poulter? Frances?" Katie called softly and when there was no reply she tiptoed up to the chair and laid her hand gently on the bony shoulder.

Miss Poulter opened her eyes and looked up. "Hallo, Katie," she said weakly.

"Are you OK, Miss Poulter?"

"Yes dear, I'm not in pain. I just don't see the point any more," and she sighed.

"Are you worried about the move?"

"Not for myself. I can end my days anywhere but poor Gladys has taken years to get used to the routine here and now they are going to change it. She'll be lost you know."

"No she won't, Frances, she'll have you with her. That will be a familiar face. You can help her settle in."

"I'm not sure I'm up to it, Katie."

"The staff will help. I'm arranging a visit. You might even prefer your new room."

"I'm afraid it's a long time since the word *new* held any charm for me," the old lady smiled.

"Can I get you anything?"

"No thank you, dear. Just seeing you has helped. Are you going somewhere else, too?"

"Yes, but I don't know where. Let's hope there's room for me at Evergreens."

"That would be nice."

But Katie knew all the staff except the nurse lived out. There were very few homes with rooms for staff. It was more economical to let the rooms to patients.

She sat on the bed in her tiny attic and took out the box Ned had given her. She knew he was fond of her but the tender way he had held her and the look of devotion on his face as he gave her the locket made her realise how special he had become to her. Was it possible that they could be happy as a couple?

No matter that he couldn't read – she could do that for both of them.

No matter that he needed to be spoken to in short sentences. She did that with the people here, already.

No matter that, to him, Long John Silver was more real than all the disasters going on in the world. It made for a happier life.

She had soon found out that if anything was repeated often enough it remained secure in his memory. It was even better when a task could be demonstrated. He had even come on a trip to the dog track with the residents of the home – pushing Mrs. Baker in her wheelchair and joining in the betting. When Katie saw how gentle and patient he was with the old lady she loved him even more.

They came home three pounds richer after a tiring but enjoyable day out. From then on she had stopped worrying about their differences. Ned didn't argue with her – or threaten her. He did not criticise or ridicule her. She thought he loved her and needed her and that made her feel like the luckiest girl in the world. Who would not like to be seen out with a tall, handsome hunk with perfect manners and a genuine smile?

Not for her a sly and slouching youth who thought insults were attention and a can of coke a symbol of affection. When Ned folded her into his arms and buried his face in her curls she felt valued, safe and grateful.

Would he consider getting married? She would have to take a picture of him to keep round her neck and find some way of telling him how she felt.

She had promised to go with Eliza to the solicitors tomorrow and she hoped the old woman was strong enough to walk. She seemed very frail since the vandals had attacked her and Ned had been re painting and smartening up the houseboat so that he was near at hand.

They would tell him she needed to get away from the smell of paint. She had implied that she was taking Eliza to see the doctor but she had yet to convince Eliza. She had a horrible feeling that the old woman had come to terms with her own mortality and was getting her affairs in order.

The walk back was exhausting. Eliza was leaning on Katie the whole way and they had to keep stopping for her to catch her breath. When they reached the houseboat the old woman squared her shoulders and strode aboard but once inside she flopped on the bed, her face grey with effort.

"You'll look after him, dear, won't you," she whispered as Katie took off her coat and shoes and propped her up against the pillows

"He wanted you to go and see the doctor," said Katie, trying to do as she had promised.

"There's no point. I know I haven't got much longer. I just want Ned to be all right. There's nobody else."

"We'll be fine, Eliza. You rest and I'll make some tea." But by the time it was ready the old woman was asleep.

"Did you get some pills?"asked Bernard as she took him a cup.

"She has to carry on as she is," replied Katie.

Bernard looked puzzled. "But she's not getting better."

"She's old, Ned. We just have to make her life as comfortable as possible."

Bernard fell silent. He was already doing that – but there was something Katie was not saying. Instinct told him the answer but he would not accept it. He was not ready to lose another important woman in his life.

Bernard dressed carefully on Saturday. He put on the new clothes Eliza had bought him for the museum opening and topped them with a padded jacket he had chosen himself from the garden centre. Eliza had trimmed his hair and he waited apprehensively for Katie to meet him on the quay. She had said they were going to meet her mother and that there would be a bus journey but reassured him that they would be out in the country, away from crowds and could come away as soon as he felt uncomfortable. "She's a warm, cosy lady, my mum. I know you'll like her," she had told him.

He saw her hurrying along the waterside and marvelled at how the sight of her made him want to sing. Instead, he held out his arms and she ran into them.

"You do look smart," she said when he eventually let her go. "You've had a haircut – my, you are a sight for sore eyes."

"They hurt?" queried Bernard. "Have you got something in them?"

"No. It's just an expression. If they **were** sore the sight of you would heal them!"

"Oh," He frowned. He wished people didn't talk in riddles.

"It's not important. How's Eliza?"

"She's quiet. I think she's got some more work to do. She's started drawing again."

"That's a good sign. I'll race you to the bus stop," and she clattered off down the road.

5

The single-decker bus drove along by the seashore and then cut inland through a town. Bernard realised that some of the shops here were familiar. He had been this way before with his mother, not often, but enough times to recognise the big Post Office, the Town Hall and the railway station.

He hugged his coat round him. He wasn't usually travel-sick but he felt rather queasy now. It seemed the bus was going nearer and nearer to the village he had known as home, taking him back to a life he hoped had gone for ever.

He ran his sweating hands through his hair and twisted his fingers together. At the next stop he had to resist the impulse to jump up and get off the bus and run and run, anywhere, just so he did not have to face his past, but the bus carried on up the hill, out into the country and stopped by a public house.

"Here's where we get off, Ned. Are you all right?" Katie had been looking out of the window and not noticed his distress.

"Yes, just a bit hot."

"Fresh air will do you good. We've got a bit of a walk."

The pub was set back from the dual carriageway. It was a large, ugly building – its pale walls criss-crossed with what appeared to be dark oak beams. The sign had a bearded face wearing a crown. It must be *The King's Head*, thought Bernard.

He nearly tripped because he wasn't looking where he was going. The footpath was so narrow they had to walk in single file.

Katie suddenly turned and stepped across a tiny bridge and preceded Bernard into a muddy lane. He knew this lane! He knew the wide gate half way up the hill and the stone wall at the top. He knew the double cottage and braced himself for the sound of Jenny, the collie.

"Come on, slowcoach." Katie was pushing open the gate and holding it for him to enter.

Bernard did not know what to do or say. He felt a mixture of fear and belonging. He had enjoyed his time here at Lane's End Cottage – but the thought of meeting Tim again terrified him.

"Ned – it's only my mother," Katie said, as if reading his thoughts – and he was encouraged to see Rose come to the door to greet them. She paused and her hands went to her mouth as if to stop a scream. Her eyes were wide with shock like the drawings in a comic. Katie ran forward and grabbed her mother by the arm. "Whatever is the matter?"

"Oh," gasped Rose. "Let me get sat down. Oh, I never thought…"

Bernard followed them both inside where they all congregated round the table.

"Katie, Bernie" Rose was looking from one to the other.

"What are you on about, mum?"

"Bernie. This is Bernie, our lodger."

"No it's not. His name's Ned."

They both stared at Bernard. He shook his head, trying to keep his thoughts in order.

"I'm not really Ned," he said at last. "That was a mistake. Eliza called me Ned. She said it was a good name for an artist so I let her. I'm sorry, Katie."

"Then you are Bernie?"

"Bernard."

"Not only Bernard," interrupted Rose, "but James Bernard Longman. That's your full name, isn't it, Bernie?"

"Yes."

"Then why don't you use James?"

"My father was James. He stopped everyone calling me James or Jim when I was little. He didn't like me."

"Oh, Ned." Kate flung her arms round him. "I'm so sorry."

"I don't really remember him. Mother and I were fine on our own."

"I put her photograph away," said Rose. "All your things are in the suitcase in the cupboard under the stairs. The vicar told me he had some more of your belongings, probably stuff like your birth certificate. You'll have to go and see him sometime. He was worried about you."

Bernard frowned. "Would you come with me, Katie?"

"Of course. There's nothing to be afraid of. Thanks, mum." She put her arm round the older woman's shoulders and they moved into the kitchen.

Bernard sat with his head in his hands. He was glad Katie's mother was someone he knew and liked but he was nervous about being back in the cottage. The lorry driver had suggested that Tim wanted rid of him because of the stores in the caves. Bernard would have kept them secret if Tim had asked. His head thumped. He wanted to run away again but Katie and her mother were chatting happily together so how could he?

He could not imagine life without Katie and he felt that Rose understood him. He would have to show Tim that he meant him no harm. Perhaps Rose could help?

He collected his suitcase from under the stairs and was ashamed to see the bag of material he had cut up ready for making the collage. He would have to take it home and finish it there. He began to design a picture in his head. There was only one form his present could take. It would have to be a rose.

He was sitting on the floor collecting various shades of pink and red when Katie kissed him on the top of the head and asked if he would like a coffee. Bernard blinked. He had been in a world of his own.

"I've told mum about Eliza," she continued and showed him a jar of apple chutney. "She's made this for us to take."

"Thank you, Rose," he said, scrambling to his feet. "Can I have the case when we go?"

"Yes, I suppose so – but I hope that doesn't mean you aren't coming back?"

Bernard looked at Katie.

"Of course we'll be back, mum. If only for your flapjacks," and she laughed.

Bernard completed the rest of the trip in a daze. He hardly noticed the snow falling as they waited for the bus. He didn't recognise the shops as he went through town. He and Katie did not talk and he had to force himself to concentrate on the present as they got back to the houseboat.

"Bernard, can I still call you Ned?" asked Katie wistfully.

"I'd like that. It makes me feel different."

"It's a cowboy sort of name, isn't it?"

Bernard laughed. "I'm not a cowboy."

"No, you are my man, and I love you." She reached up, wrapped her arms round his neck and kissed him full on the lips.

Bernard felt himself respond. "I wish you were with me all the time," he said.

"So do I – but now we've got Eliza to consider."

They crossed the gangplank and entered the cabin. The air was warm and moist. Eliza was sitting at a table, drawing, her head only a few inches from the paper. Katie put her hand on her shoulder and she jumped.

"Oh – I didn't hear you come in."

Bernard took his case through to the next room and tucked it under his bunk.

"Ned – put the kettle on, there's a dear. How was the visit?"

Katie answered, "Wonderful. Ned already knew my mother. He'd stayed with her."

Bernard made the tea and sat silent while Katie talked to Eliza. He was tired, so tired that he fell asleep and only woke when Eliza shook him and suggested he walk Katie home.

They shivered when they got outside and Bernard held Katie's hand.

The snow, such as it was, had settled. He had known only one really cold winter in his life, when he and his mother had been forced to dig their way out of the front door to the gate, the snow was so deep. Now it seemed as if it only lasted a few hours. Instead of the layer of white icing like the illustrations on Christmas cards the delicate flakes powdered the ground and then melted away.

"It's a stupid time to move anyone," grumbled Katie. Bernard waited for an explanation.

"The old folks – they have had six weeks notice – and I've got to look for another placement."

"You won't be there any more?" He was beginning to feel afraid. He could not bear to lose her now.

"No – but don't worry – there are plenty of vacancies. I just might have to live at the cottage for a while."

"I don't want you to go."

"Something will turn up. Look at Eliza with the new job."

"I don't know about that."

"You'd dozed off. She told me all about it. An infant school is expanding and Eliza and you have been asked to design a wall mosaic. She's been working on a pantomime theme. It sounds like fun."

It did indeed. It could be something Bernard would enjoy. He began to relax and by the time he had said his goodnights to Katie and returned home his mood had lightened.

The commission would take at least two months. Eliza and Bernard worked together on the designs, Cinderella, Aladdin, Jack and the Beanstalk and Peter Pan. They had promised to work in term time so the gardens could be completed by September.

"We need to start before the Easter holiday," said Eliza, "Will you be able to cope with the children?"

Bernard wasn't sure. He'd never had to deal with little children, but as it turned out the teacher found the answer. "Why don't you give the older ones a part to do themselves?" she suggested and that is what they did.

Dividing the panel into four sections they designed four different floors. Cinderella's floor was yellow, like a golden ballroom, Aladdin's floor was every colour under the sun, like a treasure trove of jewels, Jack's floor was green and Peter Pan's was blue. Four children were allotted to each section and Bernard demonstrated how to place the little tiles close together without touching. When the teacher was sure they could all carry out the task she allowed them to come out of the classroom in pairs to help.

Bernard would work from the top down on the section next to the children and became adept at answering their questions.

"When are you gong to do the crocodile?" one little boy would ask every time.

"When I reach that bit."

"Will it have big teeth?"

"Yes."

"What colour?"

"White."

"I've got white teeth," and he opened his mouth wide to show Bernard.

"I've got bigger teeth," replied Bernard and gave a low growl.

The boy giggled and jumped away, pretending to be frightened.

"Kevin – watch what you're doing," snapped his partner, a red-headed girl in a pink overall.

Bernard looked at their rows of tiles. They were almost perfectly straight whereas the other children's efforts were higgledy piggeldy. For the Peter Pan section the effect was wave-like and Bernard had introduced coloured shapes in the Aladdin picture to symbolise the piles of jewels and golden ornaments. He wished he could spend the rest of his life doing this.

But while for Bernard it was the happiest time he could remember, Katie was finding her life most distressing. The son of one resident was threatening to sue. Another resident had suffered a heart attack and was in hospital.

Katie was glad she wasn't the manager but she still had to cope with staff who were growing careless as the time to leave drew nearer.

One morning she arrived to find an angry exchange taking place in the hallway.

"My mother is too frail to move! She's been here eight years and thinks of it as her home. How would you like to be shifted about when you were 89?"

"Please Mr Wright. There is nothing we can do about the closure – but if you'll come into my office I'll tell you what we are doing to find the appropriate placement for your mother."

The manageress looked past him at Katie and tried to convey something with her eyes then, turning to her angry companion, ushered him down the corridor.

Katie wondered what she had meant. Something else was bothering her, something that she had been about to deal with when the visitor arrived. Katie went towards the kitchen and immediately discovered the problem. None of the breakfast dishes had been washed and the place was empty. There was no cook. Hoping she had just called in sick Katie went in search of other staff and found two cleaners huddled outside the back door. One was smoking a cigarette and the other was grumbling about her increased workload.

"Sorry to interrupt your break," she began, "but do you know what has happened to cook?"

"She walked out. She said she couldn't work in this atmosphere any more but I think she's been offered a better job."

Katie thought quickly. What did they do when cook was on holiday? There was an agency they used – but the details were in the manager's office. She would have to hope that things had calmed down. Meanwhile she could organise a washing up rota and maybe buy in some lunch. There were just not enough staff left to carry out all their duties and she couldn't blame them for feeling unsettled. She missed Bernard being in the garden and she missed the feeling of teamwork and continuity that the home had possessed. Still, she couldn't give in now. She had work to do. While she was here she would do all she could to keep the residents happy.

She had two interviews to attend but both posts would require her to live elsewhere.

Bernard had completed the first section. Tinkerbell had been the most difficult part of the design. They had chosen reflective tiles for her wings and she glittered as she flew above the pirate ship. Katie had lent him a camera and he had taken photographs to show Eliza.

He entered the cabin as quietly as possible and went through to her room. Eliza was asleep, her breath rasping and her cheeks hollow – but as he turned to leave she woke.

"Ned," she said, "Is that you?"

"Yes, Eliza – do you want anything?"

"Just water, please, dear."

He brought the drink but her hands were shaking so much he had to hold it to her lips. The effort of sitting forward seemed to drain her and she leaned back on to the pillow.

"Katie knows," she whispered and closed her eyes.

Katie knows what? thought Bernard. Should he telephone her and ask, or should he call out the doctor? Eliza looked more ill than he had ever seen her. He did not want to leave her but he needed advice.

Leaving the boat he hurried to the nearest surgery and burst inside. Several people were sitting round in a large room and a lady behind a desk looked up, a welcome frozen on her lips as she saw the concern in his eyes.

"The doctor must come," blurted Bernard. "Eliza is very ill."

"Please calm yourself," said the receptionist. "If you tell me your name and give me your address I'll see if anyone is free."

"There's no time. It's a houseboat."

"Please sit down, Mr?"

"Longman – Bernard, but it's not me – it's Eliza." He stood in the centre of the room, turning from one person to the other, looking for understanding, trying to impress on them the seriousness of the situation.

The receptionist went along the corridor and knocked on a door. A few moments later a short, dark man followed her out.

"Did Eliza fall? Does she need an ambulance?" he asked Bernard.

"No. She's ill. She needs a doctor."

"Well, if you just wait for twenty minutes I'll finish seeing my patients and come with you. Fiona, take the gentleman's details, please."

Bernard answered her questions as best he could but he could not sit still and wait. He went outside and walked up and down the tiny car park until the doctor emerged.

They walked to the waterfront, Bernard trying to shorten his stride so that the doctor could keep up. He climbed aboard in front of the doctor and led the way to Eliza's room.

Holding back the curtain that separated her sleeping area from the rest of the boat he let the doctor step through. Eliza lay immobile on the bed, her eyes closed and her mouth in a slight smile. The doctor reached down and lifted one hand. Then he turned to Bernard. "You were right to call me – but we are too late. She's passed on."

"She's died?"

"Yes. I'm sorry. Is there anyone you need to inform?"

"Katie. Katie knows what to do."

"Would you like me to call her?"

"Yes please. Her number is on our message board." He led the doctor through the boat and indicated the pin board on the wall.

"Katie Smith?" asked the doctor, and once she had replied proceeded to outline the situation. Then he turned to Bernard. "Will you be all right here on your own if I finish my examination and return to the surgery?"

"I just have to wait?"

"Yes. The young lady is on her way."

Bernard could feel his head getting heavy. He had to hold it in his hands. He sat and closed his eyes, waiting for the grey blanket that was smothering his thoughts to lift.

He was only vaguely aware of Katie's arrival, a discussion about a funeral plan, the doctor's place being taken by two more soberly dressed men, more people in overalls, lots of movement and bustle and then, at last, peace.

Katie was sitting next to him, her arm round his shoulders, her hair tickling his neck.

"I don't know what to do, Katie."

"I know, love. You don't have to do anything today. Eliza knew what was going to happen. She was prepared."

"I didn't want her to go."

"She was old, Ned. She had a happy life. Her body was worn out."

"What must I do?"

"You have to finish the project at the school. It will be a memorial. The other arrangements are taken care of. The funeral will be next Tuesday. We'll go together."

"Where?"

"To the crematorium. She wanted her ashes scattered over the river. We can do that for her too."

Bernard was silent. He knew when people died they were put in a coffin. He understood that they were buried in the ground in graveyards but he didn't know what a crematorium was. Katie obviously thought he understood and he didn't want her to think he was ignorant. For some reason the image of the social worker who had spoken to him before he left home came into his head. A sharp pain in his chest made him gasp. Of course, his mother must have had a funeral, and he had not been there. He didn't even know where she was buried. It was as if not seeing her in the hospital had meant he had not accepted her death. Sometimes he even spoke to her, asking for approval or sharing a new experience.

Now he felt he was going to have to say goodbye to both his mother and Eliza, but first he had to find out what happened at a crematorium.

6

Bernard could only remember being in a taxi once before but the driver had seemed friendly and knew where to go so he sat back and tried to relax.

They skirted the town and drove out into the country. A winding lane led to what appeared to be a well-kept park. The taxi drove up to a low white building with a pillared porch and carved wooden doors.

"Do you want me to wait, sir?" asked the driver.

"Yes, please."

Bernard got out and stared around. There were tall, elegant trees, beautifully tended lawns and beds of crocus and daffodils.

A figure came out of a side door and turned towards him. "Bernard!" he exclaimed, "I'm so happy to see you."

Bernard was happier too, now that someone he knew was there to guide him.

"Hallo, vicar," he said, "Is this a church?"

"Not exactly, come inside and I'll show you."

They sat in the pews while the Reverend Baines explained the committal to Bernard. At first he was aghast at the idea of cremation but when it was explained that the body felt nothing, that the spirit was set free and that the ashes were saved he grew calmer.

"Your mother's ashes are at the vicarage," said the vicar, "I kept them for you," but Bernard did not respond. He was looking around at the room, the stained glass window and the vases of flowers.

"This is a nice place," he said. "Eliza is coming here."

"A friend of yours?"

"Yes. Katie said she had it all planned."

"And Katie is?"

"My girl friend."

"She'll be a comfort to you. It is wonderful to see you looking so well. Do bring her to see me sometime. You remember the way to St Luke's?"

"I think so."

The vicar held out his hand and Bernard shook it. He couldn't remember ever doing that before. The whole day was so full of unusual occurrences that he felt strangely exhilarated. Why were people suddenly treating him differently? It was as if they respected him. Had he changed that much?

He returned to the waiting taxi.

"All fixed up?" asked the driver.

"Yes thanks."

"Back to the harbour?"

"I suppose so." He was reluctant to leave. So many questions had been answered here that he had felt the joy of achievement. Now he felt as if a candle had suddenly been snuffed out. He had to return to the houseboat and stay there, alone.

Kate's first interview was in a large mansion. Her feet crunched on the gravel as she walked up the long drive. The house was encased in Virginia creeper and the massive double doors had the usual communication system. She spoke into the apparatus and there was a buzz as the doors opened to let her in.

The entire foyer was carpeted in oriental style. The

walls were wood panelled and a chandelier hung from the ceiling. A young woman in a white coat came to greet her.

"Katie Smith?"

"Yes."

"I'm Rowena. Would you like to follow me?"

The long corridor had maroon wallpaper and prints of country scenes. She was shown into a waiting room with leather chairs and a low coffee table covered with magazines. They all seemed to be about country houses and antiques.

She had only just sat down when she was called through to an office. Behind the desk sat a middle-aged lady in a tweed suit. Katie disliked her on sight. There was something about her bearing, very upright, and when she spoke it was in short, abrupt sentences.

Katie felt insignificant but she went through the motions. She recounted her experience, the courses in First Aid and Dementia Care that she had taken.

Then she followed her companion as she was escorted round the building and given an example of the week's menus. She saw very few residents. They all seemed to be in their own rooms.

Finally, she was offered a position at a salary identical to that she was earning at present. "Of course, we have no rooms for staff – but we do include meals when on duty," said the manageress.

"I do have one other post to consider – but I can let you know by the end of the week."

"Please do. You won't find another situation anywhere with a higher reputation than ours."

Katie could hardly wait to get outside. The contrast

between that place and the relaxed homeliness of her present home was horrifying. She hoped Evergreens would be more welcoming.

At first sight Evergreens was just one in a long row of large Victorian detached houses but once inside she could see it was a hive of activity. A table in the porch had a pile of brochures and one pale green wall had framed certificates, while the other was taken up by a notice board with posters and a timetable of trips, art classes, keep fit sessions, a chiropodist, hairdresser, postcards and photographs.

A young woman in a blue overall came down the stairs.

"Oh, Have you come to see Margery?"

"Yes, Katie Smith. It's about the vacancy."

"She'll be in the conservatory. I'll tell her you're here," and she bustled off.

Margery proved to be the manageress. Her first question was, "Would you like a cup of tea before we do the grand tour?"

"No thank you." Katie was too nervous. She already felt she could be happy here. The rooms were small but bright – some with their doors open and others where she was shown inside but the occupants were not at home.

"Beryl is playing cards. Doris and Joan are watching television in the lounge. We won't bother Elsie. She'll be dozing."

"Do you have any gentlemen?"

"We only have one single man, but we also have Mr and Mrs Page. There's twelve residents at present but we are getting two more from your home which will make us full."

Katie was admiring the garden. "Can residents use the greenhouse?"

"Yes. Everything this side of the trellis is for their use. Mark, the gardener, has his own shed down the end, with the vegetables."

"Well," said Margery when they returned to the conservatory and had been served a pot of tea and a plate of scones. "Would you like to join us?"

"I'll have to ask about wages."

"You know the standard rates – but we are allowed to give bonus's for extra qualifications and experience. I would estimate that you could improve on your present salary by 20%, especially as you would not be resident."

There it was again. In a few weeks she would be homeless. Yet she needed the job. She liked the home and if she was forced to she could go back to Lane's End Cottage. She might even get herself a little scooter to get to and from work. She would be mad not to accept the offer.

"I'd very much like to come here," she said, with sincerity.

Bernard had completed the third of the four panels. Cinderella's pink meringue of a dress glowed in the afternoon sunlight. The children crowded round him, reluctant to go home, marvelling at the golden coach and the white ponies. In a few days he would have finished the ogre who was staring down from the top of the beanstalk and his time at the school would be over. What would he do then?

"Ned?" the headmistress was at his elbow. "Could I have a word with you when you have finished?"

"Yes, of course." He packed away tidily and entered the school. It was quiet once the children had gone home. He felt uncomfortable, as if he was an intruder.

"I need your advice," began the headmistress. Bernard waited, astonished.

"We are going to turn that piece of waste land into a sensory garden. Do you know what that is?"

"No – I'm sorry."

"That's OK. Not many people do. It's a garden full of things to smell and touch – for people who cannot see or hear, but also for anyone to enjoy. We have someone to choose the plants, rosemary and lavender, and someone to find the wood, but we need some textured paving stones and areas of wall – do you think you could do that?"

"You'd show me the design?"

"The landscape gardener would do that. You'd have to work with him."

"Would he pay me?"

"Well, we could do it like that if you wanted. Eliza handled all your finances, didn't she? Wouldn't you prefer to be paid direct?"

Bernard frowned. He didn't know what to say. He'd come to realise that people did not always pay with cash but he had been content with his money belt and the tea caddy he had started to use for his savings.

"Can I think about it?"

"Of course, but let me know before the holidays."

The word *holidays* remained with Bernard as he walked home. Should he go on holiday? Where would he go? He would like to go somewhere with Katie. He would like to be with Katie all the time. How could he make that happen? He would think about it after the funeral.

The little chapel was full. Bernard and Katie sat together in the front row, Bernard feeling awkward and exposed. They had followed the coffin as it was carried in and placed on the dais. To Bernard it represented not only Eliza but also his mother.

When he had tried to imagine her dead all he could see was an image of Sleeping Beauty in a glass coffin but now he had witnessed the slow progress of the wooden casket with its gold handles and bunch of flowers he felt an overwhelming sadness that he had not been present for her. No one had told him what to do or where to go. They had frightened him by suggesting he would lose his home. Now all he could do was mourn his mother at the same time as Eliza. He was glad the vicar had told him he had her ashes. She would not want to be scattered on water like Eliza. He would keep them with him until he found somewhere he wanted to stay for ever.

The music confused him. He had been in church before – but only on special days. His mother had gone without him early on Sunday mornings. She understood his fear of crowds and difficulty following the service.

Katie squeezed his hand and nudged him to sit. The elderly man who talked about Eliza's life was familiar to Bernard but the picture he painted of the old lady was a fascinating surprise. In her youth Eliza had been a peace campaigner, then a green warrior before it became fashionable. She had been a partner in a pottery business until a devastating fire had ended the venture. The riverside community had loved and respected her and much mention was made of the legacy of mosaics she had left in the district.

Bernard shuddered when the curtain was drawn and the music signalled the end of the committal. However it was explained to him he still found it hard to come to terms with the idea of a furnace. He had to cling to the image of a spirit - a soul – flying like a bird into the sky – free and without pain – and able to watch over him. This thought had kept him calm – and the feeling that his mother and Eliza could now be together.

He clung to Katie until she gave a squeak of pain. He had nearly crushed her fingers.

"We'll get home as soon as we can," whispered Katie and the next hour passed in a blur. He stood in the pub with a sandwich and a glass and let the noise wash round him. At last she grabbed his arm and led him outside. "I think I've seen everybody. You were great, darling." He didn't feel great but he loved her for saying so.

They were sitting together in the houseboat when Katie said, "I've got a new job at the Evergreens – it's another care home – near the beach. I start next month."

"You'll still come and see me?"

"Ned – we are a couple. Of course I'll still come. In fact I think we ought to make plans for the future."

"What kind of plans?"

"I wondered if you had thought of getting married?"

Bernard's mouth dropped open and he blinked. Then he stared at her as if she had changed into some creature he did not recognise. Finally he struggled with this new concept – Bernard – the married man.

What would that mean? Married people lived together didn't they? That would be fine. That was what he wanted, he and Katie together, but there was more.

In stories they always got married and lived happily ever after, but his mother and father were married and they didn't stay together. What was it about being married that made people happy?

"Ned, you didn't answer the question."

Bernard focussed on her face. "I need time to think," he said.

"Well, don't take too long – I'm going back to live at Lane's End next week so I'll only see you on my days off."

"Don't leave me."

"I'll stay tonight. I'm sorry I sprang that on you. I'll put the cushions on the floor and be here next to you."

Bernard felt more miserable than ever but he didn't know why. Something in Katie's voice saddened him. Life was just too complicated. He needed to sleep.

Rose greeted her daughter with open arms. "Your room is ready. There's a couple booked in for the weekend next door but no one else yet. It's wonderful to have you back."

"It's only temporary, mum. Just until I get settled in my new job."

"How's Bernard?"

"He's still getting over Eliza's death. I want to marry him, mum."

"I did wonder if that was going to happen. What does he think about that?"

"He's not like other men. I'm not sure what he thinks. He needs time to get used to the idea."

"Are you sure that is what you want? I think you'll have some problems."

"I know. Here comes the first one."

The two women waited as Tim wiped his feet and entered the kitchen.

"Back again?" he said.

"Yes, she's staying for a while," Rose returned.

"Out of a job?"

"No," Katie bristled, "but my new post doesn't include accommodation."

"I hope you'll give your mother enough for your board. That room earns money." He strode past them towards the stairs.

"Keep the chickens in tomorrow morning," he ordered. "George is bringing the sprayer for the apple trees." The bedroom door slammed.

"Well at least he's letting me stay."

"He will – as long as you are useful, but don't tell him about Bernard."

Next day Rose waited until George and Tim were busy in the orchard and, ignoring the plaintive barking from Jenny's kennel, walked down to the bus stop. If Katie was really serious about marrying Bernard she needed to know more about him.

First she went to the day centre and spoke to the people in charge. To them Bernard was a success story and to her surprise they had articles about his work and photographs of the mosaics on the walls. She was shown examples of collages he had created and she understood why he had asked her for the material. But when she tried to ask about his disabilities they would not discuss them with her. Who could tell her how disabled Bernard really was? Could he get better? Would any children be like him?

She would have to find someone else who knew him well. Someone not bound by rules of confidentiality. The only person she could think of was the vicar. Dare she bother him again? A doctor might be more useful but the Reverend Baines had seemed so sympathetic. She needed to discuss the possible marriage with someone and who better than a vicar?

However the Reverend Baines was not at home. Rose returned, frustrated, to Lane's End Cottage.

Bernard stood at the front of the school hall while the children clapped and cheered.

He knew he was blushing deep red and his skin felt prickly with heat. The sea of smiling faces made him feel as if he was floating on goodwill. He had never been praised for an achievement in public before and it was an overwhelming experience.

The staff had invited him to a party later in the evening and he was reluctant to attend but Katie had insisted. "You can do it," she said and, in an echo of his mother, "Just smile and nod, most people want to talk and you just have to listen. I'll stick by you."

He was wearing a tie that Katie had tied for him and he felt stiff and awkward as they took a detour to admire the completed wall.

The moonlight shone on the gleaming tiles, picking out the fairy and the cave full of jewels. "I love the way you've got the necklaces and jewels tumbling out of the treasure chest," said Katie.

"It was like that in a picture I saw, only then it was gold, lots of gold."

"Your version is better. Come on, let's go and circulate."

It was too much for Bernard. The crush of people, the constant questions, the perpetual offers of glasses of wine that he felt impossible to refuse – all combined to unsettle and depress him. It was still only half past nine when Katie realised how badly he was affected and led him outside.

"I'm sorry, Ned – do you want to go home?"

"Yes, please."

"They all liked you, you know."

He didn't care. He just wanted the pain behind his eyes to stop and his feet to go where he meant them to. He felt as if he was going to be sick and reached the river just in time.

"I should have known parties were not your thing," muttered Katie.

He drank a glass of water, washed his face and hands and collapsed on the bed.

Katie stood over him, her sleeveless dress showing her bare arms. He had to touch them to pull her towards him. He felt as if all the blood in his body was rushing towards his extremities. "Ned, you are crushing me." He released her – as if the touch of her had burned him.

"You made me hot," he cried, trying to shake off the discomfort.

Katie moved away from him. "Ned, how much do you know about sex?"

"It's rude and it makes babies," Visions of boys with magazines showing naked females, girls who giggled when he looked at them, his mother with warnings of people, *in trouble*, a soup of memories, none of them explaining how he felt now.

"Ned, it isn't always rude, only with strangers. With someone you love it is natural, as natural as the plants grow, as natural as the rain falls and the sun shines, as natural as laughing and crying. It is something we were born to do and that hot feeling means it would be natural for us to do it together."

Bernard looked apprehensive.

Katie laughed, "Don't worry. I'm not going to jump on you now. I just don't want you to be afraid of touching me. I couldn't bear that."

Bernard sighed. He needed to be alone to adjust to all that had happened today.

As if she read his thoughts Katie said, "You get some rest. I'll see you tomorrow," and kissing him lightly on the forehead, left.

Next morning Bernard determined to complete the present for Rose. He bought some glue, paint and a sewing set from a handicrafts shop that Eliza had favoured and painted the side of an old cereal box pale blue. Then he found a picture in one of her books to copy.

The only books Eliza had were about birds and flowers, trees and insects. At least there were plenty of illustrations and one, of a deep red rose, was ideal for his purpose.

He curled a small piece of pale pink silk into a tiny tube, threaded a needle with pink cotton and made a hole in the centre of the cardboard. Then he tied the cotton into a knot at the back.

Taking the larger petal shapes of crimson jersey he stuck a ring of them to the backing, leaving the outer edges free. Inside this ring he stuck rose-red petals and inside those a paler pink. The illustration had a leaf and a rose hip so he added them to his picture. He wasn't completely satisfied. It looked flatter than he would have liked but he framed it with parcel tape and waited for Katie to return. He wanted to ask her how to write ROSE.

He could recognise the words POLICE and BUS STOP and POST OFFICE but, until now had no compulsion to read or write.

Seeing Katie again made him feel shy but she did not refer to their last conversation and was enthusiastic about his gift for her mother.

"Do you want to give it to her or can I take it tonight?" she asked.

"You take it."

"You know I'm going to be staying there, don't you?"

"Yes. When will I see you?"

"Next Thursday – but I might drop into the school one day before then."

Bernard looked concerned, "Drop what?"

"Oh Ned, I don't mean drop, like fell. I mean a quick visit," she laughed.

"Can't you come and live here?"

"Well, I could if we were married."

"Then you would be here all the time, like Eliza was?"

"Yes, except when I was at work."

"You'd sleep here?"

"Yes. We'd be able to cuddle up together."

"Then when can we get married?"

"Well, there's a lot to arrange, but I'd like it to be soon, then we could go somewhere warm for our honeymoon."

"What's a honeymoon?"

"It's a holiday that two married people go on so that they can get to know each other better."

"I'd like a holiday. Would it be expensive?"

"It wouldn't have to be. It's the wedding that could cost a lot. I think mum will help."

She looked so happy he had to kiss her and once she was in his arms everything felt so right he was content.

It was a long time since Rose had upset her husband but now she was expecting trouble. Katie had telephoned her with the news and asked her to prepare Tim in the hope that he might help with the nuptials. She knew what the answer would be.

Rose waited until after the evening meal, cleared the table and, leaving the dishes in the sink, approached her husband just as he was about to move into the lounge.

"Katie has some news," she began.

"What now – lost another job?"

"No – she and Bernard want to get married."

At first she thought there would be no explosion – then she saw the struggle Tim was having to control himself.

"That idiot! She wants to marry a man like that? I knew she was stupid but not that stupid. What's got into her?" He took a step towards Rose. "Did you have anything to do with this?"

Rose ploughed on, although she felt the menace in her husband.

"No. They met somewhere else. She likes his gentleness. He's very artistic." Every word she said only seemed to inflame the situation. Even as she was justifying her daughter's choice she was aware of the implied criticism of her husband.

"Artistic! What use is that? He's thick – his children will be thick – our grand children will be thick. I'll be a laughing stock. There's no way that girl will marry him. This time I'll make sure of that." His fists were clenched and his face crimson.

Rose was afraid for Katie. She knew Tim's anger would be volcanic by the time she got home. Her husband's attitude infuriated her. He was happy enough to have Bernard around when he was useful. Was he blind to his qualities? If he cared so little for Katie what did it matter who she married? He was just being selfish and vindictive.

Katie had hardly got in the door when Tim stormed out of his office.

"Sit down there, young lady," he hissed, pointing to the settee.

Standing facing her he held up one hand – while using the other to point to his fingers.

"One – You are an awkward, stubborn, ugly little leech. You don't know how to dress, how to behave, how to earn a living or how to respect your parents.

"Two – That Bernard is not all there. He should never marry anyone. People like that should be castrated, or strangled at birth.

"Three – You are never to see him again. The whole idea of getting married is utterly ridiculous."

Rose stood in the doorway, frozen to the spot and watched while Katie opened her mouth to protest, but clearly thought better of it.

"Four – While you are under my roof you do as I say and don't expect anything from me after I have gone.

"Five – If your mother does anything to help you marry that man I'll make her sorry."

He didn't wait for a response. He grabbed his coat and slammed out of the cottage.

"Phew!" Katie was white with shock. "I didn't realise he hated me so much."

"I'm sorry, pet. He just wasn't cut out to be a father. He couldn't bear to see how much I loved you."

Rose sat down next to her daughter and tried to warm her with her body.

"He called me a leech, mum – why?"

"He didn't know what he was saying. He wanted a son."

"Then when I bring him one he's not happy." Katie was crying now.

"Bernard's not his type of man."

"What did he expect?"

"Someone into football or rugby; someone who liked a drink; someone like himself.

"Darling, you must admit Bernard could be a bit difficult for anyone to accept at first." She held her daughter's tear stained face in her hands and searched her eyes for understanding.

Katie shook her head. "But not when you get to know him. He's changing all the time. He may not be into team sports but he does swim. He told me he swims in the sea."

"So that's where he gets his broad shoulders." She tried to make Katie smile and it worked.

"Mum – you like him, don't you?"

"Of course – but the only way we can get you what you want is to trick your father."

"How?"

"We'll have to make him believe he has won. If we pretend that Bernard has called off the wedding he would believe that."

"Why would Bernard call it off?"

"Perhaps to please your father? Maybe he has to go away? That would protect him. Tim seems hell bent on getting him out of your life. Does he know where Bernard lives? He might be in danger."

"I don't think I've ever mentioned the houseboat to him."

"Well let's hope he's too busy to do anything. You come back tomorrow with the news that Bernard has run away. He's done it before. If you bring a travel brochure for Ireland and say you found it in his room it should convince him."

"If he makes enquiries everyone at the harbour knows him as Ned."

"Your father's not the enquiring type. I think we'll get away with it. You'll have to act devastated."

"I can see this will be the quietest wedding on the planet."

Rose looked at her daughter's sad face. This was not how she had imagined Katie's wedding to be. She had expected a joyful occasion, Tim a proud father at last – with another man in the family and herself looking forward to grandchildren before she grew too old to enjoy them.

"Don't worry. We'll make it special." She rubbed Katie's hands between hers for comfort.

"Have you the vicar's telephone number?"

"Why? Are you planning a church wedding?"

"No, but Ned is going to need his birth certificate."

The word *birth* rang a bell in Rose's head. She had been so concerned about Bernard she had nearly forgotten.

"Good, heavens, that reminds me. It's your father's birthday next week."

"You're not going to get him anything, are you?"

"I'll make him a chocolate cake. He's not always like this. He'll calm down when you've gone."

"He doesn't get violent, does he?"

Rose could not bring herself to say how she really felt about her husband. It would make their whole life together seem a sham. She tried to be honest.

"Not really. He's a little – inconsiderate – at times, but I'm used to it. He works hard Katie. He's in charge of all the finances and he's quite generous with the housekeeping."

"For all you know he's got a tidy sum squirrelled away."

"I wouldn't mind if he had as long as you get it eventually."

"He doesn't deserve you. Oh. I forgot. Ned made you a present."

Katie unwrapped the collage and held it out to her mother.

"Well I never. It's a rose, isn't it?"

"Yes. He made it from those bits of material that you gave him."

"He's actually got talent. It's a pity he can't make a living out of it."

"He's earning money doing the sensory garden for the school. He's not a shirker mum."

Rose was surprised at the defensive tone and responded in kind. "I didn't say he was. I'm just concerned for your future."

"Don't be. Eliza left Ned the houseboat. We'll be fine." Katie went into the kitchen, poured a large helping of cereal into a bowl, covered it with milk and took it upstairs.

Rose hesitated. She had not meant to make her daughter angry. She was undecided whether to follow her or stay up. She wanted to erase the distant memory that Tim had provoked - herself, as a new mother, gently cradling their daughter as she was feeding at the breast. She had glanced up to see her husband aghast with revulsion as he witnessed the scene. He had said nothing then, just turned and left the room, but never again had she let Katie suckle in his presence.

Now she dared not put on the television. It would look as if she didn't care that her husband was troubled. She began to doodle on her shopping list. What style of outfit should she get for the wedding? The back door opened and she swiftly hid the paper in her apron pocket.

Tim ignored her. He went through the dining area and up the stairs. She would give him twenty minutes and then go up herself. There really wasn't anything to say.

7

Bernard was absorbed in learning about the textures that were required for the sensory garden. The landscape gardener was a tall, pretty blonde with a wide mouth and an infectious laugh. She seemed ready to spend extra time with him, searching for the ideal materials. She drove him all over the county collecting flints and cobbles, bricks and stone. She taught him how to recognise different trees by their bark alone and he enjoyed closing his eyes and handling the variety of items before they made their selection. It became a game – she would bring him a bag of nuts or seeds and he would have to guess what they were just by touching them.

They were trying out different vegetables and Samantha was laughing hysterically as Bernard rolled a turnip round in his palms.

He was blindfolded and his shoulders were shaking with amusement when the shed door opened and someone else entered the room. Immediately Samantha stopped laughing. Bernard waited, puzzled, but did not remove the blindfold.

"Having fun?" Katie's voice cut the air.

"Well – it's all part of the planning," stuttered Samantha.

"What's this got to do with Ned's work?"

Bernard uncovered his eyes. He'd never heard Katie talk like this before.

"He's testing things for me."

"We have chestnuts and beech nuts and acorns here, Katie. Come and have a go."

"No thanks. I've not time. I'm in between shifts. Can I talk to you?"

That was a strange question, thought Bernard, as he answered, "Sure."

"I mean alone."

"I'll just go for a walk then, shall I?" said Samantha stiffly.

Bernard was more concerned about Katie. He turned to look at her. She sounded different.

"What's up?"

"Nothing. I've been back to St Luke's. The vicar has your birth certificate, some photograph albums and your mother's jewellery. He's been told he has to move. Can we go and collect your stuff?"

Bernard frowned. She had told him too much at once. "Where do we have to go?"

"To St Luke's vicarage. The church your mother used."

"Her jewellery is there?"

"Yes. I said so. I can't go until next Thursday. Can you get the day off?"

"Yes – if I work Saturday instead. Samantha doesn't mind what days I work."

"Well – sort it out with the blonde bombshell and tell me next time you see me. Bye," and with a cursory wave she was gone.

Bernard felt sick. He didn't know what had happened to make her act so strangely. He didn't know why she mentioned a bomb. He felt guilty and muddled. His mother would have calmed him down and explained. The only good thing to have come out of the conversation was that he was going to get her jewellery box. He was sitting down, trying to remember what each piece looked like when Samantha returned.

"She was a bit uptight, wasn't she?"

"Katie? I think she was in a hurry."

"Well, she sounds a bit bossy to me – I hope you know what you are doing."

If only he did.

The visit to the vicar was not as difficult as Bernard had anticipated. He had forgotten how understanding the Reverend Baines could be. He remembered how happy his mother had been when he visited and he seemed to have a similar effect on Katie. Her recent cool attitude began to change in his company and she listened attentively as he spoke about Bernard's mother. The two men went through the papers and then the vicar produced the photograph albums. Katie took them eagerly.

"Did you want to look at them now?" she asked Bernard.

"No. I'd like to see the jewellery." He turned to the vicar.

"Ah. That's in the other room. Come with me."

Out of sight of Katie the vicar put his hand on Bernard's shoulder. "I'm sure you have already thought of it – but I'd like to help you choose which piece to give to your fiancée."

Bernard had not thought of it, but it seemed like a good idea.

"What should I give her?" he asked as they sat opposite each other with the box between them on the table.

"Well, an engagement ring would be perfect. Your mother had lots of rings. Maybe you should pick two or three and let Katie choose."

"What shall I say?"

"Tell her your mother would have liked her to have one. I promise you, she'll be delighted."

Bernard would do anything to make Katie pleased with him again. He picked out three rings, a diamond, one with a blue stone and one with different coloured stones. They took the box back to the study and Bernard began to show Katie the brooches, necklaces and earrings.

"These are so pretty," said Katie, holding up a pair of pearl earrings, "but I haven't got pierced ears."

The vicar nudged Bernard, who brought out the three rings.

"Would you like any of these?" he asked.

"Oh, Ned. Are you sure?"

"Mother would have loved you," said Bernard from the heart.

"That looks like sapphires. I've always loved sapphires, and look, it fits!" The ring was on the third finger of the left hand. She flung her arms round Bernard and hugged him fiercely. "I'm sorry I have been such a bear – I was jealous."

"What?"

"It's because I want you all to myself. I'm being silly. I'm sorry vicar. I didn't mean to be so emotional." She was laughing and crying at the same time.

"It's an emotional time, but you can both come and see me any time if anything is worrying you, bearing in mind I shall be a little busy at Easter."

Katie turned to Bernard. "Ned – your birthday in May – would you like us to get married on that day. It's a Friday, but that doesn't matter." She turned to the vicar. "I'm afraid it will be at a register office. We are keeping it small and private."

"That's fine – but the church is always here. If you want a blessing later we'd be happy to see you both."

Katie was delighted to discover the register office had a vacancy at 12 noon on the third Friday in May. When Bernard had given her the ring she had realised how stupid she had been to be jealous. He was probably more likely to be faithful than any other man she had met. She couldn't blame him for being happy and she knew he would take his wedding vows literally, just as he did everything else.

The next thing they had to decide on was the honeymoon, which they both called, "our holiday," as the idea was familiar to Bernard.

Katie could not remember ever having a proper holiday. The family had been on day trips and once she had been away for a week with the school but her father would not leave home and did not let his wife and daughter go without him. This would be a real adventure.

Bernard had expressed a desire to go on a ship but a cruise would be far too expensive. She had a better idea – and arrived at the houseboat with details of boating holidays on the rivers and canals of England and Wales.

Bernard sat spellbound as she turned the pages. There were sleek motorboats, sturdy narrowboats and barges. There were scenes of locks and country pubs and pictures of cabins so smart they looked brand new.

"It all depends on which river we would like to explore," Katie was saying. "I think one not too far away. The train fare will be expensive. We'll have to go into London and out again - this one on the Thames looks ideal."

"The boat would go along the water? Who would drive it?"

"We would. That's what we have to decide. Which would be the easiest for us to steer? Oh, Ned, isn't it exciting!"

"It would be just me and you on the boat?"

"Yes, but it wouldn't be like work. We could eat one meal out each day and stop and explore the countryside whenever we wanted."

She watched Ned turning the pages and hoped she had chosen something they could both enjoy.

Katie's ring had given her an idea of what to wear for the wedding. She had to buy something she would wear again. They could not afford a dress for the day only. She would buy some material in palest silvery blue and make a simple sleeveless shift with a bolero jacket.

She'd get one of those hats that weren't a hat – just dangly bits on a headband – and Ned would have to have a suit, navy would be nice, and some proper black shoes instead of the boots he always wore.

They'd also have to get a new bed for the houseboat. Katie could not bear the idea of sleeping in the one where Eliza had died. She'd like a new cooker too – but that might have to wait until Christmas. She already had plans for redecorating. She was so excited she hardly slept.

Evergreens had proved to be as welcoming as she had hoped. The rooms were adequate and well heated and the manageress efficient. The only thing that let the place down was the food. The portions were enough for the residents but the menu was repetitive. She brought pasties and sandwiches from home. She missed having a room of her own and dreaded going back to the cottage where, although Tim seemed to have accepted her explanation, the atmosphere was strained. The larger bedroom was occupied by a young couple who were walking the Downland Way for charity and Rose had felt obliged to contribute. When Tim found out he was seething.

"What's the point of taking money for bed and board only to give it back to them."

"It was only five pounds." Rose sounded tired.

"Well that's five pounds less you spend on their breakfast."

Rose did not reply. Katie could see that she found it hard to be civil to her husband these days. They all had to pretend, in front of the guests, but there seemed little joy in the house.

Tim had found a shifty looking lad from the village to help with the grass cutting and pruning. He spoke even less than her father and when Tim left him alone had a music player plugged into his ears and bounced to the beat while he walked.

Katie moved some of her valuables to the houseboat. She did not feel comfortable with him around. Besides, she had to transform the interior of the boat into a home for the two of them that reflected their tastes. Out went the tapestries and the beaded curtain. There were no more fancy lights and fringed throws. She wanted the place to look light and modern. The walls would be light peach and all the inside woodwork would be white. Bernard had said he was happy with whatever she chose so she spent as much of her free time as she could transforming their home.

The sun shone on their wedding day. Katie was accompanied by a friend from Evergreens and Bernard had asked the headmistress and her husband to act as witnesses. The small party had a drink afterwards at the Ship and the celebrations only ended when Rose said, "I'll have to leave. Our guests are moving today and I have to get the room ready for the next lot."

"We'll see you when we get back. Thanks for everything, mum." Katie gave her a hug.

"Bye, darlings. Enjoy yourselves."

Katie turned to look at Ned. He had been drinking too much. He wasn't used to wine. His face was flushed and his eyes glassy.

"Come on, Mr Longman. I'd better get you home. We haven't finished packing."

The guests took the hint and departed. Bernard tried to get to his feet but failed.

"You sit still. I'll catch Paula and get a lift. Don't be sick."

But sick is just how Bernard felt. The thought of going in a car made him feel worse. He staggered to the gent's and vomited down the pan.

Swearing never to touch wine again, he washed his face and looked at himself in the mirror. He was a married man. He'd got a lovely wife and work he enjoyed. His life was complete.

The holiday turned out to be as successful as they had hoped. The pleasure they had exploring the country was only excelled by the delight they had in exploring each other. They took dozens of photographs – Ned opening locks, Katie steering the boat, birds and views they saw along the way.

"We'll make a big album," said Katie as they climbed back aboard the houseboat. "Good grief – look at all this post."

One letter in particular looked ominously official.

"You've got to go for an interview," read Katie, "They think you are working without paying tax."

"What do I have to pay?"

"You don't. You don't earn enough, but they have no record of you. How did your mother manage?"

"She got some kind of benefit. I don't know. They said I'd never work."

"This needs sorting out. I'll come with you. The garden people pay you in cash, don't they?"

"Yes."

"We need written confirmation of what they have given you."

"Will I get into trouble?"

"No. It's just that you probably haven't got a National Insurance number. I'll put them straight. Now we are married it might affect the tax situation. Don't worry. I'll pop and get some milk. I won't be long."

When she returned the cases were still not unpacked. Instead, Bernard was sitting on the bed looking through his mother's old photograph album. She sat next to him as he went backwards from his twenties to his teens and then as a little boy.

"Your mother was very pretty," she said softly.

Bernard turned the page and there was a seaside shot with a man and a boy making sandcastles. The boy was Bernard.

"Is that your father, Ned?"

"Yes."

"Do you remember him?"

"A bit."

"What was he like?"

"Tall – with blue eyes."

"What did he do?"

"He was a decorator. He painted the inside of our house. He liked things tidy."

"He went away?"

Bernard wriggled. "Yes. It was my fault."

"How?"

"He wanted me to read. He wanted me to be clever. I made him cross."

"Do you know where he went?"

"No. Please stop."

He looked so unhappy that she took the book from him and lifted up a suitcase.

"Here's something to take your mind off it. Find everything that needs washing.

"I'm back to work on Monday."

It was weeks before Katie at last found someone who would discuss her husband's situation with her. Time and again she was shunted from department to department and told they could not investigate Bernard's circumstances without his presence.

Eventually, with the help of his previous social worker and after a distressing interview where Bernard became so confused that they had to leave before anything had been decided, they received a letter insisting that Mr James Bernard Longman attend the Job Centre the following Monday morning.

"I can't get any more time off," said Katie. "You'll have to go on your own. Make them write everything down for me and don't agree to anything you don't understand."

Bernard looked apprehensive. At the previous interview he had felt so ignorant that all his old fears had returned. Seeing himself through the eyes of people who expected him to be able to read and write and understand his finances brought back all his old feelings of inadequacy. He wanted the world of fairies and giants, knights and princesses, back. How could he ever have imagined that he could be a part of this complex society?

He had bought himself a large story book full of familiar illustrations and would sit on their bed with the page open at a picture, retelling the story from memory. Yet even the tale of the Ugly Duckling could not comfort him now.

"You can do it," said Katie, "Remember – you are Ned Longman, the artist. I've told them how much you have been paid this year. In fact, they probably owe you money. You haven't had any incapacity benefit since your mother died. You don't owe them any money at all. Remember that."

To Bernard's relief the interviewer was a slim young woman with honey-blonde hair and rimless spectacles. She gave a sympathetic smile and waited for him to sit.

"May I call you James?" she asked.

"No." replied Bernard. "That's not my name. I'm Ned," but he couldn't help adding, "or Bernard," as he could see she was looking puzzled.

She scrutinised the form in front of her. "Oh – Bernard – your second name."

"Yes."

"Well, Bernard – it seems you have been able to find employment."

"Yes."

"And you look fit and healthy."

"Yes."

"So there is no reason for you not to have a job."

Bernard had nothing to say. He did have a job, even if only for the summer. What did she mean?

"You haven't had any further education, have you?"

"My mother taught me."

"So you could have a grant for training."

"What kind of training?"

"What work are you doing now?"

"Working in a sensory garden."

"Do you like that?"

"Yes."

"What do you do there?"

"I make paths and plant bushes. I'm learning which flowers have a strong scent so that blind people can know they are there."

"Well, the ideal training would appear to be in horticulture – otherwise you will have to find full time employment. You can't rely on casual work. Would that suit you?"

"Would you write that down for me?"

"I'll send you all the details in the post. Is your address still the houseboat?"

"Yes."

"Wonderful. I'm so glad you came in, Mr Longman," and she rose and held out her hand to shake. Bernard was uncertain as to what had been decided but he had escaped without having to pay any money so he was satisfied.

He still had time to check on the progress in the garden. It was perfect weather for laying flagstones. Perhaps Samantha could tell him what *horti-whatever it was* meant?

8

Once Katie had moved out, Rose considered telling her husband the truth, but the pattern of their lives had changed so much she dared not risk it.

Each morning he ate his breakfast alone, before anyone else was up, and then expected bacon and egg roll for his new sidekick. Neither of them returned for lunch and in the evening he had his meal in the lounge, on a tray.

Why didn't she trust the newcomer? "What's his name?" she asked while Tim waited for her to wrap the extra breakfast.

"André, he's French."

"Where's he staying?"

"I've found him somewhere but they don't feed him well. Why all the questions?"

"I'm just interested. He doesn't say much."

"Not like twittering women."

Rose watched him go round the house towards the kennel. He would spend more time with Jenny now, practising for the sheep dog trials. The dog followed him everywhere, devotion in its eyes.

Rose sighed. There was something odd about this André. She supposed he was living in the village, but if so why did he always arrive from over the hill instead of using the road and coming through the orchard? Still, she and Tim had actually exchanged a few words without rancour. She had feared her husband might quiz her about Katie's move but he hadn't. *Out of sight, out of mind,* she supposed.

They had concocted a cover story with the help of her friend and there had been no reports of the wedding in the local paper that he might have seen in the pub.

She turned her mind to breakfast for her guests. Both rooms were occupied this week. She set the table and filled the kettle. Breakfast would be a jolly affair with everyone discussing where they were going. If only she could have a holiday, a holiday from Tim, but then life was full of 'if only's'.

Bernard was in bed, but still awake, by the time Katie came home.

The first thing she said was, "How did it go?"

"It was OK. She didn't talk about money. She wanted to know what work I had been doing."

"That figures. Did you tell her it was only part-time?"

"She knew that. She said I was fit and healthy."

That sounded ominous to Katie. "They aren't going to force you to get another job, are they?"

"No. They want me to do training."

"What kind of training?"

"Gardening." (Samantha had, indeed, known what horti-something was and had been very encouraging about the course.)

"Will they pay you?"

"I'll get a grant. I don't know any more. They are sending me details."

Three days later a fat envelope arrived for Mr. J. B. Longman. As Katie's shifts allowed her to be home some afternoons he did not open it until they were together.

Inside were a colourful booklet, an application form and a return envelope. Katie read the covering letter.

"It's in the next county," she said, "Five days a week at a kind of college. They expect you to stay there in the week and come home at weekends. It's for 30 weeks and you get a qualification at the end. They say students are guaranteed jobs in parks, nurseries or for local councils."

"Can I see?"

She handed him the booklet. The house was old and classical, the gardens dramatic, the students all looked busy and happy. She knew how he would react.

"I'd have a certificate?"

"Yes. If you completed the course."

"And they'd pay me to go there?"

"They pay the usual dole money and the course is free. You'd like to do it, wouldn't you?"

"Would I have to read?"

"That's what we have to find out. They mention provision for the disabled but I don't know if that will handicap you too much. Shall I ring them?"

"Yes please."

It was next morning before Katie could dial the number in the booklet and tell them about Bernard's difficulty.

"They say they are used to non-readers. They just pair you with a student who can read and you help each other. She sounded very nice."

"When would I start?"

"This September. Good, we've got the rest of this summer."

Bernard was happy now he had something to do once the sensory garden was finished.

Katie filled in the form and he added his signature. "You are nine years older than me," she mused.

"Is that good or bad?"

"In your case it's perfect." He loved it when she talked like that. She made him feel special, brave and ready to try something new.

In reply to the application form they had a welcome letter with a list of requirements – clothing, washing necessities and personal tools if preferred.

Samantha advised Bernard to have his own secateurs and suggested a mini tape recorder. "You'll need some strong Wellingtons. I know where to get those, otherwise just wait and see. I'm really envious. You'll learn all the latest methods. You'll have to come back and teach me."

The sensory garden was almost completed. He would not be around to see the pupils' reaction when it was opened but Samantha promised to let him know how it was received.

His mobile phone was set with all the numbers he might need and he had practised calling his wife until they were both sure he was confident. This was even more of an adventure than leaving home the first time.

By the time Bernard was settled on the train with the name of the destination station in capital letters on a card in his pocket he was breathless with excitement.

"WESTVALE – the next station is Westvale."

Bernard and five other people alighted. There were three men and two women. All exhibited various shades of apprehension. Bernard followed the group out of the station to a waiting mini-bus.

The driver counted them in, calling each by name and they sat crowded together in the vehicle. Bernard had to bend forward as he was too tall to sit upright. He had a seat to himself but the girl across the gangway smiled widely at him.

"I'm Petra," she said.

"Bernard." He had decided to leave Ned the artist behind at the harbour. He wanted to be a success as himself and not to have to explain why he was using a different name.

"Are you in rehab? They said this was my last chance. Funny sort of place, but it's nice to be in the country."

"I'm just here for training."

"Oh, sorry. I just wondered how everyone got here. It's not like you'd choose to do this, is it? Although someone has to do it. Don't mind me. I guess I talk too much."

Bernard was puzzled. What was rehab and why did the assortment of people look so concerned? He worried that perhaps the illustrations in the booklet had not told the whole story. He patted the phone in his pocket.

If he didn't like it he would ring and tell Katie. He wasn't going to prison – just a college in the country. On Friday he would be home again. There was nothing to fear.

Bernard was escorted to a room with two beds. They were arranged against opposite walls with a table, chair and cupboard grouped alongside each. One half of the room already had an occupant. A small man in a wheelchair was arranging papers on the bed. He had thick curly hair and a neat pointed beard. His tanned features reminded Bernard of an illustration. 'Mr Tumnus,' he thought as the man turned to greet him.

"Hallo. It seems we are sharing. My name's Zak." He held out his hand. Bernard clasped the delicate fingers in his large paw.

"Bernard," he replied. "Is that my bed over there?"

"Yes. We are lucky. Some people are in rooms of three or four. What course are you on?"

"Gardening."

"Yes, but what is your specialist subject? I'm down for Business Studies - more the management type than the dig-a-hole-and-plant-a-tree brigade," he laughed.

"I don't know," said Bernard. Katie had filled in the form and he just signed it. She had read it to him first but he could not remember.

Next morning at breakfast Bernard sat silent and was rewarded with the explanation. Although all the students studied horticulture they each had to choose a specialist subject. As well as Business Studies there was Parks and Gardens, Walls and Fences and Fruit and Vegetables.

The students congregated in a large room. Each had their name pinned to their chest.

"I'm afraid some of you will not get your first choice," announced the lecturer. "There were too many names in the walls and fences group so Bernard Longman and Graham Pace will have to make a second choice."

"I'd like Parks and Gardens," came a voice from the back.

"Right – that means you are in Fruit and Veg. Bernard, is that OK?"

Everyone turned to stare at Bernard.

"Yes, thank you," he muttered into his shoes. He was already beginning to feel overwhelmed and now he had to try to keep up in a subject he knew nothing about. He felt his hands getting clammy and his scalp prickled. He forced himself to stand still.

"Well, the timetables are on the table. Group leaders are here to show you the rooms we shall be using. We have two lectures each morning and practical every afternoon except Fridays when we have visits or videos in the morning and the afternoons are free. Your first lecture will be after coffee this morning. That's all ladies and gentlemen. We hope you enjoy your stay with us."

The students drifted towards the four corners of the room.

"Are you lost?" It was Zak.

"Which one is Fruit and Veg?" asked Bernard.

"The table with the picture of the tree," answered his friend. "Each group has a logo, mine's a pound sign, parks and gardens is a daisy and walls and fences is a brick wall. I think you'll find all your files and overalls are the same colour, too. I hope you like green," and he drove away.

Bernard stood at the end of the queue by the tree table. The man behind it was handing out workbooks and at the same time trying to answer questions from the people crowding round. "We meet in Room 5 after coffee," he said, "and I'll take you on a Grand Tour. There'll be no practical this afternoon. You can have the rest of the day to settle in. There's a TV room, a games room, a gym, a pool and a laundry. My name is Malcolm Price. Be back in Room 5 at 11am tomorrow, with your workbooks, please. The 9 o'clock lecture is in the big hall."

After drinking his coffee, and vowing to stick to tea in the future, Bernard took his things upstairs and changed into his overall and boots.

When the group congregated later he found he was the only one in an overall.

"Good idea, Bernard," chuckled the lecturer, "but the overalls are for the afternoons."

Some of his companions sniggered and he blushed. He was so used to changing his own clothes when he went around the garden at the school.

Once outside the size of the grounds became obvious. The group were led between rows of runner beans, past lines of potatoes and among bushes of raspberries, gooseberries and blackcurrants. They saw greenhouses full of different tomatoes, large, small, red and yellow and they spread out in the orchard where there were not only many types of apple but pear, plum and damson.

Bernard bent to pick up an apple from the ground.

"That's a Discovery," said a voice at his shoulder. He turned to see a tall, thin, blonde man with a very pale face smiling at him.

"I'm Paul – you're Bernard, aren't you? I think we're in the same corridor."

Bernard looked round. He wouldn't have called this line of trees a corridor. Then he realised, "You mean, in the house?"

"Yes. I saw you arrive. I think we've got the most interesting subject, don't you?"

Bernard wasn't sure. There was so much more to Fruit and Vegetables than there would have been in the Walls and Fences group. "There's a lot here," he said weakly.

"I'll help you. My family run a nursery. I know stacks of this stuff already."

Bernard was uncomfortable. Paul seemed to be looking at him as if he expected something. He began to retrace his steps but his companion ambled casually beside him.

"Naturally – not everyone will be able to make a living from this course," he began. "Some are just here because their doctors have sent them. I think they believe gardening calms people down."

Bernard said nothing. He did not want to argue with his companion but he too felt more at peace in a garden, as long as he was alone, than anywhere else. A cliff-top was uplifting and a woodland fascinating but the sense of beauty combined with order that existed in most gardens was reassuring in a way that he could never explain.

"You look like the kind of person who would really make a career out of it. You are strong, and easy to talk to."

Bernard walked faster. He was not used to compliments, especially from someone he had only just met.

"What does your family think of you coming here?"

Bernard had had enough. "I just need to work," he said, "I don't have a family."

Paul smiled, "Well, friends, then?"

Bernard did not answer. Something about Paul made him want to keep his distance. His questions seemed like prying – too personal, too soon. He didn't like people making assumptions about him but he didn't feel ready to discuss his life outside college with a virtual stranger.

They had at last caught up with the rest of the group and the lecturer was showing them the long greenhouses.

Bernard bent his head to enter and worked his way up to the front of the line.

What constituted a family? he wondered – Was Katie a family - or Rose and Tim? He had answered as truthfully as he could. Until recently he would have said his mother and himself were his only family but now he was not sure.

He was glad to get back to his room. Zak was nowhere to be seen and he sat at his table and opened the workbook he had been given. There were passages of print, followed by lots of little boxes with a few words next to them. Every so often there was a picture or a diagram. Bernard was worried. How was he going to cope with this?

After touring the grounds and meeting the others he had felt ready for a new chapter in his life. But the sight of the workbook brought back memories of the short time he had spent in school. How he had tried so hard to learn the letters of the alphabet, only to find he was expected to fit sounds to a lot of little symbols that looked so alike he confused them. He had felt safe with the solid, regular shapes of capital letters but the flash cards and reading books used small letters. He had retreated into silence and became the class dunce. Now he was back in a very similar environment. Why had he thought anything would be different? He was running his fingers through his hair in desperation when Zak appeared.

"Hi, there. How did you get on?"

"It was very interesting, but I won't be able to stay."

"Why not?"

"I can't read this." He pointed at the workbook.

"You can't read that, or you can't read, full stop?"

"I can't read. I know some letters and I can remember some words but I can't read something I have never seen before."

Zak gestured to the open book. "Do you know what that is?"

"The word at the top?"

"Yes. The title of the chapter. It says SOIL. Repeat after me, SOIL"

Bernard laughed. "OK. SOIL."

"Now, I'll ask you after dinner and see if you remember."

"Oh, I'll remember, but we can't do that with the whole book."

"You can manage the lectures, but not the handouts. Do they know you can't read?"

"Yes. They are going to give me tapes."

"If they give you CDs I can play them on my laptop. Otherwise, don't worry. I'll read you the questions and answers and you can tick the boxes. We all have the same basic book. We can help each other."

Zak sounded so calm and confident that Bernard doubted that there was anything he could do for him. "How can I help you?"

Zak hesitated. "My legs don't work," he said. "If you could help me move about I'd be really grateful. That is, if it wouldn't upset you. I'll try not to be a bother."

"You mean getting dressed and washed and things?"

"You've got it. This place is fine with all the ramps and door handles but it hasn't got all the facilities I have at home."

"Did you stay indoors today?"

"Yes, but we'll get the chance to go outside. They've got a brilliant computer suite- all here on the ground floor. I'll show you after dinner if you like."

Bernard felt at ease with Zak and suddenly realised how hungry he was.

"How are you at telling the time?" asked his friend.

"I've got a digital watch," replied Bernard, "It's five fifty five."

"Almost six. Come on – Show Time!"

While Ned was at home she'd put it off, but as soon as he was away Katie went to see the doctor.

Her examination over, he asked, "How long since your last period, Mrs. Longman?"

"Four months, I'm afraid."

"And you didn't think to come and see me before now?"

"I went on the pill as soon as we came back from holiday."

"Holiday? You mean honeymoon?"

She blushed. "Well, yes – but I didn't think we'd get intimate so quickly."

"Mrs Longman - you should have known better. Your husband may appear child like but he's a grown man."

"I know. I've been telling myself that for weeks. Then when I started being sick I stopped taking the pill. I haven't harmed the baby have I?"

"No. In fact you appear to have got through the most anxious time. I'll send you for a scan and we can take it from there. Congratulations."

Katie left the surgery in a daze. She was pregnant. She and Ned were going to have a baby. It was about six months too soon but she hugged the idea to herself like a secret.

She sat in the café staring at a mug of hot chocolate until it grew cold. She would love to tell her mother, but should she wait until Ned came home at the weekend? He hadn't rung – but she didn't really expect him to if everything was going well.

'I'll go to Mothercare,` she thought. 'I can tell them and they'll understand. I can soak myself in baby atmosphere.`

The scan was booked for Thursday. She had two working days until then. She could just about keep it to herself for that long. She knew she had a silly grin on her face but she didn't care. Little memories, like the new swimsuit she'd had to buy this summer, the way she fancied grapefruit all the time and couldn't drink tea any more. It all made sense now.

She climbed onto the houseboat and suddenly saw it differently. Was this a safe place to bring up a child? Blocking out the thought she went inside and tried to imagine what she could do to accommodate a baby. Once Ned had a trade they might be able to save for a flat- but until then this was home and she was going to make sure it was perfect.

She began to empty cupboards and pile clothes on the bed. Had anyone ever really cleaned these shelves? she wondered. Anything they had not used for a while was out – they were going to need the space.

Bernard sat on the train and stared out of the window. So much had happened in one week. He was grateful for the time to sit quietly and give his brain a rest. There were few people in the carriage and he felt almost alone.

He knew Katie would ask about the course and he dreaded having to tell her. He wanted to keep the two places separate. He didn't want to tell her about Pests and Diseases or explain why he did not do Walls and Fences.

He hoped she would understand. He just wanted to be with her, smell her and be soothed by her. She could make him laugh so easily. He hadn't laughed much while he had been away. If it hadn't been for Zak he might have left mid-week, but Zak needed him and read to him so that everything he was told was repeated the same evening.

He'd get the CD's at the end of each module, they said – but he had to fill in the workbook from memory. It wasn't an exam – just a record of what they were telling him. He and Zak ticked the boxes together. It was only when he came to the Fruit and Vegetable section he was lost. He accepted the handouts but hoped he could learn all he needed from the practical sessions.

He must ask Katie if she could get some soil samples from Lane's End cottage, and some apples from Rose to see if he could identify them. He didn't want to go there himself. They still hadn't told Tim they were married. His eyelids drooped. He hadn't been sleeping well. He had time for a doze.

Katie was waiting for him at the station. He bent down to hug her.

"I've taken a shift off – I'm working Sunday night instead," she explained as soon as he let her go.

Bernard just stood and stared at her. She looked so lovely, so familiar, so HIS – of course she was family, all the family he ever needed. She looked so happy to see him a great wave of pride washed over him.

"You'll not believe what I've done to the boat." She was gabbling. "I've cleaned all the inside. We've got new curtains and mats. I tried to varnish the window sills but it made me sick so I just polished them."

She was hopping from one foot to the other, not walking in a straight line but going backwards in front of him, then dodging to the side to grab his arm and tug him along.

He was puzzled. Was it just because he was back that she seemed in such a hurry?

"Would you like coffee?" she asked as soon as they were inside.

"Yes please, Katie. Are you all right?"

"Yes, fine – more than fine. I've got some news. I've just got to tell you."

"Go on then."

She stood still at last and took a deep breath. "We are going to have a baby."

Bernard remained silent. He could not believe what he was hearing.

"I'm four months pregnant, Ned. I know it's a bit soon but isn't it wonderful – please say you are happy about it?" Her eyes wide, she was pleading with him.

Bernard fought his way out of a fog of shock. "We made a baby? When will it come out?"

"Not for months – sometime in February. Ned – we are going to have a baby!" and she flung herself at him, kissing him all over his face.

He held her tight, trying to absorb her happiness, but he just felt puzzled and afraid. He had known that what they did could make babies but she had said they wouldn't start a family until he had a regular job. He had trusted her and forgotten all about it. Now he felt that something had happened without his permission. Yet if she was so happy how could he spoil that? He kissed her back.

"Are there any chocolate biscuits?" He had to get back to the present.

"Mind reader – you guessed I'd be celebrating."

He couldn't be bothered to work out what she meant. He just wanted something sweet.

She climbed off him and turned to the cupboard. The place did smell fresh and clean. He was glad to be home and he had months to get used to the idea of being a father. Him a father! "Is it a boy or a girl?" he asked.

"They aren't sure. Do you want to know?"

"I think so. Can they tell before it is born?"

"Yes – but I would rather it was a surprise."

"What do you want me to do?"

"Just complete the course. Tell me what it's like. I want to hear all about it."

That was what Bernard had feared. He told her about Zak and the house and gardens but as soon as she began to ask questions about the lectures he stopped her.

"I want a rest from all that," he said firmly. "I'll tell you later."

It worked. Katie looked abashed. "I'm sorry," she said, "I'm just too excited – would you like to go out?"

"No, I just want to be here with you. I've missed you so much."

Later they washed and dressed and had dinner to the accompaniment of the radio and Bernard began to relax. The urn with his mother's ashes sat on the shelf by the window. He felt comforted by their presence, as if the past had merged with the present. *Look at me, Mum*, he thought, *I'm a married man. I'm going to have a job and my wife is going to have our baby.*

9

It was November. Zak and Bernard were comparing notes on the final project for the term. Each student had to design a garden and then they would be allotted a strip of land to show their design. At the end of the summer term the gardens would be judged and prizes awarded.

"I'm going to need your help, Bernard," said Zak. "They've given the wheelchair students raised beds, but they are all circular. I'm much better at thinking in rows or blocks. What do you think I should do?"

"How about a wheel?" replied Bernard. "If you put a small, slow growing conifer in the centre and then have flowers to make the spokes."

"I don't want all flowers," his friend interrupted, "Everyone will do that. I want to mix in herbs and salad stuff, just what I'd like if it was mine."

"You could make the spokes with marigolds and fill in the spaces with herbs."

"That sounds right."

"Rosemary smells nice but it can get straggly." Bernard could remember the way he had to trim the little bushes that lined paths in the school garden.

"I could combine it with radishes and lettuce."

"Slugs love lettuce."

"I'll fill in the spaces with grit. That will stop them."

"White would look nice. I wish I was doing your garden."

"Is yours so difficult?"

"Yes. It's long and thin and has to include a path, a water feature and at least one bush or tree."

"No instructions about a lawn?"

"No – but we have to say what kind of customer we are designing for. What do you think?"

"It sounds like it belongs in a terrace. How far have you got?"

Bernard laid his design on the table. He had used coloured paper to show the different areas of his garden. Instead of labelling the beds he had designed them so that the path was yellow paper, grass was green, flowerbeds were red and the water feature was blue. At the end of the garden was a white strip with red spots on it.

"What's that?" asked Zak.

"We aren't allowed to fence the sides but we can show a boundary at one end. I'm making a wall."

"Why has it got spots?"

"It's something I have been doing for a while. I make mosaics. I thought if I could collect enough bits of broken pot I could decorate the wall."

"Knock out! No one else will think of that."

Once again Zak had made him feel capable and in control. Just as when he brought seed packets and they practised reading them. Bernard had learned so much and yet it had not felt like learning. His friend had made it into a game they both enjoyed. He was looking forward to getting his CD in a fortnight's time. Katie had promised him a player for Christmas. Then he could listen to the lectures over and over again. How lucky he was to be able to spend his time doing what he loved and if it hadn't been for Katie he might never have got here.

Students were encouraged to start laying out their gardens once the change had been approved and Bernard wanted his to be terraced so he began transferring soil as soon as they had a dry afternoon.

Paul wandered up, his hands in his pockets, and walked along the edge of the strip.

"What are you doing, Bernard?"

"I'm moving soil. I want three levels."

"Who's the garden for?"

"A young couple. It feels the right shape for a town garden."

"I'm stuck. I can't make up my mind about decking. I haven't given mine in yet."

"Is it a garden for you?"

"Yes. I'd like low maintenance sophistication."

"Why not use grasses?"

"Bernard – you are brilliant. That will solve my problem – a kind of urban jungle – absolutely perfect!"

"Glad to help." Bernard began to secure the levels with miniature walls of grey textured brick. Then he would ensure that the soil was fertilised, preferably with fresh manure, and select the gravel for the section that, in theory, would be next to the house. The tree and some bulbs could go in before Christmas but everything else would have to a wait until next term. He'd chosen a cherry tree in spite of the fact that it would need protecting from birds. It was something he would like to take away with him at the end of the course. Hopefully Rose would find a place for it among the Laxtons, Bramleys and Discoverys in the orchard.

It was when he was putting his tools away in the communal shed that he noticed the graffiti. THIS PLACE

IS A SHIT HOLE + THE TEACHERS ARE CRAP, was scrawled the length of the building in white gloss paint. Who could have done that, and when?

"Can't spell Lecturer, eh, Bernard?"

The voice behind him made him jump. He turned to see Malcolm standing behind him, staring at the shed.

"I was just putting my tools away."

"I didn't think it was you – I was only kidding."

"I know what the first bit says but I can't read the last two words."

"*Are crap* – but the interesting thing is, who thinks of us as teachers? It must be someone pretty young. Who else was out here this afternoon?"

Bernard tried to remember if he had seen anyone other than Paul. He knew his fellow student would not have done this – he loved the place too much.

"Well, I'll just have to start playing detective. Let me know if you think of anything." Malcolm marched off towards the house.

The mood at dinner that evening was uncomfortable. Rumours of Bernard's involvement with the graffiti spread round the dining hall. Some said he was the culprit, others that he had accused fellow students. Someone had photographed the message on their phone and everyone had theories about the perpetrator. One wag even suggested getting everyone to write out the sentence and compare the handwriting.

Bernard finished his meal as quickly as possible and went to his room. The noise in the hall had made his head ache. He didn't know anything but he felt guilty. Should he say he'd seen Paul? Everyone in his group seemed happy on the course. There was nothing he could do.

"You are getting quite notorious," joked Zak when he came in, but seeing the misery on Bernard's face, paused. "Hey, what's up?"

"I can't think. I didn't see who did it."

"No one knows for sure – but there are a couple of candidates. I think someone has run away. We'll find out tomorrow."

As it turned out no detective work was required. The girl Bernard had met on arrival, who had been in the floral group, had been reprimanded so many times for non-attendance and unruly behaviour that she had abandoned the course and returned to London. Not everyone, it seemed, could be tamed by contact with nature.

The Thursday before they left for Christmas the students were given preliminary assessments. Bernard was embarrassed and surprised to find that he had the highest score in his group.

Paul sidled up to him in the lunch queue. "Turkey dinner, smells good," he began.

"Yes. I didn't know they would do this."

"It's a wonder they haven't put crackers on the tables."

"No," came a voice behind them, "The crackers are in the queue," and a couple of them laughed.

"Don't mind them," said Paul. "I've been meaning to ask you something."

"What?"

"I'm having a party tonight – as it's the last night. Would you like to come?"

"I'm not very good at parties." Neither the party at the school nor his wedding reception had been enjoyable for

Bernard. Crowds and alcohol confused him. Yet it seemed impolite to refuse.

"Please, Bernard. You have been such a friend to me. It wouldn't be the same if you weren't there."

"OK. What time?"

"Not 'till after supper – about 9pm suit you?"

"Does it matter what I wear?"

"Oh it's quite casual – anything will do – see you then."

He took his tray to a table where other students were waving wildly.

Bernard went to sit with Zak. He was reluctant to leave him on his own for the evening.

"Paul's having a party tonight," he said.

"Oh yes. Well, be careful of that one. I don't trust him. He's a bit too desperate for friends."

"I won't stay long. I can't wait to get home to Katie."

"When's the baby due?"

"In February – but she won't tell me if it's a girl or a boy."

"What are you going to get her for Christmas?"

"She only wants things for the baby, but after it's born she wants driving lessons."

"She's really got her head screwed on, that wife of yours."

"What?"

"It's a figure of speech, Bernard. It means she's sensible."

"I know. I'm very lucky."

Bernard felt guilty about his friends at the college. He hadn't bought cards or presents for any of them so joining Paul for his party, even if only for a short while, was something he could do to show he was prepared to join the festivities.

Nine o'clock, on the dot, Bernard knocked on Paul's door. Paul shared a large room with three other students and the sound of modern jazz wafted along the corridor.

When Paul opened the door the room looked hazy as if it was full of smoke. The only lights were tiny candles set all around the room. The four beds had been pushed against the walls to make seats and a large table was covered in bottles and packets of crisps.

"Welcome," said Paul effusively, flinging his arms wide to embrace Bernard.

Once he had been released he was ushered to the table. "What's your poison, Bernard? Beer, rum, wine? Take your pick."

Bernard was determined to avoid anything that could be poison but he recognised a familiar brand of beer. "I'll have one of those, please."

"Crazy K for the man," said Paul, "and a chaser – you must have a chaser."

"What's a chaser?"

"Essential, my man – can't have a beer without a chaser," and he filled a tiny glass from the whisky bottle.

A can in one hand and a glass in the other, Bernard looked round for somewhere to sit but all the places seemed to be taken so he swallowed the contents of the glass and stood with his drink, watching the other guests.

Two girls were trying to dance in the centre of the room but the music was so complicated that they ended up just swaying together. Everyone else seemed to be male.

One man was dressed extravagantly in a floral shirt with yellow trousers and was wearing a long dangling earring. Bernard could not remember seeing him before. His hair was bleached into stripy spikes and he was arguing with his host. By the time Bernard had finished his drink he had left.

A short, squat man with bad breath tried to engage Bernard in conversation.

"I do think they should spend more time emphasising the ecological benefits of organic agriculture, don't you?" he said and then, without waiting for a reply, "and GM foods must be the most disastrous thing on the planet."

What was he talking about? thought Bernard, unsure how to respond. "We haven't got that far yet," he muttered, hopefully.

"My dear man – you must read the papers – we all need to keep abreast of modern trends."

"What's that about breasts, Carlisle?" Another guest joined them. "You can't expect Bernard here to know what's in the papers. He can't read."

Unfortunately there was a lull in the music at the same time as this comment and half a dozen faces turned towards Bernard. He blushed and stared at his feet.

"He can so." Paul came to his aid. Picking up a folder he pointed to a chapter heading.

"What does it say, Bernard?"

"Brassicas and Root Vegetables," answered Bernard. Thank goodness he and Zak had rehearsed the titles. If they had asked him to go on reading he would have been lost but he had shown he was comfortable with key words when working in the group.

Paul's gamble that he would know what appeared to be a difficult chapter heading had paid off.

"Now leave him alone. Come on, Bernard. Have another drink," and two more glasses were thrust into his hands.

There were mutterings about favouritism and recordings but Bernard did not hear them. The party was in full swing and the music drowned out the complaints. His legs seemed weak and he stumbled around the room until he reached a vacant chair.

He felt he really ought to leave but his eyesight seemed blurred. There was a sweet smoky smell in the room and he didn't want to get up in case he was sick. He'd just close his eyes for a moment and wait for his stomach to settle.

Gradually people tired and left until there were only four people left in the room. Bernard watched Paul go over to the remaining pair and pat them on the back.

Turning to Bernard, eyes shining, he said, "Time for a nightcap, Bernard?"

As usual, politeness ruled – and as he was thirsty for a coffee he agreed – but the nightcap turned out to be a fiery drink he did not recognise and when Paul changed the music to a mournful saxophone and started swaying in front of him he began to feel dizzy again.

"Are you hot, Bernard?" Paul's voice seemed to come from a distance.

Bernard nodded.

"Take off your shirt – there's no one here to care."

Bernard started to obey but the memory of Zak's warning stopped him just as he had bared his chest. Paul was close to him – stroking the hairs on his body as if he was a pet animal.

"Don't do that."

"Why, don't you like it?" Paul's voice was slurred and he had a vacant grin on his face.

"No. No-one but Katie can touch me like that."

"Katie? Who's Katie?"

"My wife."

"You never told me you had a wife."

"We never talked like that."

"But you were so nice to me I thought I was special."

Bernard fought against the peculiar feeling that being upright had caused. He could not balance. His ears heard what Paul was saying but he did not want to listen.

He did not want to talk at all. He just wanted to lie still until the room stopped spinning and he felt normal again.

"I'm sorry, Paul – I think I'd better go." Bernard tried to move towards the door.

"No – wait. I can show you a good time. Katie need never know." Paul was gabbling now, spittle coming from his mouth, desperation in his voice, his hands clawing at Bernard's shirt and moving towards his belt.

A sudden rage flooded through Bernard. He'd never felt like this before – as if he wanted to hit and crush this person who was too close to him. With a tortured, "No!" he wrenched himself away, pushed Paul to one side and hurtled out of the door.

Zak was still awake when Bernard stumbled into the room and rushed to the sink for some water.

"Don't drink it too quick," he advised.

Bernard sat down heavily on his bed.

"Are you all right, Bernard? I was going to give you until two o'clock and then send out a search party."

"I'm OK but I'm not sure about Paul."

"I tried to warn you about him."

"He was acting like a girl."

"Not like a girl, Bernard – like himself. He prefers men."

Bernard said nothing for a while. What else went on in the world that he was ignorant about?

"I'm such a wally."

"No you're not. You are learning every day. You just didn't see the warning signs. You are too kind- hearted."

"You could have told me."

"I didn't think he'd try it on with a room full of people."

"I feel sick."

"Well, use the toilet."

Bernard made it just in time.

When he returned Zak said, "Forget Paul. Focus on Katie. Have you decided on a present?"

"I don't know. I was going to look round the shops when I got off the train. She's at work until the evening. I can't afford much."

"Has she got a camera?"

"Yes, quite an old one."

"Why don't you get her a digital one? That could be for the baby – you are all bound to want to take photographs."

"I did think of jewellery, but that's a much better idea. Thanks Zak."

"Sleep on it, mate. Everything will be clearer in the morning."

For the first time Bernard felt that someone was as comfortable with him as his mother. Maybe it was Zak's wheelchair that made the difference – but while she had made him feel like a prince – with Zak he felt like the squire to a knight.

The Knights of the Round Table had been one of his favourite stories. He had lain in bed imagining himself in shining armour, wielding a sword or thundering on horseback over a drawbridge. Castles excited him, the tall towers, the slit windows, the very size of them. Ruined ones made him sad but the complete one, set on a hill in the County Town, gave him a thrill each time he saw it.

He dreamed that night that he was in a tall tower. His hands were tied but his feet were free and he could just see part of the outside wall through the slit window. He felt cold with fear as he watched a giant spider with long thin legs crawl slowly up towards him. He had to block the gap – but how? Turning he saw a fully made up bed. He ran across and grabbed the pillow. It only blocked part of the window and the spider was nearly there. Panting, he bundled up the blankets and flung them into the space.

He woke, shivering, with the sheets tangled round his wrists. If this is what happens after a party, he thought, he'd not go to another one.

Christmas would be very strange this year, mused Katie. She had arranged to have a Christmas meal with Bernard on the day itself and then spend Boxing Day with Rose and Tim at Lane's End Cottage, leaving her husband on his own until the evening.

She wished she had been able to afford to learn to drive before she became pregnant. She would have to get a taxi both ways.

Rose had said that she was sorry she could not make it a real occasion but there would be Christmas pudding and mince pies after the cold meat. Tim always insisted on Christmas lunch on the correct day, in spite of often being too drunk to appreciate it.

Katie had surprised Bernard by asking if they could have nut roast for their dinner. She was never happy eating poultry although she knew some would say she was being over sensitive. She was getting tired easily now and finding bending to the oven, carrying and shopping more difficult. Her ankles ached after a shift at work and she wished she had put more thought into her parents' presents. She had bought her father a new torch and her mother a book about herbs and a set of towels. She had noticed that, while the guests were given fresh new linen, her parents' was old and frayed.

At Lane's End Rose was finding preparations for Christmas even more difficult. She had to time her conversations with Tim very carefully as he spent so much time at the pub that when he wasn't drunk he was hung over. One afternoon she finally broached the subject that had been bothering her for weeks.

"If Katie was pregnant you would rather she was married, wouldn't you?"

"Has that stupid girl got herself in the club?"

"Yes, but she's married to the father."

"How could she do that without telling me? Are you keeping secrets from me, woman?" This from the man who hardly spoke two words to her, nowadays?

"I think you probably keep some from me, Tim."

His face flushed and he stared at her intently. "So, who's she married?"

But as the words came out she could see he knew the answer.

"Bernard."

"So we have a nincompoop for a son-in-law and now we are probably getting a moron for a grandchild. Well, I want nothing to do with it."

"I have asked Katie over for Boxing Day. You won't have to see Bernard, although you'd be surprised how he's changed. I'll let her tell you."

"I'm going to my office. Don't bother me until tea is ready."

He went through to the front of the house and slammed the door.

Rose felt lonely. She hadn't put a name to this feeling before, but now she recognised it. The feeling of frustration at not being able to welcome Katie and her husband and enjoy what should be the happiest of family celebrations was all the more intense because her daily life held no joy. Making meals for Tim and finding ways to use the apples from the orchard had been a means of connecting with her husband. Early in their relationship she had gone with him to the Sheep Fair and watched him win trophies with Jenny's father, a dog called Max. Now Jenny was getting old Tim really ought to have begun training up a new dog but he seemed to have other interests, interests that involved people she never saw and which kept him locked away in his office for hours on end.

She smiled at the memory of the time she made a hundred toffee apples and sold the lot in two hours. She couldn't do it now – too many rules and regulations. She shook herself out of her reverie. She would have to pull herself together and try to make Boxing Day as enjoyable as possible. Perhaps, in the New Year, she could spend a few hours a week helping out in the village. She couldn't go on like this – not for the rest of her life.

10

Christmas day was as enjoyable and relaxing as Bernard and Katie had hoped. Katie was delighted with the new camera Bernard had given her and Bernard was at last ready to show her what he had been learning. They snuggled together on the settee after lunch, each lost in their own thoughts – until a ringing on Katie's phone broke the mood. It was Rose.

"Katie, darling – your father has asked me to invite Bernard to come with you tomorrow. I'm not sure what he's up to but let's hope it's seasonal goodwill."

Katie didn't really believe that but she accepted without reference to her husband.

"Who was it?" asked Bernard.

"It was my mother. She said they would like you to come with me tomorrow. I said yes – is that OK?"

Bernard felt a cold shudder. What if Tim still wanted to get rid of him? Yet how could he, with Rose and Katie there? Could he have forgiven Bernard for finding his boxes and marrying his daughter? Perhaps the fact that Katie was having his grandchild had changed his attitude?

As usual he did not object to a decision already taken, but he was not happy. The Christmas cake Katie had made seemed dry in his mouth and he had a disturbed night.

"I'm glad you're coming with me," said Katie next morning. "I had too much to carry and I didn't really want to leave you on your own."

"It will be nice to see Rose," replied Bernard, trying to put a brave face on things.

When they arrived Rose was the only person home and gradually Bernard began to relax. His host, when he returned from the pub, seemed more inclined to ignore him than refer to their past association. Even the meal was pleasant enough, with Tim saying very little but replying civilly when spoken to.

After lunch Katie said she felt like a walk. "Let's go to the village," she said to Bernard.

Not wanting to stay in Tim's presence any longer than necessary Bernard agreed and it was only when she climbed over the stile with some difficulty and set off up the hill that he realised where she was heading.

"I thought the village was the other way," he protested.

"No – this is the quickest way. Then we can come back through the orchard. Come on, slow coach."

He reluctantly followed her along the path until they reached the fence and then down the steps to the gate that led to the road. Instead of turning right they then went left to a lane Bernard did not know.

"Katie?"

"Yes."

"Why did the sign on the fence say DANCER?"

"You were close. It said DANGER because there is a drop on the other side. It's an old chalk pit. That's a word you need to know."

"I don't remember seeing it before." Why hadn't his mother taught him that?

"Look – there's the church. That's where I'd like our baby to be christened."

"It looks very old."

"I bet it's locked." But it wasn't and the pair went inside.

It was tiny and quite dark with worn wooden pews and a single stained glass window over the altar.

"Isn't it just perfect?" whispered Katie.

Bernard looked at the narrow sills decorated with holly and ribbons. In one corner was a nativity scene arranged on a table with a single candle enclosed in a stone cup. Behind it was a board with pictures of the stable and angels, shepherds and the three kings, all drawn by children.

"It's beautiful," sighed Katie, turning to hug her husband. "Have you thought of a name, Bernard? If it's a boy I want something strong."

"Cliff," answered Bernard immediately.

"Cliff. Clifford Anthony Longman. Anthony was my grandfather. That sounds great. What about a girl?"

"I don't know. You decide. Something pretty."

"You like jewels, don't you? Pearl? Ruby? Too old fashioned. This needs more thought."

They wandered out into the churchyard and Katie pointed out the general store and the old village school, now used as a community centre. Then they walked slowly back the way they had come.

Passing the road to the quarry they continued until Bernard could recognise the straight rows of apple trees over the fence and realised they had reached the orchard.

A wooden gate with a PRIVATE notice on it led to the trees.

"That's another word I can't understand," said Bernard, "and I've seen it lots of times."

"Private. It means it isn't open to everyone. You don't go there without permission of the owner – that's my father."

"Private," repeated Bernard, "Private and Danger."

"There's no danger here," said Katie as they walked through.

Immediately a loud crack echoed across the orchard. Particles of bark sprayed Bernard's face. Katie screamed, "I've been shot!" and staggered sideways against a tree, sliding to a seated position, holding her arm. The shoulder of her coat was torn away and her arm was bleeding. She was shaking and gasping for breath.

Bernard shook the bark out of his eyes and looked to see where the shot had come from. There was no movement and no sign of an intruder.

He turned his attention to Katie, who was huddled on the ground, breathing quickly. He felt sick that someone had done this to her. Someone had harmed her in her own garden and they could be waiting to do more.

"You must get up, Katie. It can't be far to the house. Please, lean on me."

"Who would shoot at us here?" she puzzled as she got to her feet. "Who would want to harm our baby?" Her voice strengthened. "It's probably a mistake. Nobody else should be here except my father." Her voice tailed off. "Perhaps it was someone messing about."

Bernard was surprised at how quickly her tears had turned to anger. Katie was holding her arm stiff to her chest and occasionally winced, but her face was grim and she forged on faster than he thought possible.

Together they came out into the garden of the cottage and up to the door. Rose must have been looking out for them because she opened the door with her finger on her lips.

"Shsh," she began, "Your father's asleep – oh my God."

"It's OK, mum. It's not as bad as it looks. It's ruined my clothes."

"Don't worry about that. Come upstairs and we'll get it washed and see the damage. Can you move your arm?"

"Yes – but it hurts."

"Bernard – find the first aid box – in the cupboard next to the sink. Come on, lass, upstairs with you."

Rose managed to extract two shotgun pellets from her daughter's arm, cleaned and disinfected the wound and made the bandaged patient go to bed.

Bernard, reassured by her efficiency, made them all a cup of tea but by the time he took it upstairs Katie was asleep. He was sitting in the dining room with Rose when a bleary-eyed Tim wandered in.

"Oh. You still here?"

"There's been an accident," Rose replied, anger making her face red.

Tim looked round to see who was injured. "Katie? Is she all right?"

"No thanks to you. She's been shot."

Bernard had never heard Rose talk like this to her husband and, for the first time, saw a look of guilt on his face. "I didn't – oh."

"Yes. I'm betting it was your gun. You lent it to that witless foreigner, didn't you?"

"Only for rabbits. I didn't tell him to shoot anybody." Tim was blustering, now.

"Well – he can't be trusted. Get it back off him. He could have killed our daughter."

"I'll go now." He grabbed his coat from the hook and left.

"I thought someone was shooting at me," muttered Bernard, suddenly drained.

"You? Why?"

Bernard shrugged. There was no way he was going to upset Rose after all she had done for him. He was sorry he had ever suspected Tim. The whole day had been ruined.

"We were having such a nice time," was all he could say.

"You'll have to keep an eye on her, you know. If she shows any signs of being ill take her straight to hospital. I know it's Christmas but you must insist it's an emergency."

That night Tim drove them back to the harbour. Katie had promised not to take the matter further and Rose had declared herself satisfied with the wound. "I'll never let that gun out of my sight again, I swear," were her father's parting words. "I've given that André his marching orders. You'll never see him again."

Bernard shivered but Tim slapped him on the back almost as if he had accepted him. Was it because he was doing something practical with his life or because he had kept his mouth shut? Whatever it was Bernard was grateful he no longer had to fear his father-in-law. Nevertheless Christmas had been a disaster. He now had two lives to care for and he felt incapable of protecting them.

Once back at the houseboat he began to realise he no longer wanted to return to college, although Katie had encouraged him to describe his designs and watched while he chose some pebbles from the beach to complete his wall. She had been to hospital for a check up and both she and the baby were declared fit.

"I still don't want to leave you," said Bernard.

"It won't be for long, darling – and it's my birthday next weekend. I hope you don't mind. I've organised a treat for us both."

Bernard had been so preoccupied with Christmas and the preparations for the baby that he hadn't realised Katie's birthday was so soon.

"You are wonderful," he replied. "What is it?"

"Nothing to be nervous about. A matinee performance and a take-away meal. I'll tell you on Friday. You'll love it."

What was a matinee performance - some kind of show? He would ask Zak as soon as he got back to college. He was excited about his design for the garden and pleased that he seemed able to remember much of what was on last term's disc.

This was the term they concentrated on seeds, tubers and customer satisfaction. He already had experience of designing a garden for a specific group of users but he was not used to working within a budget, someone else had always done that.

The practical work at the college had always been easy for Bernard and he had enjoyed planning the wall to go at the end of his strip. He had picked up lots of pieces of broken terracotta and was going to decorate it with a mosaic of four large ladybirds. The pebbles he had collected were for the shiny black spots. With Katie's words of reassurance ringing in his ears he boarded the train.

At the first outdoor session he found Paul had attached himself to someone else and he could work alone. Next day he was once more isolated and when he went to the lectures he was, again, ignored. At first it was a relief but soon he began to notice that when he moved close to a group they would fidget and snigger and then disperse. His discomfort grew worse when he noticed some of the branches snapped off his cherry tree and the carpet-like evergreen he had chosen instead of grass had been dislodged and was turning brown. When the rustic fencing that he was using to edge the path had been disturbed he knew it was sabotage but who was doing it, and why?

One morning Bernard was surprised to see a new lecturer – a tall, elegant lady with dark hair pinned back from her face and a wearing a light grey trouser suit.

"I'm not going to do much talking today," she said, "I'd rather use the time in workshops. Could you form yourselves into groups of five or six and move the tables so that you can exchange ideas. Pick a leader and I'll give each group a different scenario.

"There's a pensioner couple, a self sufficient household, a working couple with plenty of money and a family with lots of energetic children and a dog."

People began drifting towards the corners of the room until there was a core of four people left in the centre.

"Right, you four are group five," called out the lecturer, "You have a childminder. She looks after babies and toddlers."

A short, plump student with crooked teeth took charge immediately. "Kay – you start. Bernard- you take notes."

"I can't." Bernard blushed as all eyes in the group turned towards him. Now he was letting a team down. Why did he have to choose him?

"I forgot you were so bleeding useless. No wonder everyone hates you."

"Shsh, Raymond. Just because Paul said he couldn't be trusted you don't have to be so spiteful," the girl interrupted.

"I heard he was teacher's pet," sneered another man.

Bernard looked from one to the other. What had he done to deserve this? Did they really hate him?

Seeing their impasse the lecturer came over. "What's the problem, folks?"

"Bernard here can't read or write."

"Then give someone else the job. You've wasted five minutes already."

"I'll do it," said the girl, "Let's draw a spider and brainstorm."

"Safety." "No prickles." "No pond." "Tarmac for big toys." The ideas came thick and fast but Bernard sat silent and miserable. If this was the reaction in a protected environment how could he ever hope to make a living outside? How could he expect to be a father when his child would see that no one respected him? It was no good being able to do one thing well if as soon as you were asked to do something else, something everyone else found easy, you failed. Would he always be mocked and despised?

He went back to his room at lunchtime more isolated than he had ever been.

Bernard was relieved to escape from the poisonous atmosphere of the college and return to the harbour for the weekend. He bought Katie a bunch of flowers on the way home from the station, telling himself he had to hide his feelings and try to make her happy. He was greeted with thanks and eager chatter.

That night he fell into a deep sleep very quickly but was awakened at four in the morning by a restless Katie.

"I'm sorry love. I'm just too hot. I can't seem to get comfortable. Go back to sleep."

He closed his eyes and pretended to go off but his mind went back to the tensions at college. How could he carry on for seventeen more weeks, knowing he was needed here?

Why should he stay somewhere he was hated when he would rather be somewhere he was loved? What would Katie say if she knew the truth? Daylight came before he closed his eyes again.

Katie was absorbed in her plans for the afternoon. She made him wear a proper shirt and she was dressed in a long tiered skirt that he hadn't seen before. Lunch had been cheese salad, after which she linked arms and marched him along the promenade to the pier. Crowds of people were milling about outside the theatre and when they went inside the foyer was full of children.

Katie showed their tickets and they were directed to their seats. "Have you ever been to a theatre before?" she asked.

"No. It feels like the cinema."

"It is a bit. Only the actors are all here, on stage – not on a screen. Are you OK Ned?" He was about to say yes when they had to stand to let a family past.

"I got you the aisle seat. I thought you'd prefer that."

"Yes. I see. Hold my hand, Katie." He sat waiting for the next surprise.

A number of people with musical instruments appeared in front of the stage.

"They are the orchestra. It will be starting soon." She gripped his hand firmly.

The chattering and fidgeting in the audience subsided. The lights changed and the music began. They were about to be transported to the magical world of Aladdin.

Katie watched as her husband took in the colours and drama of the pantomime. His tired features became animated. The worry lines in his face were replaced by the creases made by laughter. His sad eyes began to gleam with the attraction of the energy and excitement generated on stage. He was entranced by the performance and carried along with the participation of the audience. His response was more than she had hoped and she was glad she had planned to take home a Chinese meal, rather than eating out. Ned would need some time to get over the buzz the pantomime had engendered. It was a wonderful birthday and seeing him happy had made it perfect.

She had begun to worry that the course was too much for him. He didn't tell her much about it but she felt that it was vital to their future. If they were going to have a child he needed a secure job. She had seen how well he could work when given practical tasks that he enjoyed. Once he was qualified she was sure he would be happy again.

Bernard woke on Sunday morning with a new determination. Katie needed him to complete the course and earn money. There was no magic lamp in their lives. They had to rely on hard work.

Back at college he found Zak in a similar mood. "We don't have to spend every evening studying," he said. "Let's use the gym and the pool."

The gym did not appeal to Bernard but he had been in the pool a few times.

"Can you get into the water?" he asked.

"Yes. There's a special hoist. I'll show you. How about I meet you there at 9.15?"

"I hope there won't be many people there."

"That time of night? I doubt it."

He was right. The gym overlooked the pool and Bernard could see through the large windows to where the treadmills and rowing machines were in action. There was only one other person in the pool, an older man that Bernard recognised as a member of staff. He let himself down into the water and swam a few lazy lengths. When Zak arrived he showed him how he transferred himself from his own chair to the pool's special lift that lowered him down to the shallow end. In spite of having no strength in his legs Zak had a strong upper body and struck out for the deep end fearlessly.

Bernard was amazed at how well his friend swam. He dived under the water and surfaced beside Zak, who was breathing heavily.

"That was terrific. Now let me watch you," said Zak.

"I don't do anything fancy. I just go up and down."

"I bet you're quite fast."

"There's no need to go fast. It's more fun going under the water." He kicked out and dived to the bottom. "Here." He held out a button. "It's amazing what you can find down there."

Zak laughed. "I'll do one length. You start from the other end and see if you can do two." Bernard grinned at the challenge. He was sure he wasn't twice as fast as his companion. Zak was waiting for him as he completed his languid crawl. "You weren't trying."

By ten o'clock they were getting cold and left the water. After a warm shower Bernard returned to the changing room to find Zak, track suited, sitting in his chair, combing his hair. "I just need a hand with my shoes, please, Bernard," he said.

Bernard hitched up the towel he had round his waist. "Hang on while I get my kit," he said, going to the door of the locker where he had left his clothes. It was empty.

He was certain he had put them in the end one on the top row. He opened the adjoining doors. None were locked and all were empty.

"My clothes! They've gone. Someone must have taken them."

"It must be a prank. I'll go and check outside. You look in the rest of the lockers. Did you see anyone?"

"Only a lecturer. Not one I know."

"That was Mr Clark. He swims every day. He wouldn't touch your stuff."

Zak wheeled himself out into the corridor and up the slope to the gym. There was no one to be seen. By the time he came down Bernard was shivering in the corner of the changing room.

"Did you have anything valuable with you?" asked Zak.

"No, not even the room key. I was relying on you for that."

"Well, let's go back, then. I've a feeling we may not see your clothes again or, if we do, it might be embarrassing."

Holding his towel round his waist Bernard followed Zak back to their room where Zak made some coffee while Bernard put on pyjamas and a robe.

"Some of them have really got it in for you, haven't they? I think it's jealousy. We need a plan. If only we knew who the ringleader was."

"It isn't Paul - if that's what you're thinking."

"No. He's not the type. It's someone who is struggling with the course, someone in your group. Don't give them the satisfaction of knowing you are rattled. I'm sure they'll give themselves away soon."

"Rattled?" queried Bernard.

"Worried, concerned, upset."

But Bernard **was** rattled. What would they do next?

Over the next few days it was obvious Zak had problems of his own. This term required more research, more essay writing and more physical activity. Zak, who was happiest on the computer, was getting tired and going to bed earlier and earlier in the evenings. When the students were required to give a talk to the rest of their group the two friends felt under real pressure.

"I'm going to do Bonsai," said Zak. "We haven't covered exotics yet so it won't look as if I'm rehashing something we have been taught."

"I can't look anything up," said Bernard. "I'll have to talk about something I know."

"Use your experience, Bernard – What was that garden you worked on?"

"The sensory garden. I could do that – and include a bit about mosaics. I don't want to upset the walls group by stealing their ideas."

"They won't be there, will they? Go for it."

Each speaker had to talk for five minutes on their chosen subject and, if possible, include visual aids or examples. The student before Bernard spoke on the history of the plum and went on for twice as long as expected. He had written out his speech and passed round examples of different varieties for people to taste.

Bernard only had a card with a few headings in capital letters to remind him of the sequence of his talk. He had tried it out on Zak the evening before but had the unhappy feeling that it would not be well received.

He was right. As soon as he rose to his feet there was a low mutter from the back of the room. The lecturer frowned and turned to watch him.

"Last year I helped to make a sensory garden," he began, but there was a low, constant hum in the room. "When people cannot see or hear they need to use their other senses. So we planted lots of scented plants like lavender and rosemary and trees with unusual bark, like eucalyptus." He paused. The humming was swelling and dying like waves of sound. He felt he was battling against an ocean. He looked towards the lecturer for help.

"Please stop that," she said sharply.

There was a snort of amusement from one of the group. They were silent for a while until Paul spoke up, "Did you plant holly?"

"Yes," answered Bernard.

"And ivy?" asked another voice – "and dandelions?" "and thistles," "and stinging nettles?" The questions overwhelmed him. Bernard had no time to reply to one before the next. He stood, helpless, as his tormentors continued. He felt cornered, he could not speak or move. Somehow they seemed to grow larger and louder as he felt himself shrink.

"Gentlemen, please. I'm sorry Bernard. We have run out of time. Perhaps we can hear the rest another day."

The others filed out, laughing. His ordeal was over, temporarily.

11

It was February and the start of a new week. Bernard had just unpacked his things and was ready to go to supper. The weekend had been strained – two days of waiting for something to happen. Katie had backache and was impatient and irritable and Bernard was feeling useless and miserable. Neither had seemed able to console the other.

Bernard's phone trilled in his pocket. His heart beat faster. Was this the news they had been waiting for – or was something wrong?

"Bernard – it's Rose – don't worry. There's no panic. Katie has gone into labour. She's at the hospital but nothing will happen for a few hours yet. Can you get time off?"

"Yes. I warned them this might happen. I'll come straight away. What ward?"

"Milne Ward – I'm staying, so I'll be here when you get here. She's fine, Bernard - everything's under control."

Bernard repacked his bag. He needed to tell Zak what had happened. He tore a page out of his notebook and drew a picture of a woman in bed and wrote BABY SOON under it and left it on Zak's table. Then he left a message at reception for his tutor and started for the station. If only he never had to come back, he thought.

Katie wasn't sure she wanted Ned there to witness the birth. She had been shouting more than she had meant to and was afraid she might scare him. He might be a whiz with plants but he didn't show much interest in animals. She hoped Rose would keep him busy until it was all over.

The pain made her cry out again. 'Come back and help me, you useless lot,' she thought, 'I can't manage this alone.'

By the time the baby was ready she was not alone and her healthy daughter was delivered at 1.15a.m. weighing 7lb 2oz. The news was conveyed to the waiting father and grandmother who had been calmed with the usual, "Everything is progressing smoothly, thank you."

Finally they were allowed to view the infant in her plastic crib, from a distance, and report to the new mother.

"Are you OK?" asked Bernard.

"Yes, fine. Isn't she beautiful?"

"I suppose. Why didn't they let us in?"

"I'm sorry. There were enough people around me. It was a bit frantic. I wanted you to see me calm." She smiled at Bernard and he bent to kiss her.

"She's a fair size, darling," said Rose. "Have they let you hold her?"

"Just for a moment. I'm going to feed her later."

"What are you going to call her?"

"We hadn't decided, had we, Ned?"

"Heather," said Bernard – "I'd like her to be Heather."

"Heather. What was your mother's name, Ned?"

"Anne."

"Heather Anne Longman. That's really pretty. What do you think, mum?"

Rose smiled. "I've always liked flower names. I think it's perfect."

"Would you like to stay at the houseboat with Ned until the morning?"

"That would be lovely, if the new father doesn't mind. We ought to let you get some rest. We'll phone Tim and see you tomorrow. Good night, love."

"Goodnight mum, Ned – I love you both."

Together they gravitated towards the nursery on their way out and this time they were allowed closer. Heather was asleep, one tiny fist near her mouth, her pink cheeks invitingly soft. "I hope they let me hold her tomorrow," said Rose, longingly.

Bernard was suddenly overwhelmed by this new responsibility. Katie and he had been mutually supportive – but this little thing – this needed all the strength and wisdom he possessed. It was his job to protect and guard his new daughter. He should be the provider – and what was he doing?

He was about fifteen years behind everyone else and not doing very well at catching up. When he returned to the college he must stand up for himself. He needed a job, a career, a life.

His garden was wrecked.

Someone had simply deluged the upper level with water – probably with a hose – and soil, bushes and plants had all ended up on the gravel below.

The curved, slabbed path was still intact but his flint wall had been pushed over and rolled down until it reached the cherry tree, uprooting it and leaving it in the little fountain he had installed in the water feature. There was scarecrow standing where the wall had been and the clothes it was wearing were familiar to Bernard. They were torn and dirty but they were the ones he had worn to the pool.

Bernard stared at the devastation. It only confirmed what he had been thinking – that he should no longer be here. However much care he had put into his design it was still only a garden, and a pretend one, at that. Next year it would be dug over for another set of students. He retrieved the clothes and left the rest.

He would not make a fuss. That was what bullies enjoyed. Maybe there was an easy way of making sure they did not win. Meantime he would carry on as if it did not matter. After all, what had just happened at home was so much more important.

There was an investigation but no one admitted seeing what had happened. Although everyone knew it could not have been an accident Paul had a perfect alibi – he had followed a personal tutorial with an early night. All three of his room mates confirmed this and Bernard himself was inclined to believe them.

"Is there someone else who might be jealous of you?" asked Zak.

"I don't know. I don't study people like you do."

"Well the main thing is to re-design the garden. Why not do a copy of your sensory garden? You could get cuttings from home. It could be quicker than starting from scratch."

"Mmm. I did think I might try a dry weather garden. Instead of trying to separate the soil and the gravel I could mix it all together. Then I'd change the gravel area to bark."

"Try it. I'm sorry I can't be more help."

"I might come back early next Sunday. My mother-in-law is staying at the houseboat and I feel as if I'm in the way."

"How's the baby?"

"She cries a lot – but when she's asleep she's beautiful."

"And Katie?"

"She's different. She's not so sure about things as she used to be. We don't seem able to help each other."

"Change does that. I've got to go to hospital for an operation next week."

"For your back?"

"Yes. It's been so painful they are going to try something new."

Bernard had noticed his friend was moving more stiffly but had not realised it was serious enough to take him out of the course. This was an extra problem he would have to face."How long will you be away?"

"Until after Easter. I'll be here for the summer term."

"I don't know if I will." The more he thought about it – the more he knew he did not want to stay.

"Don't let them beat you, Bernard."

"I won't. I just wish I knew who it was."

"You're too good, that's the trouble."

"Good for nothing, you mean."

"Who told you that?"

"It was one of my father's sayings. I didn't know I'd remembered it."

"I think this incident must have stirred up memories of your childhood. You're not the same now, Bernard. You have achieved so much. I'm sure he would be proud of you."

But Bernard wasn't convinced. He had to think of a way of confounding the vandals or the whole time at the college would be wasted.

The next morning the answer came to him. He went to the nursery before breakfast and bought fifty packets of seeds, some jumbo sized periwinkle and a five-foot buddleia.

With three sacks of poor quality topsoil and a large pyrocantha he was happy that his purchases would serve his purpose.

He would make his garden look as neglected as possible. He would have to go without the water feature until the last minute. Perhaps an upturned dustbin lid would be appropriate. If it looked abandoned no one would try to spoil it.

That evening he scattered most of the seed over the soil, but kept some back to grow in the greenhouse in case anyone guessed what he was doing. He planted the buddleia in the centre of the, now flat, garden and put the periwinkle round the edges.

Finally he re-erected the remains of the wall, placing the pyrocantha up against it. He then set about convincing the other students that he had given up entirely and would no longer compete for marks. Only Zak knew that he hoped the poppies, cornflowers and grasses that he had sown would become a perfect wild flower garden in the summer. Even if he wasn't here to see it his would be the only insect friendly meadow on the course and, with luck, the other students would just think it was wasteland until it was too late.

Once Zak had said he had to go into hospital Bernard knew he could not continue on his own. His problem was that he had to convince his wife and that proved to be the hardest battle he had fought yet.

That weekend he got the reaction he had feared.

"What do you mean – you're not going back?"

"I'm staying home with you and Heather."

"Why – for goodness sake? Whatever's the matter?"

"I don't see the point. It isn't doing me any good. It's making me ill."

"Making YOU ill! Ned – it's the only chance we have of ever having any future.

"How can you be so selfish?"

"I'm going backwards. I can't explain." He shook his head from side to side.

"But Ned. There's no money. We can't afford for you to stop. They won't give you any dole if you don't finish the course. You'll have made yourself redundant. It's bad enough as it is," and she burst into tears. With Katie sobbing hysterically Heather began to whimper and then squall. Bernard couldn't stand it. He jumped off the boat and raced along the quay. Not only was he useless at earning a wage he was a useless husband and father. They would be better off without him.

He walked down to the beach and followed the seashore until he reached the town. It was night by the time he got to his old home. He had been walking for hours and his feet were sore.

Someone had changed the front door. It was no longer painted green; it was white with an oval glass panel. He felt nothing. He was cold and tired and his steps slowed. He didn't know why he had come or where he was going.

He sat on the wall of the vicarage garden and stared at the gravestones in the churchyard. It would have been better for everyone if he had died when Tim had wanted him to. What had he done to Katie? Just brought her unhappiness.

Light streamed past and the sound of laughter and goodbyes was carried on the air. Caught in the beam from the doorway, Bernard stood and blinked. The couple leaving the house walked past him and a voice called out, "Bernard? Is that you?" It was the vicar. Should he run or stay? The man was coming out of the door now and striding towards him.

"Bernard? Come inside – you look exhausted."

Bernard obeyed.

With a mug of hot chocolate and two slices of fruit cake inside him Bernard began to unburden himself. As soon as Katie's name was mentioned the vicar asked, "Does she know where you are?"

"No. I've got my phone but it is turned off."

"Let me see."

Bernard gave the vicar his mobile. There were three messages from Katie, each more desperate than the last. "She's number three." Bernard mumbled.

The vicar pressed a button and a voice answered immediately. "Ned – I'm worried about you. Where are you?"

"It's the Reverend Baines, Mrs Longman. He's here with me."

"How did he get there? It's nearly ten miles."

"I think he walked. Don't worry about him. He can stay the night. Would you like to speak to him?"

"Yes, please."

The vicar passed the phone to Bernard, who held it gingerly to his ear.

"Ned – I'm sorry. We need to work this out. Please come home. I love you."

"I love you too. It's all my fault. I don't know what to do."

"Tell Reverend Baines. He'll help us I'm sure."

"Yes. I will. I'm sorry I made you cry."

"Don't – or I'll start again. I'll see you tomorrow."

"Good night." Bernard handed the phone back to the vicar. "You don't need to contact anyone else?" he asked.

"No. I'm not due back until tomorrow night – but I still don't want to go." He began to tell the vicar about his experiences at the college. When he had finished the Reverend Baines patted him on the shoulder. "There must be a solution to this. How many more weeks to the end of term?"

"Two – with the exams."

"How do you manage those?"

"I'm allowed to tell the examiner the answers. There's another student who does it that way too."

"I expect the others resent that."

"Maybe. I had the best result in our group last term but that won't happen again."

"The course is modular, isn't it?"

"Whatever that means."

"Each third is marked separately. So by Easter you will have completed most of the course and been judged on it."

"I suppose so."

"I'll phone them on Monday – or are they there at weekends?"

"Someone is. They do day courses."

"Good. I'll find you some pyjamas and you get a good night's sleep. We'll sort this out tomorrow."

It was gone midday before Bernard awoke. He lay looking at the ceiling, not thinking, just waiting for instructions. A knock on the door elicited a quiet, "Come in."

"Would you like a cup of tea – or a shower?" The vicar was still in his church robes.

"Could I have a bath, please?"

"Of course. Here's a towel. The bathroom is next door. Come down when you are ready. Lunch is at two o'clock."

After lunch Bernard sat in one of the vicar's deep armchairs, sipping coffee. Conversation over the meal had been minimal. He felt detached from the world, his movements automatic, his brain shut down.

"I have had a talk with someone from your college," began the vicar. "They confirmed what I thought. You could do the final module at any time in the future."

"I don't have to go back?"

"Not once you have done those exams. Not with this group."

"But I could complete the course another time? I don't have to pay back the grant?"

"Not now."

"But I would still need to get a job."

"I'm afraid so."

"I wish I had never started."

"Bernard – you can do this. You may even be able to complete your course from home if you go back some weekends. They say you are an excellent student."

Bernard shook his head. "I'm no good for Katie and Heather."

"You need to discuss all this with your wife. I can take you back this afternoon. I'd like to help."

Katie was relieved to see Bernard arrive in the vicar's old Rover. After putting Heather in her cot she hugged him fiercely. "Don't ever do that again. I was worried sick."

Bernard bit his lip to stop himself crying.

"If I could have a word?" said the vicar.

"Of course. Thank you so much for taking care of him."

Once inside, the vicar outlined the problem and the possible solutions. The young couple sat holding hands, listening intently.

"Can you bear to go back for two weeks?" asked Katie.

"I think so. As long as I know I am coming home to you."

"I have arranged for Bernard to stay for his final weekend. If he does his tests then he would not have to do them among the people who were bothering him."

"I'm sorry. I have been so caught up with the baby I didn't understand. Please, Ned- cheer up. This does sound like the answer. Thank you vicar."

Once the vicar had left her husband still looked forlorn. She had a lot of thinking to do to resolve this situation.

When Heather cried she pretended to be busy.

"See if she's wet, darling, will you?" she called.

Bernard hesitated. "The baby," she continued, "She shouldn't be hungry. I'll get some water. Just see if she needs changing."

She watched as he picked up the whimpering child and held her up against his shoulder. An idea was forming in her head. If they could manage financially until August perhaps SHE could go back to work – but could she trust Ned to look after the baby?

Bernard and Zak worked hard to rehearse the answers to the questions they expected in the tests. Bernard left his garden alone and worked on the communal vegetable patch and in the orchards. He was silent in lectures and ignored during meal times. The atmosphere was uncomfortable but bearable.

The weekend was a revelation. A busload of disabled adults arrived on Saturday.

Bernard was informed that his ground-floor room was to be occupied so had to lock away his belongings and use the second floor room of another student.

The lecture rooms were transformed into art studios and craft rooms. Some people were studying creative writing, some photography and others art and craft.

Bernard felt energised by their enthusiasm and when he came to do his exams on the Sunday actually enjoyed telling the lecturer what he had learned.

It was on the Sunday evening when he forgot he was not in his own room and, seeing a key left in a drawer, unlocked it and found a diary.

The student who used the room, Graham Dowling, had filled pages with a large loopy scrawl, which Bernard could not read, but every now and then there was a cartoon with a bold heading. He recognised LONGMAN IS DEAD and FAIR PLAY and closed it quickly, feeling guilty. As he did so a photograph dropped out from between the pages. It was a picture of Bernard's garden with two figures sitting on the remains of the wall, giving the thumbs-up sign. Bernard put the photo in his pocket. He would show Zak tomorrow. It looked like evidence of who had trashed his garden.

Monday morning the usual students were in class. Bernard sat at the back of the room while the lecturer explained the day's activities. "Bernard," he called out, "While the others are sitting the first test – you are wanted in the greenhouses." All eyes turned to watch him as he left the room. He could feel their resentment like darts in his back.

He was sweating by the time he reached the corridor. Why the greenhouses? No one used them in the mornings.

When he arrived he understood. All the seedlings he had nurtured were scattered across the floor. Something, or someone had knocked them off the shelving and trampled on them. The tutor was waiting for him.

"We take this very seriously, Bernard. Did you do this?"

"Certainly not."

"Well yours are the only plants damaged. Do you know why it happened?"

"Some people don't like me. It could be them." He produced the photograph.

"Where did you get this?"

"In Graham Dowling's room. I had to stay there over the weekend and he had left the key in the lock of his desk drawer."

"Oh dear. Leave it with me. He's a sad young man. We hoped doing something creative would help him sort out his problems. He's in your group, isn't he?" He looked at the picture. "Do you know the two in the photo?" he said, "It's that pesky pair from room 21, the ones that don't know what the word, 'work' means. They are in Walls and Fences, but they might as well be in Beer and Barbeques. Their garden strips are just the other side of the greenhouses. They are almost identical, with loads of decking and water features bought from the nursery down the road. I'll be glad to be shot of them."

"I'm leaving on Wednesday," said Bernard.

"No. Don't do that. If we get rid of these you can come back next term."

"I've made up my mind. I need to be at home. I may finish the course another time."

"You must. You stand a good chance of getting a distinction."

"Watch my garden for me. There may be a surprise." Bernard smiled.

Although he was nervous of causing trouble he felt that he was, at last, winning the war.

The following morning Bernard was summoned to the Director's office.

"We have this term's CD for you, Bernard. Would you like us to make one for you next term?"

"Yes, please."

"There is a way you could finish the course this year."

"How?"

"Come back at weekends – and complete your exams in the summer holidays. I think Mr Brown has an offer for you."

Bernard had not noticed the other lecturer waiting silently in the corner.

"We'd like you to come and help our paraplegic students with their weekend activities. We'd pay your expenses. It would be a mixture of helping them physically and buddying them when they needed encouragement. Zak said you were a great help to him. You could keep an eye on your own garden and one of us could take you through the workbook."

"I'd have to come Saturday morning and go home Sunday evening?"

"Yes, of course. See what your wife thinks of the idea."

"We'd rather have seen the other three leave," continued the Director, "but we are supposed to be helping to try and rehabilitate people like them and we need to give them a chance to redeem themselves before we let them loose on the public."

"We won't let them think they have won," added Mr Brown. "Be certain of that, Bernard."

"Thanks. I must go and tell Zak. I owe him a lot."

Zak was sitting in their room, a picnic of quiche and salad and two glasses on the table in front of him.

"A farewell feast," he announced, "Salad and champagne – followed by raspberries and cream."

"Zak – you are the best," exclaimed Bernard. He was going to miss the company of his friend. He took a sip of the sparkling wine. If this was special he didn't know why. It was too sharp for his taste but he did not want to seem ungrateful.

"What did they say?"

"They asked me to come back at weekends to finish the course and help as well. They really think I can be useful."

"Useful? – You are unique! Come on, tuck in. I still have a practical test this afternoon."

"Is it OK for you to drink?"

"One glass won't do any harm. It might steady my nerves. When do you leave?"

"I was going tomorrow but I think I'll go tonight. I don't mind missing supper."

"Well, here's all my details, including my mobile number. Keep them safe and let me know how it all works out."

Bernard waited until Zak had left and then he set about packing to go home. Everyone had been so helpful. He could not imagine how his life was going to work out but the overwhelming feeling was one of relief, relief that he would no longer be among people who resented him and relief that the last few months could be salvaged and he could still get a certificate and a job. Somehow he had to convince Katie that the new plan would work.

12

Katie was in despair. She knew tiredness was making her irritable but she was worried sick about the bills she had been keeping from her husband. They had a sizeable overdraft and she had been buying things for the baby that they could not really afford. Now she was desperate to learn to drive but had no way of affording the lessons. She wouldn't ask her father. In fact, she fancied being taught by a lady driver.

Yet she had neither the funds nor the time. Baby Heather was alert, active, noisy and demanding. Katie's one afternoon a week at the clinic was her only relief from the constant one-to one. She felt scruffy, disorganised, inefficient and lonely and now Ned was throwing a wobbly just when she needed his support and understanding.

She rang her mother. She had to talk to someone who would know how she felt.

"Why didn't you tell me sooner?" Rose said, "I could have given you some money."

"No. We can't borrow from you. We must manage. I just can't see how at the moment."

"What do you want most?"

"Apart from getting control of our finances? I want to learn to drive."

"Yes – it's best to learn while you are young. I did, before I met your father."

"I never knew that. You don't drive now."

"I haven't done for over 30 years. I don't think Tim would like it. But if it would help you I can take a new test and start again."

"You mean, teach me to drive?"

"I don't see why not – but we'd have to buy you a car."

"That's put an end to that, then."

"Not necessarily – leave it with me. Did you say Bernard was coming home?"

"Yes."

"Then he might get a job in no time."

"I doubt it. He's in a very funny mood."

"We all have our ups and downs. How's Heather?"

"Beautiful and exhausting. I'll bring her to see you at Easter."

"Lovely. I may have some news by then. See you, love."

Katie looked round her little home. There was no way of making money while she was imprisoned here with her daughter. It was Ned who was the creative one.

Her skills lay elsewhere. She heard Heather cry out and her heart sank. How could she be so patient with older people and yet find her daughter's demands so irritating?

She was surprised by the depth of feeling she had for her daughter. Sometimes it seemed as if she had been cloned and the child was just a repetition of herself, while other times it felt as if, to make Heather, Katie had been drained of all individuality and life force.

Her love for her mother and her connection with Ned paled into insignificance compared with the overwhelming necessity to do anything to ensure the health and happiness of her tiny charge.

Yet here she was, actually contemplating leaving her daughter in the care of her husband. If it worked out it would bind the three of them together but if it didn't she would have destroyed the foundation of their marriage. If

Ned failed at this fundamental task the trust she had placed in him and the confidence he had built up over the last year would be irrevocably shattered.

She had to make sure he was as secure in the role that she was planning for him as any new parent could be and that would take time and patience. She knew he could be better than her at the mundane, repetitive tasks but how would he react to the unexpected?

There was no doubt he loved his daughter but could he ensure her safety? Maybe the fact that the baby could not talk was, while to Katie a disadvantage, to Ned something that allowed him to work on an instinctive level. Maybe he would not feel the doubts and frustrations that often assailed her. She hoped so.

Rose woke with a start. It was dark. Her husband had not come to bed, but that was not unusual. What was surprising was that something had disturbed her. She was notorious for sleeping through thunderstorms.

There were shouts from downstairs and then a flashing light penetrated the flimsy curtains. Jenny was barking and scratching at her kennel. She could hear voices – men calling Tim's name and her husband shouting back – calling out a warning.

She leapt out of bed and went through to the hall. As she peered through the window she could see shadowy figures round the edge of the lawn. Who could be surrounding their home at this time of night – and why?

There must have been a car in the lane with a bright searchlight shining along the side of the house, but it was unable to reach Tim's office.

"I'm not coming out," yelled Tim. "You've got the wrong man. You should be at the pub."

"We know everything," came a voice from the shadows, "Don't do anything stupid. We don't want anyone hurt."

"Someone will get hurt if you come any nearer," shouted Tim and, as if to emphasise the point, there was a loud explosion.

'My God. He's shooting at them,' thought Rose and raced back to the bedroom, grabbed her dressing gown, shoved her feet into her slippers and started down the stairs. As she did so she heard a muffled thump and the sound of ripping wood coming from the back of the house. Someone was smashing their way through the kitchen door.

"Police!" yelled a loud voice. "Keep back."

She knew where they would go next – through the lounge to Tim's office. She had to stop them before someone got killed.

She raced into the kitchen to be faced by a figure clothed all in black with a black helmet. The voice that emerged was female although the image was military.

"Mrs Smith, don't go any further. We need to talk to you – but we must stop your husband first. He's a danger to himself and others."

"Why are you here? What has he done?"

"I can't say, but keep calm. I'll wait here with you," and she gestured to Rose to sit at the table. Rose became aware of more banging and thumping, fighting and swearing but, thankfully, no more shooting.

It seemed as if they had taken Tim out through the front door because the noises died down and the policewoman took off her helmet and switched on the light. Two more black-suited figures came into the room, followed by a grey-haired man in a brown suit.

"Sorry about the door, Mrs Smith. We'll get it fixed for you – but we'll have to ask you to stay in here while we search the rest of the house."

"What for?"

"We have reason to believe your husband has been involved in illegal activities. We need to check for evidence. We'll be taking his computer and papers – we'll give you a receipt."

Rose sat, bemused, while they searched upstairs and then moved through the downstairs rooms, opening drawers, tapping walls, lifting carpets and even looking in the refrigerator. "Have you any other buildings, Mrs Smith?"

"Apart from the garage and the hen-house? Only the stables in the bottom field."

"Right – we are finished here, for now. Constable Hales will stay with you tonight. We'll be in touch."

"The room's only free for two nights. I've got visitors coming next week."

"You can't put them off?"

"No. We need the money."

The two officers exchanged glances. "Have you a separate account from your husband, Mrs Smith?"

"The money from the rooms is kept separate, yes – it's the only account I manage. Tim does everything else."

"I should take the money in cash from now on – just until we confirm that. Thank you, Mrs Smith."

The policewoman turned to Rose. "Shall I get us a cup of tea?"

"No. I'll do it – but I'm worried about the dog, Jenny." The dog's barking had turned into a croak.

"She'll calm down once they have gone."

"I'd like to bring her indoors but Tim wouldn't allow it."

"Why don't you leave her tonight and see how she is in the morning?"

Rose looked at the kitchen clock. It was 4 am. "It's morning now," she said. "I'd never sleep if I did go back to bed. What will happen to Tim?"

"He'll be charged with resisting arrest and the other offences they think he is guilty of."

"You can't tell me what they are?"

"Not until we've established how much you know."

"Will they let him out on bail?"

"I don't think so."

"I'd like to phone my daughter."

"Now?"

"No – later. I wouldn't disturb their sleep." Rose thought for a moment. "Is it anything to do with that shifty young man, André, who came to help us? Tim wouldn't say where he was staying."

"Have you been down to the stables recently?"

"No – but Bernard has. Goodness, if Tim is away the horses will need taking care of."

"Is there anyone else who could help?"

"Only George or the farmer over the road who looks after Tim's sheep."

"George?"

"Tim's brother. He owns the King's Head."

"Ah yes."

"Don't say he's involved, too?"

"Very much so."

"Oh dear, this is awful." But even as she said it Rose realised that, in a strange way, she was beginning to taste how it felt to be liberated. Without Tim in the house the rooms seemed lighter, she could breathe easier. After all if Tim really was a criminal he deserved to be put in prison and she deserved to have escaped from one.

Katie was washing when her mobile phone started to ring. Her hands in the suds, she felt inclined to leave it but it could be Ned, who was out with the baby, so she dried her hands and picked it up.

"Katie – are you busy?"

"No – Ned and Heather have gone to the park. What's up?"

"It's your father. He's been arrested."

Katie's first feeling of shock was replaced by a sense of satisfaction.

"I suppose he's been fighting."

"No, worse than that. He shot at a policeman. They came to ask him about stuff he had got from abroad – for the pub, I think. I'm not sure of the details."

Katie's hatred of her father suddenly seemed justified. Would he at last be seen for the monster he was? Why hadn't she realised that he was probably involved in some dodgy money-making scheme?

"I did wonder about his enthusiasm for fishing. We never saw the fish. Are you OK?"

"Yes. A policewoman stayed with me last night. Then today I had to give a statement. I've three guests coming tomorrow. I haven't time to worry about Tim."

"Do you need help with anything?"

"Poor Jenny is still shut in her kennel. I'll get her out next. I should be able to manage until after the weekend. Can you come then?"

"Of course. Ned has given up his course. We may have a few changes to tell you about. See you on Monday. Love you, mum."

She sat down heavily on the bed. What had her father been thinking of – to fire at the police? Whatever else he had done, that was the stupidest. He would go to prison, for sure – but would they let him out before then? Sometimes these things take months, or even years and in the meantime could she and Ned put into action the plan they had discussed?

Her two favourite people arrived then, glowing with fresh air and ready to eat. "It will have to be soup and sandwiches" she said, "Ned – will you make some sandwiches while I feed Heather?"

Bernard washed his hands carefully and began to prepare lunch. "We kept meeting people who wanted to see her," he said proudly.

"Something's happened, Ned."

"What?"

"My father has been arrested."

Bernard did not look as shocked as she had expected. "What for?"

"He shot at a policeman who was coming to see him about stuff belonging to the pub."

"Ah."

"What do you mean, Ah?"

"Had they been to the chalk pit?"

"What do you know about the chalk pit?" She was beginning to feel frightened.

"That's where the stuff was."

"Don't say you were involved." She felt as if she had swallowed a block of ice.

"No. I didn't know it wasn't his stuff."

"You saw it? What was it?"

"Boxes and bottles. I was just going for a walk. It was a long time ago. I didn't touch anything. What should I do?"

"Keep quiet. Wait and see. I expect the authorities found it. Just don't tell anyone."

"Oh Katie, could I go to prison?"

"Not if I have anything to do with it – not after what we decided."

"Heather! What will happen to Heather?"

"Nothing. You will stay home and look after her as we agreed. She loves being with you. You are calmer than I am. I'm going to start back at Evergreens sometime whatever happens – but Monday we must go to Lane's End and see if we can help mum."

When they got to the cottage Jenny was sitting across the back step. She wagged her tail when she saw Bernard and Katie but only moved when they pushed the buggy towards her. It was a beautiful sunny day and Rose waved at them from the open kitchen window. "The walkers have gone out with packed lunches," she said, "We've got the day to ourselves."

"I'll see to the ponies," offered Katie, "and arrange for Sheila from the farm to keep an eye on them. Anyone booked?"

"I cancelled them all," said Rose, "Luckily Tim had a chart on the wall of his office that the police left behind."

"Ooh – you went into the holy of holies, did you?"

"I had to – but all his papers and the computer have gone. It feels very empty."

"Heather's outside asleep in her buggy. I'll let Ned tell you all our news." Katie went out to the outhouse for some Wellington boots and left them together.

"What happened at college, Bernard?"

"I didn't get on with someone – but I'm going back weekends. There's a boy there who is brilliant at carpentry and we are going to make bird tables."

"What about Heather?"

"I'm going to be home all week and Katie is going to get weekends off."

"You won't mind caring for the baby?"

"I love it. She's such a happy thing. I love showing her things. It's the best way."

"What about when she starts crawling?"

"I've thought about that. I'm going to make extra sides for the boat so there is no danger of her falling over – but I watch her all the time. There's nothing to worry about."

When Katie returned from the stables, looking pale, Rose stammered, "I'm sorry, darling, I didn't think."

"Don't worry, mum – I offered. I'm not scared of them any more. I just don't want to ride them. Sheila will come for them tomorrow. It's all sorted. What do you think of our plans?"

"If you can get back to the place you liked it should work well. Look at them now."

The two women watched as Bernard cuddled Heather in his arms. The baby stared at him as he pulled faces. They seemed in a world of their own.

"Now tell me everything that happened here," said Katie, "What made him shoot?"

"He only fired into the air. He didn't hit anyone. He was angry."

"Poor, mum, weren't you frightened?"

"It was like watching a film," Rose shuddered. "What made him like that, Katie? Was it my fault? We seemed OK until that French boy arrived. I don't think he was really French. He was staying in the huts at the chalk pit – and I don't think he was the only one. Tim suddenly got all twitchy and nervous. I didn't feel safe but I just carried on."

"But he smuggled goods before he started on illegal immigrants?"

"Oh yes, thanks to George. I think they thought it was fun – getting cheap drink and cigarettes for the pub and hiding them in the caves."

Rose saw Katie glance over to see if he had overheard but his attention was elsewhere. "Anyway," she continued, "They have been caught now and Pat and I have to carry on without them. In a way it will be easier and I'll be able to see more of you all, won't I?"

Katie did not share her mother's optimism. She had made sure her husband copied the correct procedures for feeding and bathing their daughter. She had emphasised the dangers of leaving her unattended. Yet still she felt unsure whether she was doing the right thing. Still, she would not have to worry about her mother. She looked more at peace than she had for months.

13

The summer was warm and the young family spent time together on the beach. Then, when it got busy with visitors, Katie would look after Heather while Bernard went for a swim.

The college was closing for a fortnight in August. Bernard would not be required for three weekends. He was happy he could spend the time with Katie and Heather but envious of the holidays the others were anticipating.

It was Simon Clark who came up with a solution.

"Why don't you bring the family here, Bernard? You could stay at the gatehouse, show them the grounds and keep an eye on the place at the same time."

"I don't know what Katie would say. Heather has only been as far as Lane's End."

"Well, a few days would do. I'll square it with the director. You wouldn't have to go inside the college, just keep an eye on the greenhouses."

Bernard remembered the last time he had been asked to guard a site. This would be different. Having Heather with him would make it their first holiday together. He hadn't realised how separate the two sides of his life had become. This would give him an opportunity to show Katie what he had been doing. The summer meadow still looked wonderful and the woods and hills nearby would be a change from the harbour. The village was a fair walk but once they had stocked up they were away from traffic – yet near the garden centre with its pet department and coffee shop.

"Oh, Ned. I wish you'd said sooner. I'm going to start at Evergreens in three weeks."

"Please, Katie. We haven't had a holiday."

"We've been on the beach." She looked at his eager face and relented.

"Did you ask what they'd charge?"

"Nothing. It would be free."

"I suppose I could do with a change. It would be a bit of a palava with a baby and everything. OK We'll do it – just for a long weekend – Thursday to Tuesday – and it better be fine weather."

Her husband's features relaxed into the warm, innocent smile that she loved. It was so easy to make him happy. She hadn't taken enough interest in his achievements since Heather was born – and it did seem like the ideal place for a break.

He didn't realise Heather was too young to appreciate all he wanted to show them – but if she was starting work in September she would like something fresh and new to remember. Goodness only knows when they would get another holiday.

The gatehouse was usually rented out to temporary staff. College security was managed by an outside company who had alarms in the building. All Bernard would have to do was take in any post and keep an eye on the grounds.

"All the gardens have been judged but you could water the greenhouses," Mr Clark told Bernard. Katie had asked him to ensure that the cottage contained a cot and, if possible, to look inside to see if it was clean. Bernard was sure she would be satisfied.

When they arrived on the Thursday afternoon she was pleasantly surprised. It was more spacious even than Lane's End and the kitchen equipment was up to date.

The digital television had channels they had never seen and there was also a hi-fi with a collection of CDs.

"Look at all this music, Ned," she exclaimed, "classical, country, pop – there's everything from Frank Sinatra to Ronan Keating."

Bernard didn't really like music. He found modern tunes too loud, he couldn't always hear the words and most classical music made him sad. If he had to choose he would have said he enjoyed marches – but only out in the open air – not on a record.

"I'll just go and have a look round," he said and went out through the back door to the tiny walled garden. The place was a sun-trap – with wisteria and clematis climbing up every surface, a slabbed patio and a small lawn surrounded by bushes. The narrow path took him to a wooden gate that led onto the gravel drive that encircled the grounds.

He passed the allotments that were used to provide vegetables for the college and reached the garden strips that the students had designed. Half of them had been dug over ready for the new intake but the other half still showed the remains of last year's efforts. Buttercups had invaded many of the strips and the grassy walkways between them were looking shaggy.

Bernard found his strip. The grass had seeded and the poppies were almost finished but there were still insects flying about. The blue periwinkle had formed a wild, low hedge round the meadow and the butterfly bush stood proud and purple in the centre.

He walked on to the greenhouses. They were locked and he hadn't brought the keys.

He'd been told where they were in the lodge but hadn't thought to pick them up. He would check them out tomorrow. He tried the outside tap and water spurted out. The house looked strangely empty. It was time to return to his family.

They settled into a comfortable routine. Each morning Bernard would check the grounds while Katie and Heather stayed in the house and garden. After an early lunch they would go for a walk.

They started with the garden centre, then on Saturday they went to the village. It was there that they found leaflets on waymarked trails – one along the river and another to a ruined castle.

"We'll take a picnic tomorrow and do one. Which would you prefer?" asked Katie.

Bernard looked at the pictures. The river had illustrations of flowers and trees but the castle had the greater appeal. "That one," he said.

As it turned out it suited them both as the sandy pathway led them upward through thick woodland. Bernard pushed the buggy while Katie bounced along by his side, marvelling at the light and shade, the fungi, the birdsong and the overwhelming beauty of the place. When they came out of the trees and saw the grassy hillock topped by the stone tower it seemed like a significant moment.

The sky was blue, the air still and the grass by the shade of the wall made a perfect spot for their picnic.

Bernard spread a blanket on the ground and took Heather out of her buggy. He placed her down and flopped into the space beside her. Katie sat on her other side and began to open the picnic bag.

He stretched out on his back and turned towards the wriggling child. With his hands under her armpits he lifted her up, calling out, "Heather's flying – look Katie – she's flying."

"Don't get her too excited, she's about to have her lunch." Katie's smile belied her tone.

Heather was waving her arms and legs as if she was swimming in the air. He let her down onto his chest. "Mummy wants you now." He let her reach for his nose and pretended to be hurt.

Katie passed the flask and sandwiches to him and he handed her their daughter. Then he propped himself up on one elbow to watch her feed.

The sight of the two of them so close had always seemed magical to him. He wondered if his mother had breast-fed him. He liked to think that she had. Her presence had always calmed him.

Katie shifted slightly. "Can you sit with your back against mine, please, Ned. Just till we finish."

After lunch they took pictures of each other and the castle. It had lost one side and there were no stairs so they couldn't reach the window. Katie read out the historical information on the plaque and Bernard tried to imagine the people who might have lived there. "Were they knights?" he asked.

"I don't think so. It was before that. I think they wore leather clothes and shot bows and arrows. I'm sorry, Ned, I'm not very good at history."

"It feels like somewhere important. We are high up."

"I guess that's why they built it here – so that they could see all round."

Bernard lifted Heather up in his arms. "Look, Heather – see all the sheep and the little house – look – there's a train," and although they were too far away they all waved.

It stayed dry until the Tuesday morning when Katie rang for a taxi to take them to the station.

Bernard was content. He had shown Katie his garden and she had told him how proud she was that he had been so imaginative.

"When Heather starts school you could be a full-time gardener," she said. "Perhaps you could work for someone rich and important."

"I wouldn't mind as long as I could grow things."

"Who does your friend Zak work for?"

"The council, I think. He orders stuff and works out prices."

"That sounds boring."

"I don't think so. He gets to choose plants."

"You'd like to do that, wouldn't you?"

"Yes – but I'm happy looking after Heather."

He locked the door and put the key back through the letter box. As he put the folded buggy into the boot of the taxi Katie hitched the baby onto her shoulder and looked back.

"It's been really lovely, Ned. I wonder if we'll ever have a place as nice as that."

One afternoon an unexpected visitor arrived at the houseboat. Bernard had Heather on a rug on the floor, surrounded by her favourite toys. He was sitting on the bed, sketching a design for a bird house, when an educated voice called out, "Hallo – Anybody there?"

"Yes," replied Bernard, "Who is it?"

"Barbara Phillips from Social Services. You don't know me. Can I come in?"

Bernard stepped over the baby and opened the door.

"Ah – indoors, I see."

Bernard waited for her to explain herself.

"I have just come to see baby Heather," she said. "My, she's a big girl, isn't she?"

"I take her to the clinic regularly." Bernard was beginning to feel alarmed. Why should a stranger, an official stranger at that, want to see their daughter? Was there some disease going round?

"Oh I know. Her weight and progress are fine."

"Why did you come to see her then?"

"We just like to check on the home environment. The boat doesn't move, does it?"

"No – but it's quite safe."

"And you look after Heather while your wife works?"

"She's home in between shifts and at weekends. We care for the baby together."

"I'm sure. This is all the room you have? It must be difficult to keep her amused. I notice you do not have books or games to hand."

"No – but I do take Heather out. We have been to the shops this morning."

The stranger was opening and closing doors. "There's no bathroom?"

"Only the shower, there's water and electricity." Bernard switched on the light to show her. He was getting annoyed.

He didn't like anyone criticising their home. Katie had made real improvements since Eliza had left it to them and now this stranger was sneering at the place they both loved.

"Well, thank you, Mr Longman. I see she has a cut on her finger. How did that happen?"

Bernard coloured. Katie had remarked as she left for work, "Heather has been scratching her face. Her nails are getting too long. We must cut them."

He'd tried to do it the same way he had seen her, but Heather had wriggled at the wrong moment and the scissors had slipped. The cut wasn't covered. He had cleaned it and it had dried but it must have opened up again and there was blood on her sleepsuit.

"I was cutting her nails. Katie usually does it."

"I see. Well, I think I have seen enough. Thank you, Mr Longman. I'll see myself out."

Bernard was uneasy. The visit had been unannounced and cool. Perhaps Katie could find out what the reason was.

He shook Heather's rattle and made her giggle and then, impulsively, picked her up and hugged her to him. It was at times like this that he wished he were not alone.

Tim's trial was to be in November. Katie was at full stretch working all week and trying to support her mother at weekends. Luckily Rose had completed five driving lessons and passed both parts of the test. Katie was amazed at the transformation in her mother. She seemed energised – almost blooming. She smiled to herself as she hurried along the corridor at Evergreens.

Her thoughts were interrupted by a call from the manageress. "There's someone to see you, Katie – in my office."

Katie hurried down the stairs. No one ever came to see her at work. Had something happened to her family?

The woman waiting in the office was unfamiliar. She was a little older than Katie, with untidy brown hair and a navy, belted jacket. She didn't look like a police officer.

"Mrs Longman?" She held out a hand. Katie shook it automatically.

"I'm from Social Services. My name's Barbara."

"What's happened?"

"I'm here about your husband."

Katie felt a flood of alarm. "Why? Is he all right?"

"Yes. He's looking after your daughter while you are at work, isn't he?"

"Don't tell me something has happened to Heather?" She could feel her heart beating faster. Why was the woman standing so still?

"She's fine – but I understand Mr Longman cannot read or write. How does he manage if he cannot read instructions?"

Katie began to relax. Thank goodness. They were just being careful.

"He's learnt by watching me. He's very gentle and deliberate." She smiled at the thought.

"He didn't finish his course. Why was that?"

"A clash of personalities, I believe."

"And your father – he's in jail?"

"Yes – but that's nothing to do with us." Once again she wondered where this questioning was heading.

"We'd like to do an extended visit to the houseboat with you and your husband there. Would that be possible?"

"I suppose so. I can take a day's leave."

"Good. We'll send you a date. Thank you, Mrs Longman."

Katie felt she had been dismissed. She needed to talk to her mother, soon.

As soon as she got the call Rose made up her mind to go to the houseboat. This sounded serious enough to make her leave her guests alone for the evening. She had changed the insurance for Tim's van and as soon as she had washed up the supper things she drove straight to the harbour.

Bernard was putting Heather to bed in her carrycot. "I've nearly got the side finished for the bunk," he said, proudly. "Then she can sleep there. She's growing so fast."

"How are you fixing it?"

"It will drop down on hinges and the top will have hooks and bolts so that they can't be unfastened when she learns to stand up."

"That's great, Bernard."

"I had a visitor."

"You, too?" She said it before she could stop herself but he didn't notice.

"She asked about Heather and said we didn't have many books on show."

It was true, thought Rose – but babies didn't need books – and if they could see Bernard acting out the noises of animals or turning his big, soft hands into butterflies or ducks or doors to hide behind – they would realise he had qualities that made him a perfect child- minder.

"Did you tell her you told stories from memory and didn't need books?"

"No. I just thought she meant it was tidy."

"When is Katie home?"

"About now." He was right. Katie burst into the cabin, breathing heavily.

"I saw the van. Thanks for coming, mum."

Bernard pulled the curtain round the sleeping baby. "Did you want some supper?" he asked.

"Just a coffee, please. Ned, we need to talk."

"Bernard's had a visitor."

"What, already?"

"She didn't stay long. She looked at the boat and asked about Heather."

"How dare she come without asking us. It shouldn't be allowed!"

"Why? What's wrong?"

"I had a visitor, too – from social services. They want to see how we take care of Heather. I don't like it. Anyone would think we were unfit parents."

Bernard's face showed he had caught the distress in her voice. "What can we do?"

"You just have to show them how efficient you are," said Rose. "Anyone can see how healthy and happy Heather is. You both look after her beautifully."

Bernard made them each a coffee and they tried to anticipate what the social workers might be looking for.

"The deck is safe," said Katie. "Down here is cramped but clean. We can get some cloth books and hang up a mobile. I really don't see how we can do any more."

"Nor do I, darling. I thought they were used to the idea of men looking after babies these days."

"When you think of the people they do let keep babies – they can't take her away from us, can they?"

"Shsh. Don't suggest it," said Rose. "It couldn't happen."

But Katie wasn't so sure. How could she protect Bernard from these people? She knew instinctively that their very presence would make him behave differently, especially if he thought they were threatening his way of life.

The 'inspection,' was set for ten days time and she scrubbed and cleaned, checked and rechecked, rehearsed everything that she could with her husband and spent nights tossing and turning, growing ever more frantic with worry.

When the day came Heather was obviously teething. Bernard had scraped and cut up some carrots for her to munch on but she was still wailing when the social worker arrived.

"You just carry on as normal," she said – but they couldn't. Normally Bernard would have put the child in her buggy and wheeled her along the quayside but it was extremely hot and he wasn't sure that was allowed. Katie and he seemed to be tripping up over each other. It was unusual for them to be together in the mornings and Bernard's routine was upset.

Katie tried to get Heather to drink while Bernard sat and watched. When she saw the lady making notes she shoved Heather at Bernard and rushed on deck. Bernard did not know whether to follow her or stay below.

He soothed the infant, strapped her into her bouncy chair and then, assuming the social worker was a responsible adult – went up to calm his wife.

"What are you doing here?" she hissed. "Stay with Heather."

Bewildered and upset he returned to the cabin. He usually started to make Heather lunch – a jar of baby food, followed by a yoghurt, but should he offer their guest some refreshment first? Racked by indecision he filled the kettle and opened the fridge.

"Would you like a drink?" he asked.

"Just forget I'm here. I'll get some water when I'm thirsty."

He washed his hands and tipped Heather's food into a dish.

He usually fed her from the jar, after taking the chill off in the microwave, but it seemed wrong, somehow, when someone was watching. Sitting the baby on his lap, with the plate on the bench, he began to offer her the food. Unfortunately she waved her arms and legs and sent the spoon and dish flying. Now what was he to do?

Normally he would place her in her carrycot while he cleaned up and made some more lunch. Often he gave her a bottle instead of food and left the meal until later. Should he open another jar – or would a mashed banana suffice? He was undecided.

He wanted to ask Katie - she was here, after all, but he didn't dare. He hesitated just long enough for his wife to come in and see the situation for herself. Briskly she took charge, warming a second jar and putting Heather back in her chair while she sat on the floor facing her. Bernard did not know whether to get the bottle ready or not.

Had he relinquished control or should he carry on? Which of them was going to change her and put her down? He felt useless and clumsy.

Katie seemed to sense what he was going through. "I'll wash these things up, darling," she said, "and you can see to her."

Bernard picked up the sleepy child and placed her on the bunk. Then he realised he would usually get everything ready before he put her down. He had to hold her over one shoulder while he got the changing mat and nappy bags.

Katie brought him some water and cotton wool and cream and he proceeded to clean up his daughter. He felt unusually embarrassed and wished their visitor would leave.

Once Heather was clean and resting in her cot Katie faced the social worker. "What else would you like to see?" she asked – with a sharp edge to her voice.

"I just have a few questions," replied the lady and turning to Bernard she asked, "Bernard – who is the Prime Minister?"

"What the hell has that to do with anything?" screeched Katie, a well of black hatred flooding through her. She reached out to the cupboard door and snatched at the tea cloth. Twisting it in her hands she approached the visitor.

The social worker looked up, surprised. "I only wanted to be sure…" she began.

"Sure! – sure of what – sure we can't look after our baby or sure we don't fit into some pre-conceived ideal? How would you like someone poking and prying into your private life, asking your family stupid questions to try and catch them out? That's enough – get out, get out before I throttle you!" She was wringing the cloth with vicious strength.

The social worker needed no more telling. She closed her notebook, shoved it into her bag and turned to leave.

"You'll hear from us," she stuttered as she fled down the gangplank. Katie stood watching her, shaking with anger and when Bernard came over to hug her she burst into tears. "I couldn't help it," she sobbed, "I felt like killing her. Oh, Ned. What have I done?"

"Nothing. You didn't touch her. It will be all right."

"I don't think so. I wish we could all run away."

"Don't cry, Katie. You'll think of a plan. You always do."

She smiled at him through her tears. "Thanks, darling." He was right. Already an idea was forming in her brain.

If 'They' were going to argue that Bernard was not fit to look after his daughter she would need evidence to the contrary. She would need witnesses to prove he was capable. She began to list those people she could ask – the vicar, the headmistress, someone from college. She'd have to talk to the mothers at the clinic – or would that be where the doubts about him first surfaced? Who had started this investigation and why?

"Ned, did anything happen last time you were at the clinic? How were the other mothers?"

"They don't say much to me. They talk to each other."

"What about?"

"About the babies. Some of them are not growing as well as Heather. The nurse was very pleased with us."

Katie tried to visualise the scene. Surely it could not be envy that had prompted someone to call out the authorities?

Bernard was watching her, a strange look on his face, and she realised she hadn't spoken to him for some time. "I'm fine, now, Ned," she murmured, "Ham salad for lunch?"

14

The official letter came a week later. Heather was to be placed with foster parents as, *conditions at her present address were not sufficiently stimulating, and it was felt her welfare could be compromised.* They had seven days to send in any written submission but *unless circumstances change* their daughter would be collected on November 9th.

"Two days after the trial," screeched Katie. "It's a conspiracy. They haven't even spelt out what they think is wrong. How can we fight this!"

Bernard looked on, helpless, while she fumed. A cloud of misery had settled over him in the intervening days. At home he had been an automaton – doing what was necessary but feeling nothing except a huge emptiness.

At college he had come alive. Being among people so much worse off than himself, yet positive and willing to learn was exciting and rewarding. He demonstrated his collage and mosaic work and learned more about carpentry and metalwork.

On Saturday evenings he sat with a new, young tutor who had introduced himself as John Novak. He had his hair tied back in a pony-tail and wore a baggy brown smock that almost hid the fact that he had only one arm.

"You'd never guess I'm in charge of Health and Safety," he joked. "I had an argument with a chain saw and the chain saw won."

John had been a tree surgeon and taught Bernard about trimming, pruning and coppicing as well as where to source different trees. They went slowly through the workbook, with the tutor letting Bernard answer those questions he could and discussing the others. Bernard found him patient and amusing although he felt daunted by the questions on costing and administration.

"You'll probably never need all this," John told him. "Just remember the bits you enjoy." Bernard felt guilty. Should he be enjoying anything when Katie was obviously distressed about the possibility of losing their child? He couldn't believe anyone would take Heather from them. They would realise it was a mistake and it would all come right.

At least here at college he could get a good night's sleep.

The strain of coping with an increasingly energetic child, Heather was crawling now, and an emotional and outraged wife, was beginning to tell. Katie no longer seemed in control, of herself or of events.

He could not bear to see her so unhappy and could not even comfort her at night.

Heather seemed to pick up on the atmosphere on the boat. When her mother was home she would refuse to eat and if she tried to put her to sleep in the afternoon she would rattle the bars of her cot like a cage and scream to be let out.

Katie could stay on the boat no longer. Without waiting for her mother to pick them up she grabbed Heather and a bag of necessities and jumped on the bus. She was wearing old jeans, a ragged shirt and a thick sweater. Her hair had not been cut for weeks and she wore no makeup. She didn't care how other people viewed her, now.

She clambered off the bus, struggling with the bag and child and then began the long walk up the hill. By the time she reached Lane's End her back ached and she was panting with the effort. She put Heather down on the settee and flopped next to her.

"What were you thinking of, girl?" scolded her mother as Heather began to cry.

"I don't know. I can't think any more. They have ruined everything."

"Let me just get Heather settled and then you can tell me all about it." Rose picked up the restless child and took her into the kitchen. When they returned Heather was sucking happily on a bottle.

"I'll go to the papers," growled Katie. "That's what I'll do. I'll force them to say why we can't look after her. Then we can refute what they say. I just don't know what will make them change their minds."

"Let's get your father sorted first," Rose argued, "Then if they take Heather away you can use all your energies to make a case to have her back. At the moment you don't make a very good impression."

Heather had finished drinking and was happily crawling over Jenny who had settled into life in the household. Katie ran her fingers through her hair as she watched her daughter. Her eyes filled with tears. "I may never get her back. I'm a dreadful mother, aren't I?"

"No. You are doing your best. Have you thought of getting legal advice?"

"We couldn't afford it, mum."

"When Tim's trial is over we'll look into it."

Her husband was sentenced to a minimum of ten years. Rose felt as if an elastic band that had been stretched taught was suddenly relaxed. The joy of her freedom was tempered, however, with the thought of the damage the news would do to the young couple.

Details of Heather's grandfather's activities and violence were now in the public domain and Katie had admitted she had almost strangled the social worker who had come to check on the baby. If only they could be made to detail their objections so that the family could prove them wrong. Why did everything have to be conducted in secret?

Bernard would be there when they came to take his daughter away. She would have to make sure he was not alone. Although she had never known him to be violent she didn't know how he would react.

In the event, the little boat was crowded that day. Katie had taken legal advice and the lawyer, Katie, Bernard and Rose were there to greet the car load of people who came to collect Heather. The police waited on the quay and curious bystanders were kept well back.

She did not go quietly. In spite of Katie telling her she was going for a visit and Bernard making sure she had her favourite fluffy bunny, Heather could feel the tension in the air. She kicked and screamed as the social worker tried to coax her into the child seat and Rose could still hear her wailing long after the vehicle had driven away. Katie was shaking and sobbing in Bernard's arms. "What will this do to her?" she asked over and over again.

"It could be temporary, Mrs Longman. The family she is going to have other children. They will look after her well. We'll soon get her back," soothed the lawyer

"Did you get them to declare their reasons?" asked Rose.

"They promised me a copy of the complete assessment," replied the lawyer. Turning to Bernard he continued, "Your job is to carry on as normally as possible. We must find witnesses who have had children, people who can vouch for your character and, Katie, you need people who can show how caring you are. If we find enough evidence it should outweigh the word of one person. Only if that doesn't work do we go to the press. Going public sometimes does more harm than good."

Rose stayed the night on the boat sleeping fitfully in Heather's bunk. Katie, exhausted, slept so soundly she was late for work the next day.

Once she had left Rose helped Bernard to tidy up and then sat him down. Holding his head in her hands to hold his attention she began, "Bernard, you mustn't let this destroy you."

"What can I do, Rose?"

"You must trust the lawyer to sort it out."

"Will we get Heather back?"

"I'm sure you will, but you need to fill your days. How about coming to work for me?"

Bernard opened his mouth and closed it again. Rose imagined he was picturing Lane's End cottage in his head, wondering if he could bear to return to somewhere that held such mixed memories for him.

"Tim won't be coming back," she said. "I'm going to see the lawyer about a divorce."

Bernard frowned. "You would have to pay me?"

"Yes, eventually, to make it official, but I meant just until you get Heather back. It might only be a few weeks."

"I could still go to the college at weekends?"

"Yes, of course. I'm sure they really appreciate you."

"I wouldn't have to sleep at the cottage, would I?" The bathroom fan still unsettled him and he wanted to be with Katie as much as possible.

"No. I feel quite safe with Jenny to protect me. Katie can't keep coming backwards and forwards to Evergreens from there. She needs some time to get over this. See what she says."

Katie did not come home until late. She had spent the afternoon with their lawyer. They had the list of objections the social worker had made from the apparent mental incapacity of Bernard to the antagonistic attitude of Katie. The Protection Order meant there was a likelihood that Heather would be put up for adoption.

"She said you were clumsy and uncoordinated, and that leaving Heather in your care was like leaving her with another child." said Katie, "Didn't they realise you'd be nervous? Normally you are fine. Oh, it's so unfair!"

"I'm sorry, Katie." Bernard was shaken to hear his problems spelt out so starkly.

"They said I was unpredictable and that you relied on me too much. That's because I took over, didn't I?"

"I don't remember."

"She didn't like the boat – said it was not child-friendly – what does she know?"

"Don't tell me any more."

"I know it hurts, darling – but we need to know what we are dealing with. There are other boats with children on, aren't there? We must find them."

"Rose had an idea." He couldn't wait any longer to give her the news.

"What?"

"She wants me to help her – just while Heather is away."

"Thank goodness for my mum – and she said she'd teach me to drive. All we need now is a load of witnesses and a windfall and we'll be back on track."

"Why do you want wind?"

"Oh, Ned. Sometimes I just get tired of explaining." She burst into angry tears.

Rose dressed carefully for her prison visit.

She would have to decide what to do about Tim. She did not want him to return. She had tried to imagine what life would be like if he did come back but all her respect for him had gone.

She could not envisage doing his bidding as she had before – yet she could still remember the fear she felt when he lost his temper. She would have to stifle the pity she felt for him when she saw him in jail and do what was best for herself, Katie and Heather. He must understand that when his sentence was over he could not return.

It was her cottage, her land and her decision.

Yet she needed to convince him that she did not hate him. As soon as she could she would go ahead with the divorce – but first she wanted to make sure she could help Katie and for that she needed money.

"They have still frozen your account," she complained to Tim. "The only way I can manage is to lease the stables."

"But what about the horses? My family have always had horses. The manure is good for the land."

"But Tim, no one wants to ride them any more. They are getting old and costing us money. Without you to look after them I just can't manage. Will you let me sell them – and the sheep? I can't take care of it all by myself."

"Can't you ask that useless lump?"

"Bernard? He has no idea with animals. Will you agree?"

"Oh, sell them if you must. Soon there'll be nothing left to come home to. How's Jenny?"

"She pined at first, but Katie got her eating. I may get geese. The dog would enjoy bossing them."

Tim gave a bitter laugh, "I'd like to see that."

"What made you do it, Tim?"

"The booze or the people?"

"Both."

"George got me involved, bringing in drink and cigarettes for him to sell in the pub. Then we realised there was more money in immigrants."

"They said at the trial that you used the chalk pit."

"Yes. André stayed there. If we hadn't started on people we'd have been OK."

"I'm sorry, Tim."

"Oh don't fuss, woman."

Rose closed her lips together. What else was there to say? She watched her husband's eyes flick round the room and onto the clock on the wall. What else could she ask him?

"How's the food, Tim?"

Tim snorted. "Terrible. You'd make a better job of it. That's something I do miss."

'And you'll miss it for ever,' thought Rose, but she had what she wanted, enough to put her plan into action.

Before she went to see Tim again she would write him a letter. It was the only way she could confront him with the decision she had made. She didn't want to discuss it. She was afraid he would threaten her or, worse still, plead to be given another chance.

She acknowledged that they had been together for over twenty years but the togetherness had been a sham. She had been a housekeeper – not a wife. She didn't even like the man any more and the possibilities that were opening up before her were too precious to lose.

Yet she could say none of this to his face. She would have to blame his secrecy and violence. She would have to write that she no longer trusted him – that she could not live with a criminal. It would have to be **her** fault that the divorce was necessary, her weakness, her shame. Whatever he said she would be resolute. She would not let him hurt her now.

Bernard was robotic. He and Rose had collected the cherry tree from the college in the van and planted it near the garage so that it could be seen from the kitchen window. However, it did not look well.

Bernard felt it was an omen. If that died, nothing would go right. Rose asked if he wanted to bury his mother's ashes under the tree but he decided against it.

He found their presence comforting. She was happy to let him keep them on a shelf in the little bedroom. During the week he would perform every task she set him and at the weekend he would travel back to the college while Katie stayed with her mother.

Rose was worried about her daughter. It was like living with a volcano. She could sense the rage and impotence boiling inside her and only hoped her proposition would lead to a calming down, rather than an explosion.

Christmas was horrible. The three of them went to church in the morning, each searching for peace, but the emphasis on the baby Jesus only emphasised their loss. After lunch Katie shut herself in the bedroom and Bernard went for a walk. They had been promised that their gifts would be given to Heather but it had been decided that a visit would be too disruptive. Rose suspected that the fact that Heather's grandfather was in jail had something to do with the decision. The animals had been sold and she had seen the lawyer about a divorce.

She spent the next couple of weeks searching for the thing that she hoped would bring back a sense of purpose to her daughter's life. The driving lessons had continued and Rose thought she was ready for her own car.

Katie's birthday was in the week but when Rose collected her from the houseboat the Saturday before she asked casually, "Do you want to drive?"

"Yes, I suppose so. The van knows the way."

"You sound tired, love."

"No more than usual. I hate this stupid boat. If it wasn't for that I think we'd still have Heather."

"I'm glad you don't blame Bernard."

"Oh, I do, for not wanting to fight. If I knew where she was I'd get her back."

"You know that wouldn't be wise."

"I feel so useless, mum." Katie's shoulders slumped.

"Don't. It's your birthday on Wednesday – look on it as a new beginning."

"And it's Heather's the following month – and she won't be with us," she snapped.

They reached Lane's End and had to park by the garage as a little yellow car was taking up the space by the wall.

"Must be walkers," muttered Katie as she approached it.

"No," said Rose, "It's a present. It's for you – your birthday present. I know it's not new but I've had it checked over and it's only done twelve thousand miles. Do you like it?"

Katie stared at it in amazement.

"Mum, it's beautiful. It's a funny shape – nice and high for Ned – how on earth could you afford it?"

"I've sold all the animals. Come and have a cup of tea, then we'll try it out."

"Now I'll have to pass my test." A flicker of delight crossed her drawn features.

"It's booked, isn't it?"

"Yes, I've got the theory next week."

"You'll be fine."

She had watched, impotent, as the people she loved most in the world had suffered the loss of their child. To Bernard, whose obedience to authority was total, it was a temporary setback, a mistake that their lawyer could sort out as soon as possible. He missed their daughter greatly but he lived in the present and felt Katie's pain more keenly than his own.

In contrast Katie was outraged. Rose knew that the fact that her daughter had been stolen from her was with her every second of every day. It coloured all her words and actions. She suspected that it made her less patient with the residents at Evergreens. It certainly made her less sympathetic to her husband. Misery had a way of seeping into every nook and cranny of someone's life and it was a real achievement, she thought, that at last she had made her daughter smile.

Rose was at the hairdresser's, leafing through one of the many 'True Life Story' magazines when she stopped at a half page photograph of a near-naked girl. The teenager was wearing a skimpy bikini. Her dark hair was wet and draped over one eye and she was posed like a mermaid on the sea shore.

Can the sea hide more dangers than jellyfish? ran the headline. Underneath the picture the text continued: *Seaside Sandra is a warning to girls who swim off her local beach. She urges them to beware of men who use the sea to cover unwanted sexual advances.*

'I was swimming in the sea after school last summer when he swam underwater and came up on me before I knew he was there. He was big and strong and he pulled my top away from my body and stroked my boobs. You don't expect people to be under the water, do you? You don't think you are going to get groped by a stranger under the sea.

'He didn't say anything but I thought I recognised him. I had seen him by the houseboats on the river. I don't go that way any more and I'm afraid to go in the sea.'

Have you been assaulted when you were swimming? Did you tell anyone? How can we stop this menace? If you wish to tell your story write to us at....

Rose shivered. The description sounded rather like her son-in-law. The girl did not say when or where the assault was supposed to have taken place but the picture was of their local beach. She recognised the buildings in the background.

Rose did not for a moment believe Bernard was guilty but how could anyone defend themselves against an accusation like that? What was the girl's motive? Was she thoughtlessly looking for publicity or did she have something against Bernard?

Had someone else frightened her? How could Rose find out without alarming Bernard or upsetting Katie further? This was an extra problem they could do without.

She looked round the salon to see if anyone was watching and then slipped the magazine into her bag. Perhaps she had jumped to the wrong conclusion. There were other houseboats along the coast. Maybe she had nothing to worry about.

They approached Katie first. She was leaving Evergreens to return to the houseboat when a young woman came up to her and said, politely, "Mrs Longman – are you aware of the accusations against your husband?"

"Ned? No. Ned has done nothing wrong."

"Does he often swim in the sea?"

"Yes – but not in this weather. In the summer time."

"Is he a friendly person?"

"Very. What is this about?"

"If we told you he had been accused of groping teenage girls, what would you say?"

"I'd say you were being ridiculous."

"Is your sex life satisfactory?"

"That's none of your business. Why are you saying this?"

"Read this, Mrs Longman. My name is Wendy Fell – from the local paper. If you would like to give us your side of the story, please call me."

Did she see a flash as she took the magazine? She couldn't be sure but it wouldn't be surprising if where there was a reporter there was also a photographer. She stood, immobile, in the middle of the pavement and looked at the article. The girl was definitely familiar – although she had usually seen her in school uniform. It was the long hair that made her distinctive.

The photograph looked professional and the accusations beneath carefully written to avoid legal action. Yet to anyone living by the harbour it was Ned she meant. Had they approached him? It was unthinkable that her husband could have done this – yet – he had had the opportunity. It must be a mistake - or someone being spiteful. Why? Why should anyone accuse Ned of something so sordid? Just looking at the girl filled her with rage and revulsion. She would have to be careful how she spoke to Ned about this. Until then she should phone Rose and stop him coming back to the boat. If she could keep him at Lane's End it might all blow over.

He hadn't been named. It could be someone else. If the social workers believed this about her husband they would never see their daughter again.

Rose told Bernard that Katie was spring cleaning the houseboat and did not want him back for a few nights.

He did not like the idea of spending more nights away from Katie. Although they never discussed the situation they were in he felt they both gained some comfort from their closeness. He loved the way Katie snuggled under his arm before she went to sleep and a feeling of rejection swept over him.

Rose's voice broke into his thoughts.

"Do you know any of the local schoolgirls, Bernard?" she asked.

"Not to talk to. The same ones come past most days – but I don't know their names."

"I expect you see them on the beach."

"Last summer they were there. They get a bit giggly. I try not to take any notice."

"I don't suppose they go in the water much?"

"I don't know. Not many people swim. Most just play in the shallows."

"They don't talk to you?"

Bernard blushed. "Sometimes they shout things."

"What kind of things?"

He shrugged. "Stupid things – they call me Arnold. Sometime they whistle. I can't remember." Why was she asking all these questions? He was puzzled and began to fidget.

Rose saw his discomfort and stopped abruptly. She could picture the scene. A bunch of girls, anxious for attention – a muscular man, stripped to his trunks – only interested in the sea. He would have seemed like a challenge to them. But did he really touch the girl or did she swim up against him – or was it all in her imagination? How long would it take for the rumours to spread? Even if the girl took it no further the damage was done. No one would look at Ned the artist without wondering what kind of man he was. She would have to try to find out the truth.

When Katie arrived on Friday night she looked exhausted. Her eyes were red and her lips set in a grim line. She flinched when Bernard hugged her and kissed the air by his cheek. He'd seen this side of her before – when she was jealous – but what could have brought it on now? He watched her pick at her meal and then left the two women in the kitchen. He hoped Rose would discover the problem and, if possible, solve it.

But Katie would not come to bed that night.

"I'll be up later," she said. "I've got a book I want to finish."

It was a lie. He knew it was a lie. Why was she lying to him? What had made her grow apart from him? He would try to ask her in the morning. He slept alone that night.

Next day Katie seemed her usual self, solicitous over breakfast, smiling and squeezing his arm before he set off for the station. Relieved, he hoped the weekend at Lane's End would cure her bad mood.

He felt the usual sense of anticipation and empowerment as he returned to the college. Being the guide instead of the follower, the teacher instead of the taught, gave him pleasure he never expected to experience.

Reading and writing did not matter when people asked your opinion and acted on your advice. Much as he loved Katie – she did tend to take the lead - but here he could show other people what to do and they listened to him and made him feel important.

He knew the head of the college had written a reference for him and everyone wished him well in his efforts to get back his daughter. Here they made anything seem possible. Here he could relax and concentrate on supporting the students.

It was March before Katie finally passed her driving test. She and Bernard were strangers now. Katie couldn't tell him what had made her change and hated him for being so satisfied with life. There was no route out of this mess.

She had tried not to let the accusations affect her but once she saw Ned, big, soft, Ned – she felt her limbs stiffen and a picture of him swimming underwater to undress some voluptuous teenage girl flashed into her mind and she was revolted by his touch. Pictures floated through her head like some macabre film show, the girl's long hair waving like seaweed, her arms stretched out, her hands moving just enough to keep her afloat, the tiny top of her bikini brushed aside by Ned's fingers and the two of them smiling as flesh met flesh. She was sure the girl was a local tease- but for Ned, her Ned, to be taken in by a young tramp – she shuddered at the thought.

"He's innocent," her mother had said, but she didn't know. She wanted to be 100% certain. Yet how could she ask? He would be so hurt if he knew she doubted him.

"We'll get that Sandra to tell the truth" Rose had said, "She's had her five minutes of fame. The girl didn't name anyone. We mustn't act as if we think she meant Ned."

Rose was right, of course but Katie had something else on her mind. She had to find her daughter. She had to act now. She was tired of waiting to hear the response to the character references. All she had was a photograph of Heather taken on her birthday.

Yet she also had a car – and she was parked outside the Council offices in the hope of seeing a particular young man.

He looked not much more than a boy, slim, dark and with neat, modern spectacles. He carried a backpack, more student than social worker, but she knew he had been assigned to her daughter's case.

Pulling up beside him, she flashed him a smile. "It's Peter, isn't it? Would you like a lift?"

The young man stared at her in surprise. "Do I know you?"

"Kate, Katie Longman – you are helping our family." The words almost stuck in her throat.

"Oh. I don't think I should."

"I won't bite." She tried to look innocent. "I won't discuss work if you don't want to."

That seemed to reassure him and he moved round to sit next to her.

"Where to?"

"The railway station, please. I'm going home."

"Do you have to go far?"

"Near the airport."

"I'm going that way. I'm on an errand for my mum."

"She's the one with the smallholding?"

"Yes – and she's going to buy some geese. I've heard of some for sale and I'm going to look at them."

He seemed satisfied with her explanation. They drove for a while in silence.

"Thanks for the photo," she said at last. "It's odd having to contact her through you."

"She's quite happy, you know."

"Good. How many other children have they got?" She tried to sound casual.

"A girl and a boy, both at school."

"I expect they have a big garden."

"Not massive – but it is a detached house. He's a dentist so they can afford it."

He was trying to reassure her, she knew. Dare she pry any further?

"Ned was going to take her for swimming lessons."

"That family is more into tennis."

"It will be some time before Heather can join in that." She was trying to sound lighthearted.

"Don't give up hope, Mrs Longman."

"I won't. I haven't. Circumstances change."

She let him direct her to his house and accepted effusive thanks. Then she drove slowly away. What had she discovered? Quite a lot. The family played tennis so they probably belonged to a club. The husband was a dentist and they had a boy and a girl. With that amount of information she should be able to find her daughter.

She needed to see her. That would be enough, she told herself, but part of her knew that would just be the start.

A picture of the future was forming in her head; a future without Ned, without the houseboat, even without Rose – a future where she and Heather lived together – where she could continue her work and care for her daughter, alone.

Trying to do what was best for her husband and her child had torn her in half. If she only had Heather to care for she knew she could manage. Living with Ned had sometimes seemed like living with an overgrown child but now they had a daughter she wanted him to be stronger, wiser, different. Or did she? Wasn't it Ned's unquestioning dependence that made him so loveable, and the way he would do anything to please her? Or had that changed? Had marriage stirred something in him that she had been too busy to see? Could it be possible that the story had been true? If it was she could not stay with him. She had to be strong. Her daughter needed her most. She had to find her, and keep from Ned and Rose the thoughts that were chasing through her mind.

15

Rose knew exactly who to ask about the girl in the magazine. Bernard's friend the headmistress would probably be able to identify her.

"Sandra Groves," she said when Rose showed her the picture. "I'm not surprised she was seeking publicity. She always was a little show off."

When Rose explained why she needed to know she was immediately sympathetic.

"Does Ned know?" she asked.

"No. We haven't told him and if I can talk to Sandra's mother he need never know.

"What can you tell me about the family?"

"Sandra had an older sister and her two younger brothers are still at Secondary School. Father worked in the docks but ran off with a dancer from one of the shows on the pier."

"So Mrs Groves had to bring them up by herself?"

"Well, by then the eldest daughter was working and able to help out but, yes – I suppose so."

"What's she like – Mrs Groves?"

"Friendly, happy-go-lucky, fond of her children but finding them a handful."

"I have to meet her. I don't want to cause trouble. I'll tell her I need Sandra's help."

As she stood she glanced out of the window and saw the wall of the sensory garden. Bernard had so much to offer. She could not allow him to lose everything because of one teenage girl's desire for fame.

The café was almost full but two women sat in the corner, one, all in black with dark rimmed glasses and pointed features – the other heavily built, her greying hair bleached yellow. She wore a floral dress and her coat was hanging over the back of the chair. That had to be Sandra's mother.

Rose approached the table. "Hallo," she said, looking from one to the other. "Rose Smith. I believe we talked on the phone?"

"Yes, Mrs Smith," answered the larger lady. "This is my friend Elsie. She was just leaving. Thank you, Elsie. I'll see you tomorrow."

The thin lady pushed back her chair and, with a nod to Rose, left the café.

Rose sat opposite Sandra's mother and tried to smile. "Thank you for seeing me, Mrs Groves. Your daughter is quite striking."

"Yes. She wants to be a model."

"It was the picture in the magazine that I wanted to talk to you about."

"Do you know anything about that? Were you there?"

"I'm afraid not. Would you like another cup of tea?"

Mrs Groves was smiling now and accepted readily. Rose brought the cups back to the table and continued, "You need to know about my family to understand why I am here. My daughter is married to a placid, rather slow-witted man. They have a baby daughter – but because of where they live and how they acted when the social workers came to check on them they are likely to have my granddaughter taken away from them for ever. Believe me, they are a loving, caring couple and losing their baby will devastate them."

"Poor souls, but what has this to do with Sandra?"

"They live on a houseboat."

"You mean – he's the man that attacked her?"

"No. He's the man people are saying attacked her. It's not true. My son-in-law has no interest in anyone other than his own family. Honestly, I know him – but if his name continues to be connected with these accusations their chances of keeping the baby would be nil."

Mrs Groves looked thoughtful. "How can I believe you?" she said. "You might just be protecting him."

"Are you certain every detail of Sandra's story is true? Couldn't she be trying to make it more sensational than it really was? Is she a good swimmer?"

"Sandra?" Mrs Groves laughed. "She can't swim a stroke. She hates to get her hair wet. She just poses on the beach in her bikini."

Rose waited to let Mrs Groves realise the implications of what she had just said.

"Her boyfriend's a photographer," she said, slowly. "Do you think they could have made it up?"

"Did she seem upset when she came home?"

"I don't know. I wasn't there. I work at the newsagents four afternoons a week and if it was at the weekend she spends most of it at Robert's."

"Did she tell you about it before you saw the article?"

"I don't think so. She didn't talk about it until after the magazine. Then all she wanted to do was show me the photo."

"How did you feel?"

"Angry, upset that she hadn't told me – that it was too late to do anything. Then she said they had made it seem worse than it was. She said Robert had helped her write it but the magazine had changed bits."

"Didn't Robert's reaction worry you?"

"I never spoke to him. They don't talk to me much. You know what youngsters are like nowadays."

"Did she say who touched her?" Rose was getting more and more incensed. Not only was Bernard not involved but she was beginning to believe the whole incident was a fiction.

"No. She said she didn't know his name."

"What if it never happened?"

Mrs Groves looked sheepish. "I must ask her," she muttered. "What shall I do if she's lying?"

"So far there's no harm done. But I need something to say it wasn't my son-in-law. Could you get her to write a note?"

"Saying what?"

"She doesn't have to say it didn't happen. All we need is for her to write that Bernard Longman, known as Ned, did not touch her and has never touched her. Please just get her to tell the truth. I'll give you my lawyer's address. Don't send it to me. Ask him to keep it, just in case the authorities find out about the article. The papers haven't printed anything yet so it might never happen. He'll keep it safe and only produce it if necessary."

"But people will think Sandra has been got at – that it's all a lie."

"No – it won't be brought out in public. The only place it might be seen is in the family court. They meet in secret. No one ever knows what goes on in there."

Reassuringly, she continued, "I don't think your daughter meant any harm. She's clearly imaginative and ambitious.

Just warn her – if she did have someone in mind she may have really hurt them."

"I will. I'll try to get her to understand. I'm sorry, Mrs Smith." She grabbed her coat and hurried out of the café.

Rose waited until she was out of sight and then leant back in her chair. Closing her eyes she wished, or perhaps prayed, that she had done enough to save Bernard's reputation.

For the next two days Rose was reluctant to leave the cottage. She snatched at the phone the second it rang. It was the lawyer.

"Is there any news?" she cried, breathlessly.

"An interesting development." The lawyer's voice was calm but she could tell he was smiling. "The submission by the headmistress was very helpful."

"She said how good Bernard was with the children – and the college gave him an excellent reference – but something else has happened."

"What?"

"I believe you met Sandra's mother?"

"I did speak to her, yes."

"What did you say?"

"I told her how Bernard and Katie had a baby but it was taken away from them."

"What did you say about Sandra?"

"I said I had seen the article and that she was very pretty but perhaps she had been a bit imaginative. I said people had suggested her attacker was Bernard and because of these rumours he and Katie might never see their daughter again."

"Any more?"

"I asked her if her daughter had told her who touched her. She said, no – and that she was surprised Sandra had been so deep in the water."

"But what made her contact me?"

"I did. I said if Sandra could write a note declaring that Bernard had never touched her you could hold it, in confidence. Then if it came up in discussions about Heather you could produce it. What did she put?"

"I'll read it. *To whom it may concern. Ned Longman has never touched me. I thought he looked nice but he never noticed me. This is the truth. I'm sorry.*

"It is signed and dated."

"Could it help?"

"Possibly, but let's hope it's never needed."

"It's such a relief. Katie was going mad with worry. When are they meeting?"

"Not for another month – but with all the evidence I've got things look promising."

Bernard sat in front of the television. He wasn't listening to it – just watching the flickering light and letting the hum of sound wash over him.

"Can I turn this off?" asked Rose.

"What? Oh yes."

"Bernard, I need to talk to you."

"Yes?"

"It's about the houseboat."

"Is it OK?"

"Yes – but the way you and Katie are living isn't."

"I know. I hardly ever see her."

"It doesn't have to be like this."

"What can I do?"

226

"Sell the houseboat. She doesn't have to live there any more. You could both live here, together. Now she has the car she can drive herself to work. Think about it and talk to her on Sunday night, before she goes back."

"She doesn't love me any more."

"Don't say that – and if she doesn't it's up to you to do something about it."

"They won't let us have Heather because of me. They say I can't look after her."

"That's rubbish – but we have the answer here. If you both move in with me I can help look after Heather. I wouldn't interfere – but the authorities wouldn't know that. It's your best hope of getting Heather back."

Bernard tried to absorb all she had told him. He made a mental picture of himself, Katie, Heather and Rose all together at Lane's End Cottage.

"You two will be in the big bedroom and Heather can have your old room." Rose's enthusiasm gave him hope.

"I'd like that," he said at last.

"Well, all we have to do is convince Katie."

It was late Friday evening when Katie rang Lane's End. "I'm not coming this weekend, mum," she said. "I've got to work overtime to cover for holidays."

"Oh, darling. I really wanted to talk to you."

"Is Ned all right?"

"Missing you."

"He's in good hands. Must dash. Bye, mum."

She hadn't given anything away. Now she had the whole weekend to put her plan into action. She had scoured the Yellow Pages for dentists but there were too many.

The day she had seen Mrs Burton's granddaughter come to visit her – climbing onto her lap for a cuddle and snuggling down to look at a picture book – was the day she had made up her mind she could no longer tolerate the suffering that separation from Heather was causing. It was as if all her insides had been scooped out and the hollow painted with pain. She had thought it would get easier, it certainly seemed that way for her husband, but it seemed to take over her life. If she did not do something soon she would break down completely.

She began with the County Town – making a list of all the dental practices in the area and then setting aside time to visit them. She would pretend to be a prospective patient – one with an overwhelming fear of dentists, with very specific ideas of who could help her.

The first practice she tried was in a large detached house. The reception area had a long desk with computer terminals and glass cabinets filled with toothbrushes.

There were a number of certificates on the walls and she was greeted with a friendly, "Good morning. Can I help you?"

"I'm new to the area," she began, hesitantly. "I should find a dentist but I haven't had very good experiences with them before."

"I'm sorry to hear that. Where did you live?"

"London. My last dentist was a lady."

"Well – we have four dentists, two men and two women. They are all very good with nervous patients. Would you like me to arrange a preliminary examination for you?"

"How old are the men?"

"Both newly qualified. The previous partner retired last

year. They use all the latest techniques. When would suit you?"

"I'm sorry. I really wouldn't feel confident with a young man. I think I'll leave it."

The receptionist's attitude changed. "Perhaps you had better try somewhere else, Madam."

"Yes. Thank you for your help." Katie hurried out. She had better think up a more convincing story or she would never get through the other eight practices.

Next she explained that a friend had recommended someone but she had forgotten his name. "She said he was in his early forties and had a lovely family, a wife and two children"

"I'm sorry. There's no one here answering that description. Mr Wood is 60 and his children are grown up."

"It sounds like Philip Mace," said her companion, "but I'm not sure they have any vacancies. They don't do NHS."

"I'm happy to go private," said Katie, eagerly. "Can you tell me where his practice is?"

"We shouldn't really – but he does do some root fillings for us sometimes. Here you are."

Overjoyed with her success Katie was ready to approach Philip Mace immediately but she thought it better to ring and make an appointment. They were only open in the mornings on Saturdays but they had a cancellation for the following week. If she could keep her impatience in check she could be one step nearer finding her daughter.

Once again she was seated in a dentist's chair. She had told the receptionist she was separated from her husband and given a hotel as her address.

"You won't tell anyone I have been here, will you? I don't want him to find me," she confided, "but I can't eat cold or hot things so I thought I had better get it checked out before it gets worse."

"We'll put it down as a temporary address – as long as you let us know when you have a permanent one."

A tall, well built man with a round, friendly face and wavy dark hair introduced himself. "I'm Philip. This is my nurse, Penny. You just make yourself comfortable and we'll take some X rays. Nothing we do today will hurt at all. Let me know if you don't like the music."

Katie hadn't even noticed the gentle tune playing in the background.

"It's very nice," she stuttered. Now she was here she was almost numb with excitement. Would he let her talk? How could she ask about tennis? What was it about him that made her feel so vulnerable?

He tipped the chair back and gently touched her jaw. "We'll just put this inside your mouth," he murmured. "If there is anything that makes you uncomfortable, just wave."

His eyes twinkled and she felt herself thrill to his presence. 'He's gorgeous,' she thought, hypnotised by his warm, deep voice. How could anyone not trust herself completely to someone who looked and sounded like that?

"Now – I'll go round the mouth, tapping each tooth in turn. Let me know if it is at all painful."

She felt his face coming closer to hers and fought the urge to move towards him. There was a slight twinge in one tooth and she grabbed his arm.

"Fine, that's fine. Nearly done. One filling needing replacing by the look of it. The X rays will tell us more. Would you like to make another appointment?"

Finished? But she hadn't had time to ask him anything! Quick – quick! "Yes – but it will have to be on a day I don't have a tennis match."

"Well – let the receptionist know and we'll see you again soon." She was dismissed.

She didn't know whether to laugh or cry. She had found the most attractive dentist in the county but she still didn't know if he had her daughter. She had one more chance. She would ask the receptionist. She would have to return, but then she would pretend to move house. She had known the cost of the initial check up but without news of Heather she resented having to pay.

As she wrote the cheque she commented, "Mrs Mace is a lucky lady."

The receptionist smiled. "That's what everyone says. She's a dentist too."

"Oh. I thought he had a family."

"They do, two boys, twins – at boarding school."

"I see. Thank you. I'll ring for my next appointment. I've not got my diary with me."

She nearly fell down the stairs on the way out. No – she wouldn't make another appointment. If she could remember which tooth ached she would use that for the next time but the search was proving more complicated than she had envisaged.

Still – she was not ready to give up. She hoped the dental fraternity didn't compare notes. By the time she had finished they would all have seen this strange young woman who asked them questions and then disappeared.

Her response to a man who was not her husband had shocked her. That irresistible combination of authority and consideration made him more exciting than Ned. She still loved him, in a way, but was it her idea of Ned, rather than the real man? Did she deliberately ignore the elements of her husband that she found irritating? Was anyone really a perfect match? Well, it was too late now. Philip Mace was taken and she had to live with her choice.

Over the next three weeks she covered the last few practices. None of the dentists fitted the criteria. One filled her tooth – but he was the kind of man who would not stop talking. Instead of putting her at ease it made her want to shout, "Stop – give me a chance to speak." but she couldn't with her mouth propped open.

She sat in the park trying to plan her next move. They all seemed pretty well off, she thought. If I was a dentist with a family where would I live? There were two possibilities that sprang to mind, discounting the isolated small villages. If he wanted to be near his practice and good sports facilities she thought she had the answer. Not too far away was somewhere she had always considered idyllic. That would be where she would try next.

Stenton was a large village hidden in a fold of the Downs. It had numerous antique shops, a large park, some pleasant public houses and restaurants and a well-used leisure centre.

It was almost impossible to reach by public transport but as Katie had her car she set off with high hopes. She would start at the Leisure Centre, pretend to have a raging toothache, and ask about local dentists.

Two hours later she sat in a small tea room wondering if she had made a mistake.

Her only discovery was that there were two dental surgeries in the area. She had stood outside the first, staring at the names on the plaque. Baxter and Cole. Cole? She had heard that name before. The social workers had spoken about Cole when they took Heather but she thought they meant coal. She couldn't very well march in and ask if he had two children and a new baby, could she? Her other course of action was to show an interest in the private tennis club at the end of the village. Could she pull it off?

Those sort of places usually intimidated her. Was she smart enough? She wished she had some higher heels and maybe earrings, or a scarf. She'd make a bet with herself. If she could find some attractive accessories in a charity shop she would try the tennis club. If not she would go home and think again.

It was lunchtime when she drove up to the Georgian mansion that served as the centre for the tennis club. They advertised indoor and outdoor courts, a splash pool and a restaurant and bar. She had a new plan. Instead of trying to join the tennis club she would pretend she was looking for a venue for charity event, a cheese and wine party, perhaps. She had found some chunky earrings that matched her sweater and a chiffon scarf that she hoped added a frisson of style.

The girl at reception said she would need to speak to the bar manager and directed her upstairs. When she explained that she had come to assess the suitability of the venue he brought her a function list and the programme for the next three months. She sat with a glass of sparkling mineral water and tried to appear relaxed.

There were a few people at the bar who had obviously been playing tennis. She couldn't hear what they were saying but she could see through to the restaurant and there were two children sitting at one table.

A tall, fair man peeled away from the bar and carried a tray of drinks through to their table. Was it too much to hope that she had found her quarry? There was no sign of his wife, or Heather.

She had to do something, but what? She couldn't ask the barman if the member was a dentist. She didn't want the family to know she was searching for them. She would have to get closer and try to pick up clues from their conversation.

She walked up to the bar. "Would it be possible for a non-member to buy a snack?"

"Sure. What would you like?"

"A toasted cheese sandwich, please."

"In the bar or in the restaurant?"

"In the restaurant I think – with a coffee."

"Trisha will bring it out to you in a moment," and he took her money.

Katie's heart was thumping as she sat down as close to the family as possible. She chose a chair with her back to their table in case her face gave her away. The boy was boasting about winning the match but the girl seemed fidgety and impatient.

"Can we go home straight after this, dad? My feet hurt."

"I did say we'd give your mother a bit of peace – and we still have to pick up a few odds and ends."

"Oh – not the supermarket!"

"Can I get a comic?" interjected her brother.

"You've both had your pocket money. You can spend it on whatever you like."

"I'm saving mine," said the girl.

Their conversation continued while they ate their meal. Katie tried to chew her sandwich as slowly as possible. Nothing they had said gave her a clue but if she could follow them to the supermarket she might find the answer she was seeking. She cursed herself for not buying a street map – somehow she felt she had the right family – but she needed to be certain. She felt a pain in her chest. She had given herself indigestion, eating while she was so agitated. She needed to get out before they moved and then hope she would see them in the car park.

The three figures climbed into a silver BMW which drove past her and turned left at the end of the drive. She followed to some traffic lights where another left turn took them into a one-way system. Katie swore when a white van squeezed between the two vehicles but she had no need to worry. They had reached the supermarket.

The man took a trolley while Katie picked up a basket. The two children ran off and she picked up some lettuce and tomatoes. His purchases were unremarkable until he moved to the end of the store and included baby shampoo and nappies.

'Bingo!' thought Katie. 'All I need now is to find out where they live.'

She was soon through the checkout and back in her car. When the BMW exited she settled in behind it, but this time she was not so lucky. The traffic was heavier and the man was driving faster. He turned right and she was held up behind a lorry. By the time she had made the same manoeuvre he had disappeared. She was in a maze of tree-lined avenues. The houses were large and detached. She cruised round looking for the silver car but to no avail. She parked and thumped the steering wheel with frustration. "I'll come back," she declared out loud. "I'll come back until I find her."

Shakily she drove away until she realised tears were blinding her and it was dangerous to go any further.

She stopped by the park and got out. If she could walk about for a while she could calm herself down. After all – today had been a partial success. She had chosen the right village. She had seen a likely family.

Now she needed to decide what she was going to do if she did find her daughter. Should she snatch her – or would that count against her? Could she get away? Would Ned help or would she have to leave him? She couldn't shake off the mental image of her husband under the water with that girl. She knew now that it hadn't really happened but, once she had pictured it, it was impossible to erase.

She climbed the hill and sat on a bench overlooking the children's play area.

'I want to swing my Heather and watch her come down the slide,' she thought.

'More than anything in the world I want my daughter back.'

16

Rose looked out at the long field behind the house. There had been so much going on she had done nothing with it. Now she could see that nature had taken over. Curious, she went out and walked slowly through the grass. A great deal had grown since they stopped cultivating it, nettles, holly, elder and that irritating creeper that clawed at her ankles and clung to the hem of her skirt. She had told herself that it would benefit from being left fallow but looking at the weeds that were taking hold she wondered if she had done the right thing. She could see a few wild daisies and some tiny cabbage plants trying to push between them. It gave her an idea what to do next. Instead of planting turnips or potatoes she'd consider ornamental cabbages.

If they could keep the caterpillars away she could sell them at market later in the year without having to compete with the stalls that claimed to be organic. Her smallholding was not large enough to try for a licence. Tim had been keen to use natural methods but they had never claimed their produce was actually organic – just fresh and locally grown.

Bernard was nervous. It was weeks since Katie had shown any sign of affection towards him. They were sleeping in the little bedroom. Bernard from Sunday to Friday and Katie on Saturday night. It had started in order to accommodate the visitors but, even when there weren't any, it continued. He believed she hated him for causing them to lose their child but until Rose had come up with a solution he hadn't seen a way to change things. Now there was a chance of not only getting Heather back but also the love of his wife. He'd never stopped loving her and it had made him miserable, watching her withdraw into herself. He did not know what she was thinking any more. When she spoke to him it was like a stranger. Only Rose and the people at the college made life bearable.

He had spent the weekend making bird tables and wooden gifts. The musical boxes were his favourite. They had hinged lids and a figure, either a ballet dancer or a cupid, that revolved on the mechanism inside. The students were covering them in shells and sticking mirrors inside the lids. There was a choice of two tunes, 'Edelweiss' or 'Greensleeves.' Bernard was making one for Heather but he had not chosen a tune. He wished he could ask Katie but he wanted it to be a secret.

The end wall from his garden had been saved as an example of what could be achieved with different stones and tiles.

He was pleased it would stay a permanent reminder of his time here, but if Rose's plan worked he would spend most weekends at Lane's End. He hoped Katie would agree.

"I thought with my father's account frozen you would need every penny the place would earn." Katie's voice was unusually shrill. "Now you tell me you don't need to rent out the bedrooms. How can we all possibly afford to live here? There's no sheep, no ponies and did the produce from the place ever make a profit? It's just not realistic!"

"Trust me, Katie. It is possible. I thought you'd love to come home."

238

Rose sounded beaten. Neither she nor Bernard had expected this reaction. Bernard had the strange feeling that, for once, his wife was not being honest. Perhaps she did not want to go back to living as a family? Perhaps she could no longer bear to be near him?

He thought of Rose's offer – to make him a partner – and their plans for the lower field. They were going to make it a camping site and turn the stables into a toilet and washing area. Rose said they would need a loan but that much of the work could be done by Bernard. He was really looking forward to it.

He went into the kitchen.

"She's gone for a walk." Rose's mouth was set tight.

Bernard nodded and headed for the orchard. He knew where Katie would be – talking to the chickens. She had told him about her habit of telling them her troubles.

"They listen better than the geese," he said softly as he came up behind her.

"You know what mum is suggesting?"

"Yes, but you don't want to."

"I don't know. If it brings Heather back it might work. I think I was angry that I didn't think of it first."

"What are you afraid of?"

She turned towards him and he saw her tear-stained face.

"I'm afraid of so much. I'm afraid they will still say no and I couldn't live here without her.

"I'm afraid she's changed and that she will love my mother more than me.

"I'm afraid that you'll get tired of living with a houseful of women and that the place will be a mill-stone round our necks. There's so much that could go wrong. I don't think I could bear it."

To Bernard's relief she flung herself into his arms and he held her until the sobbing ceased. He kissed the top of her head and she looked up at him and smiled.

"I've missed this," she said.

"So have I. I feel so much better when you are with me."

"I shut you out, didn't I? I didn't think you cared any more. I have been trying so hard to find the answer and now mum has thought of something so simple. If only we can really get back to how we were."

"We can. Rose has such plans. Heather would love living up here. Please give it a try."

"I need time, Ned. I've been a selfish fool. I was only thinking about myself. I'll talk to the lawyer. If he says it will work, I'll agree – but to start with we'll let out the houseboat, not sell it."

"Agreed." He hugged her as hard as he dared. He would agree to anything to have his family together again.

Rose's life changed more than she could ever have thought possible. Suddenly opportunities opened up that gave her hope for the future – for all of them. Not only had the lawyer agreed that once they were all settled there would be nothing to prevent them from being reunited with Heather, but Katie seemed to lose the brittle shell she had developed and began to take an interest in what she and Bernard were planning.

Bernard threw himself into the project. While Rose visited camp sites to find out what was required he measured the fields and drew plans. They all knew it would have to be designed by a proper architect but they needed some idea of what they wanted before they began.

Rose discovered that it was preferable to have security on site and they hoped they could get planning permission for at least two hard standings for caravans or motorhomes.

Having the stable buildings already on the back lane gave them hope that permission would be granted to turn them into washing and toilet blocks. Car parking would be from that side as Chalk Pit Lane was very narrow.

"*Stable Lane* is shorter than *Chalk Pit Lane*," she said to Bernard, "*Stable Lane Camping Site* sounds fine. I think someone on the Parish Council knows all about plans. We must do it all properly."

Bernard had taken over the care of the orchard and was rotating the vegetables in the other fields. He had tomatoes in the renovated greenhouse and let the geese run free under the fruit trees. Rose knew he did not really like the geese and determined to get rid of them before her grand daughter came home.

Jenny the collie was acting her age now but as long as she kept eating Rose would go on treating her as a precious part of the family.

Her weekends had changed, too. Now Katie was home to get the Sunday lunch Rose had given in to her sister-in-law's pleading for help in the pub. George had a shorter sentence than Tim and they hoped he could carry on when he came out.

The brewery had allowed Pat to remain in place for a probationary year, to see if she could run it on her own – and she had accepted the challenge.

"I didn't have anywhere else to go – and the customers sent in letters of support," Pat had told her, "but I want to do meals. I'm starting with Sunday lunches but I'll only need someone part-time at first. If I get a demand for more I'll have to hire a chef.

"You could do lovely home-made lunches. Please come and help, Rose – just until we see if it takes off."

"I think you'll need to upgrade your kitchen," replied Rose. "I'll do it for a month. If we can make a profit I'll think about staying on."

The month passed and Rose was enjoying herself so much that it didn't seem fair to ask for payment.

"You'll need it for the alterations," said Katie on one of their rare occasions together.

"Pat's getting a new accountant," replied Rose, "Then we'll see how we are really doing."

Pat was beaming with delight when Rose arrived the following Sunday morning.

"If we discount the cost of the new kitchen we are increasing our takings. Mr Kent suggested we try monthly musical evenings. I'm going to ask the regulars what they think."

"As long as it doesn't interfere with the darts I don't suppose they'll care. Which night is too quiet? You won't do Karaoke will you?"

"Only if the locals want it – and you know the age range we get in here. What do you think?"

Rose knew a lot of the younger element had left once the cheap cigarettes and alcohol had stopped. It was mostly farmers, salesmen and walkers, with more women now than there used to be.

"Let's get a Christmas Draw going and clear out the back room for parties. Now Tim doesn't stay here any more we can make it a proper family pub."

Pat giggled. "I wish you'd been helping us before," she said. "What idiots those two were."

"I don't like to think about it – but Tim would be amazed at how well Bernard is looking after our place. Aren't you afraid of what will happen when they come out?"

"George could be free in two years but he doesn't want to come back. He says he'd rather go on the road."

"Tim told me to stop visiting. He said it made him realise what he was missing. I don't think he meant me – more likely his big dinners. I can't help feeling sorry for him. He shuts people out."

"We are better off without them, love. Let's enjoy it while we can. Have you seen the new delivery man? He's a real hunk."

"Pat – I'm surprised at you!" But she wasn't really. Pat had always been a flirt. With her red hair and cheeky smile she lit up the bar, and always dressed to impress.

Rose was glad she could hide in the kitchen, although she was called upon at busy times to help behind the bar.

It was when she was serving drinks that she met Brian Sampson.

He was deep in discussion about a damaged roof and gestured wildly without noticing how near she was standing. The tray of drinks cascaded to the floor in a tumble of glass and beer.

"Oh gosh. I'm so sorry love. I didn't hear you coming. I'll pay for the damage."

"You're a clumsy blighter," shouted Pat and, seeing how flustered Rose was, went out the back for a mop and bucket.

By the time she returned Rose had found a dustpan and brush and everyone had moved back so the floor could be cleaned.

"Here, sit down, love – you look all shook up." Brian pulled out a chair for Rose.

"Thanks," she said, shakily. "I'm not very good at bending."

"It was all my fault. Can I get you a drink?"

"Have a brandy," said one of his mates. "Brandy is good for shock, isn't it, Pat?"

"Thanks, but I'd prefer a ginger wine." The group laughed. "The lady wants warming up, Patsy."

"Not by you lot, she doesn't."

Rose didn't know what to say. She wanted to talk to Brian about the work he did but didn't know how to broach the subject.

He turned to his companion. "I'll see you tomorrow – as long as the weather holds. Keep your fingers crossed."

"Do you work outside?" ventured Rose.

"Mostly. I'm a builder – brickwork, roofing, tiling, renovations – you name it – we do it. Have my card."

Rose smiled. That was exactly what she wanted. Now all she needed was a recommendation – or, better still, to see for herself.

"Are you very busy? Where are you working now?" She was amazed at her own impertinence.

"Bert wanted a barn turned into a holiday let. It's just up the road – in the village – next door to the church."

"That's a good place for a holiday home. I used to let rooms – but I expect you know that."

Brian looked embarrassed. "Sorry about your Tim," he said, "He wasn't a bad bloke – worked hard, didn't he?"

"Yes, that's true. He did work hard. I must get back to the kitchen. Thanks for the drink," and she scuttled away.

"You've changed, Rose," said Pat that afternoon as they snatched a quick cup of tea and a sit down. "I saw you chatting to the customers. All we need now is to get you to the shops and find some new clothes."

"Don't you start. That was business. I don't need smart clothes."

"Oh yes you do. They'll make you feel better and the customers won't treat you like a skivvy."

"Pat – they don't," she protested, but she had to admit they did sometimes ignore her as if she was just part of the furniture. Perhaps she should try to get more up to date now she did not have to put up with Tim's scorn. Whenever she had bought anything new in the past she had been ridiculed. "Mutton dressed as lamb," he had said, until she had given up trying.

"I don't expect you to glam up – just find a few bits and pieces that suit you. Come on Wednesday morning, early. We'll have a great time. We can get the eight fifteen bus."

Rose had to admit it was tempting. She had plenty of time to warn Bernard. He was working on the hedges this week and making sure the fencing round the property was secure.

"OK, I'll come – but I must be back by twelve."

"Don't worry. So must I. I don't trust Craig to man the bar by himself – even on a weekday."

Rose wasn't surprised. Pat's son was supposed to be a motor cycle mechanic, living with his partner in town – but he always seemed to be available to help at the pub. He was sullen and monosyllabic, with a group of friends who took over the bar on Thursday nights, much to the disgust of the older regulars. They didn't drink a lot, beer mostly - but Rose did worry when they rode away in the evenings. They seemed so sure that nothing could happen to them.

"I'm too dumpy for trousers," Rose complained when Pat brought a selection of items into the changing room.

"No you're not - if you buy the right shape. Look at this material – it's all soft and drapey. Try them with the top."

Rose had to agree she did look different – taller, even.

"I must get my hair done," she muttered at her reflection.

"Those grey bits look like highlights. You just need a good cut."

"Tim never wanted me to get my hair cut."

"It's a bit old-fashioned Rose, and it can't be practical."

"I've got used to pinning it up."

"Well – it's time for a change."

They missed the bus and did not get back to the pub until one o'clock but there were few customers. Rose rang the cottage and Bernard replied.

"There's been a call for you, Rose. From the prison."

Rose gulped. "What's happened?"

246

"They wouldn't tell me. They asked you to call them back."

"I'll be right home. I can't think here." She told Pat and hurried up the lane.

Bernard was hovering in the doorway and took her packages while she went to the phone. A few moments later she came into the lounge and sat down heavily on the settee.

"It's Tim. He's been taken ill. They've had to move him to the hospital wing. They say he hasn't been eating properly. Oh, Bernard – I feel as if I have abandoned him."

"It's not your fault. Should we tell Katie?"

"Not yet. They don't want me to visit. They just had to tell me. I knew he didn't like the food but I didn't think he'd starve himself."

Bernard frowned. He looked so lost and uncomfortable that she had to smile. "Thank-you, Bernard. You did absolutely the right thing in calling the pub."

His face relaxed.

"Now tell me what you have done today." She pretended to listen while he told her the tasks he had accomplished. What she really wanted to do was make a blackberry and apple pie and take it to the jail. Normally they would not let her take food but perhaps the circumstances were different in Tim's case.

Would they force-feed him? she thought. Do they do that nowadays? She hadn't seen him for weeks. She didn't feel as if he belonged to her any more. Yet they had been together for years and she had always been there when he was ill.

She needed to talk to someone who understood. She would ring Pat and ask her to quiz George tomorrow and find out how serious the problem was and then go and see her tomorrow night. Once she had made the decision she felt calmer. She was really tired after her hectic morning, tired and drained.

"I'm going for a lie down, Bernard," she said, "can you carry on OK?"

"Yes. I can finish cleaning out the stables."

"Don't do too much. I'll be up to get tea." She rubbed her eyes as she climbed the stairs. Was she being punished for thinking only of herself? Had the divorce been too much for Tim to handle? She couldn't go back on it now. She would have to wait until she could see him and play it by ear.

Pat didn't get back from the prison until opening time. Rose said she would drive down after the pub closed. She'd called Katie and told her the little she knew but her daughter's reaction was unambiguous.

"Serves him right," she had declared. "Don't feel sorry for him, mum. If he hadn't done what he did he wouldn't be there."

Rose drove slowly down the lane and waited at the junction to turn left. The lads were driving away from the pub, most of them using the gap in the dual carriageway to go south on the other side of the road. She was about to pull out when a black car slid beside her, swept left and accelerated towards the pub.

She did not see the crash but she heard the impact. Slowly, she drove up onto the grass verge and got out. She only had to walk a few yards until she could see the carnage. The black car had come to a halt among the picnic tables outside the pub, the bike beyond it, the rear wheel completely crushed and its rider flung into the carriageway. People were milling around – some trying to cover the body, others waiting to direct traffic and Pat herself kneeling in the doorway by what appeared to be the driver of the car.

"He had an airbag – the bastard. I wanted to hurt him but I can't – he's unconscious." She stood up and screamed at the form on the ground. "You, you murderer!"

It didn't seem enough, thought Rose as she pulled her away. Maybe they shouldn't have dragged him out of the car – but he only had a slight cut on his head - no wonder Pat wanted to punish him more. She hadn't seen the crash. She would be useless as a witness. It would be better if they were indoors.

"My boy, I can't leave my boy," resisted Pat, her attention turning to the prone figure in the road.

"There's nothing you can do. It will only upset you more."

A thin blonde girl was crying hysterically by the rider. His helmet was dented and his body contorted.

Someone had brought a blanket out of a car but the girl would not let them cover his face. Rose stared at her sister-in –law. She was shaking uncontrollably and Rose felt a surge of anger that Craig's death was being turned into such a circus.

"Come inside, love. I'll make us some tea. The ambulance will be here soon." As she turned a police car, followed by a paramedic on a bike, drove up to the pub. They quickly put out cones and ordered the witnesses inside. Seconds later the ambulance arrived and Pat pulled herself together enough to watch them load the two casualties.

"He was going too fast," she said, bitterly. "Craig didn't have a chance. Why did he always have to wear black!" and finally the tears came, racking sobs that seemed to come from deep inside her and make her whole body shudder.

Rose called the cottage and Katie answered.

"I'm staying here tonight, love. There's been a terrible accident. Craig had been knocked off his bike and killed. Pat needs me here. You two will be fine, won't you?"

"Of course. I'll ask for a shift off tomorrow. Give Pat my love. I'm really sorry, mum."

"Ned – the social worker came to see me again yesterday." Katie had to get her husband to think about something other than the previous day's disaster.

Bernard stared at her blankly. He hadn't known Craig, but anything that kept Rose away from Lane's End had to be serious.

"She wanted to arrange for us to see Heather. I know where she is, Ned. I nearly found her. I don't think they are going to let her be adopted."

"Can we go and see her? Can we bring her back?"

"They say it is complicated. They want to arrange a meeting outdoors, in a park or something. She said we mustn't rush things."

"She's our baby."

"Yes – but she's not a baby any more. Oh, Ned. What if she doesn't remember us?

"What if she thinks the other lady is her mummy? I'm frightened, Ned."

Bernard tried to take in what she was saying. He knew Heather had to be older but could only think of her as she was. He could not imagine that they had been forgotten but now he picked up Katie's fear. He had been so looking forward to seeing his daughter. Why did Katie have to spoil it now?

"They'll tell us what to do, won't they?"

"Yes. They want to come and talk to us. We can show them the new bed and all the toys. I want her back so much but I can't bear the thought of her being unhappy."

"I've made her a present. It's a musical box. Do you think she'd like that?"

"She'd love it. I'll tell them to come as soon as possible. We are ready, aren't we?"

"Yes – only Rose isn't here."

"I'll go down and see her. I want to know what Pat found out about my father."

"Can I come too?"

"That's a good idea. We can kill two birds with one stone."

"Katie! We are not going to throw stones at birds?"

"Of course not. It just means we can both find out lots of things in one trip."

The pub was closed but Katie knocked on the door and Rose let her in.

"Pat's resting, poor dear. She's going to need help arranging the funeral. I'm going to have to go to the prison and tell George. Come in – I've made some sandwiches."

"Did she say anything about you-know – who?"

"Not much. I didn't like to ask – but it seems he's in a lot of pain. I'll find out more on Saturday. I need to find someone to trust behind the bar. We must keep open."

"Why don't you ask the brewery – or another pub?"

"Pat doesn't want the brewery told yet. I thought Sam might do it. He used to have a shop in the village and he's a regular."

"See who turns up tonight. How long are you staying here?"

"Over the weekend – as long as you can manage."

"We are fine. We are going to find out when we can see Heather. It will come right, mum. Don't you worry."

She looked round for her husband. He was sitting in a corner with an elderly weatherbeaten man, engrossed in something between them on the table.

"I thought the pub was closed?"

"It is," answered Rose from behind the bar. "Bert was just showing me how to manage the cellar. It looks like he's got Bernard playing dominoes. Could you stay for a while, Katie? I want to put a notice on the door to say we'll re-open on Saturday night."

"Are you sure about that?"

"It's what Pat wants. She needs to be busy."

It was a relief to get on the road, away from the scene of the accident even if she was the bearer of bad news. George would know something was wrong as soon as she asked for him. He had loved his only son and been happy to have his help in the bar.

She watched his face as she told him the news. His normal ruddy features went grey with shock and his eyes narrowed.

"Who did it?" he asked hoarsely. "Have they charged him?"

"I don't know. He's in hospital. He was concussed. I didn't ask about his injuries. I'm dreadfully sorry, George."

"How's Pat?"

"I'm staying there. She's still numb. We'll look after her, George."

"And I'm stuck in this hole. Damn that bloody bike. Damn the job. I'll never go back to that again, Rose. If I'd got out sooner it would never have happened."

Rose let him rage. She wanted to reach out and hold his hand but she couldn't. Eventually he sat silent, his fists clenched on the table in front of him.

"How much longer have you got?" she ventured.

"Nine months – if I keep my nose clean. I guess they'll let me out for the funeral," and he turned away from her, choking back tears.

She waited again. There wasn't enough time.

"George – I need to know about Tim."

"Of course – I didn't think. I expect they'll let you see him but don't be shocked. He's very thin and weak. He's shrunk, Rose. He doesn't seem the same man. He can't take it in here. You might do him good. Go and see him. I'll be OK. Just let the jail know about the – arrangements." He got to his feet and a guard came over to escort him out.

Rose went back to the door.

"You going home, Mrs Smith?" asked the warder at the entrance.

"No. I need to see my husband. He's in the hospital wing."

"Well, hold on. I'll get you an escort. Does he know you are coming?"

"No. It's a family emergency."

It was bad enough coming in through the little door in the gates. The big stone walls looked so forbidding. But being escorted through the corridors, waiting while each door or gate was unlocked in front of her and locked behind her, smelling the disinfectant and hearing the echoes of footsteps as people went up and down the metal stairs, made her feel like a prisoner herself. How could anyone stand being in here for more than a few hours? she thought. It made her want to scream and run.

The last door was unlocked and she was ushered through. The hospital wing was unlike the rest of the prison. If it wasn't for the bars on the windows she would have thought she was in a real hospital. The patients were in cubicles, with only the ends of the beds open, with colourful curtains to pull across. Two cubicles were empty but she could see the two under the window were occupied. Both patients were in bed and had a table beside them with a tray on which was a cup of tea and a piece of cake. One man was awake. He had an eye patch over one eye and one arm in a sling.

"Aye, aye – woman aboard," he shouted.

The figure in the other bed rolled over and she met his gaze. If she hadn't been prepared she would have fainted. The stocky, healthy man she had known had turned into something skeletal, his cheekbones prominent, his hair almost all white and his hands, when they reached out, wrinkled like an old man's.

"Hallo, Tim," she said gently and sat down next to the bed. "How you doing?"

"Rose? What are you doing here?"

Rose felt tears come to her eyes.

"I just came to see how you were. Have a cup of tea."

He slowly hauled himself up to a sitting position and she handed him the cup and saucer. Shakily he put the cup to his lips.

"It's cold."

"It doesn't matter. It's good for you – and you've got cake."

"It's too dry. I can't swallow it."

Tim handed back the cup and flopped onto the pillow.

Rose did not know what to say. She couldn't tell him about Craig while he was in this condition. She watched him close his eyes. He looked too exhausted to continue the conversation. She sat looking at him, wondering how it was that every time life seemed ordered and happy something occurred to knock you off the rails and make you struggle to stay optimistic. Experience told her that they would get over this but at the moment she felt the burden too much to bear.

A voice behind her made her jump. "The governor would like to see you if you have the time."

"Yes, of course. Thank you." Tim's eyes were closed. She patted his hand but there was no response. She was flustered now. How did one behave in the presence of a prison governor? What did he know? Should she tell him about Craig? She wasn't prepared for this.

The governor's room was carpeted - the first piece of carpet she had noticed in the whole building. He was a tall, grey haired man with tortoiseshell-framed spectacles. He came out from behind his desk and shook Rose's hand.

Once they were seated he began, "Now, Mrs Smith, about your husband."

"He doesn't seem at all well."

"No – and it's partly his own doing. We suspect he has an ulcer. We have changed his diet and are treating it with medication."

Rose held her breath. "What can I do?" she said at last.

"He needs to have hope, Mrs Smith."

"But I've divorced him."

"You still care for him? There's nobody else?"

"No. Of course not."

"If you could visit regularly, take his mind off things. Is there anyone else you think he would like to see?"

Rose tried to imagine Tim with anyone whose company he enjoyed.

"Only George." She remembered then – "I came to tell George about his son."

"The accident," answered the governor. "The police informed us this morning. We hoped someone from the family would come and tell him. Since you saw him he has been offered some time to himself and a meeting with the chaplain. We do try to be sympathetic."

"I know. I see. It's a lot to take in. I really ought to get back to Pat, now. Thank you." and she stood to leave.

"Try to visit once a week, Mrs Smith – and we hope we will see an improvement."

"Yes, yes, of course." Now she was up she couldn't wait to get out. There was so much to do back home.

17

Bernard wanted to write a letter. If Zak had been around he would have let Bernard dictate and then written it down for him to copy, but it was Zak he wanted to write to.

He had reduced his time at college to Friday night and Saturdays so that he could have Sundays at Lane's End with Katie, but when the news about Pat's son came he knew he could not go. Now it was Saturday morning and he had no set routine. Katie had gone into the village and Rose was at the prison. He would have to phone his friend – but he felt shy. What if he was doing something important? What if he didn't want to be disturbed? What if he was driving somewhere? Finally he could bear it no longer. Thoughts were battering his head, trying to get out. He had to tell Zak.

He found the number in his mobile phone and carefully copied it onto a sheet of paper. Then he rang the number on the house phone. It was picked up after three rings.

"Hallo, Zak Portos."

"Zak – it's me, Bernard."

"Bernard – it's great to hear from you. How are things?"

"Some things are good and some are bad. Can I tell you?"

"Sure. I was getting bored adding up figures. Carry on."

Bernard told him about the motorbike accident and how Rose was trying to help at the pub. Then he told him about the fostering and how they were going to have to prove to Social Services that everything was in order so that Heather could come home.

"Your place sounds perfect," prompted Zak, which enabled Bernard to release all the fears he had about running the smallholding and opening a camp site.

"Wow. You've got a lot on your plate," responded his friend. "Is there anything I can do to help?"

Bernard hesitated. The picture of a plate full of food had flashed into his mind. That must be another way of saying he had a lot to do. He wished he could see his friend again. What would be the next best thing?

"Could I send you photos?"

"I'd like that. Tell me all your address. I don't know the postcode. Then I can write back and perhaps get down your way in the spring."

Bernard did as requested. Once the call was over he felt a weight lift from his chest. He hadn't even had to ask him. Zak would visit when Heather was here. It was a long time to wait but meantime he would have someone to tell what was going on. If only he could write more than single words. He supposed he could ask Katie but he did not like to remind her of his weakness.

She burst in through the back door.

"Guess what? They've just rung my mobile. They can come this afternoon. They wanted to see us both together. I told them Rose wasn't here but they said she could go and talk to them when she had time. Get the hoover round, Ned. I want to tidy up the kitchen. How's the bathroom?"

Bernard blinked.

"Uh – huh – too much, too soon," she laughed. "OK. You hoover the lounge. I'll see to the rest."

He was grateful he had something to do but glad she wasn't always like this. He had no need to tell her about Zak yet. He would collect some photographs and copy some designs for the camp site. Rose would understand.

Sometimes he just needed to be with different people – like Bert, who treated him as if he was just another customer. He'd enjoyed learning how to play dominoes. He hadn't won, but it didn't matter. It was relaxing. It made him forget all the problems around him. Perhaps he would go down another day and hope to do it again.

"Ned – change your trousers. Put the brown ones on – and that cable sweater. Is it warm enough in here?"

Katie glanced round the lounge. Oh gosh, they needed a fireguard. They had radiators so the fire wasn't alight but what else had they forgotten? It looked cosy – but all the toys were upstairs. Did it look too grown up? What would they say?

She didn't have long to wait. There was a gentle tap on the door and Barbara and Peter greeted her as they entered.

"Oh – both of you. Would you like a cup of tea?"

"Later, perhaps," said Barbara. "Could we have a look round first?"

"It looks great outside," added Peter. "Hallo, old thing," and he bent down to pat Jenny who was weaving round his legs.

"I'll just put her in the lobby for now," said Katie as Bernard entered the room.

"Hallo, Bernard," said Barbara. "This is Peter, my colleague. I don't think you've met."

"No. Hallo."

"We are just going on a tour round," said Katie. "You lead the way, Ned – upstairs first, I think."

They followed Bernard up the stairs, glanced at Rose's room, inspected the bathroom, exclaimed at the freshly decorated bedroom ready for Heather and hardly noted the last bedroom.

"We have a gate for the stairs," burbled Katie. "Ned is good at putting up things like that."

It seemed natural, then, to sit round the large table and Katie fetched tea and biscuits.

"I hear you have a part-time job, Bernard?" began Barbara.

"Yes – I go to the college on Friday evenings to help the students get settled. Then we make things on the Saturday and I come home in the evening."

"But he need not stay, if it isn't allowed," interjected his wife.

"No. That's fine. We understand Rose will be the chief carer. Will she move back soon?"

Katie explained about the crash, leaving out the fact that Rose had been cooking meals at the pub. They needed to convince the authorities that someone would be here all the time to look after Heather.

"We have to warn you that things could be a little difficult at first. Your daughter has been away for long enough to form attachments. We wanted her to be happy at the foster home and she has been but we think that means she may miss it."

"You mean she thinks of them as her family."

"Yes – and although we are sure she will soon bond with you and Bernard again we feel she may miss the children."

"I wondered about that. What can we do?"

"Take it one step at a time. Our plan is that you and Bernard meet up with the family, casually, in the park and become friendly. As she was so young when she left it could be that she doesn't remember you."

Katie gasped and clutched at her waist.

"Are you all right, Katie?" asked Bernard. She shook her head.

"That hurt," she whispered.

"I'm sorry, Katie," said Peter, "but you must be prepared."

"Then what?"

"Then we'll arrange a visit to their home. After that they could visit you. If it all goes well she should be back with you before Christmas."

Katie tried to imagine the children she had seen at the tennis club playing in her orchard but the picture would not form.

"Do you want to see the chickens?" Bernard was asking.

"That would be nice. I think Katie needs a few moments to catch her breath."

"Heather is walking, now, Bernard," said Barbara once they were outside. "You'll have to make sure she can't open the gate. There's no pond is there, and no vehicles in this area?"

"No. That's the garage, at the end of the field. It goes straight out into the lane."

"You don't have horses any more?" asked Peter.

"No." He nearly added the information about the camping site but was saved by Katie calling from the house.

"It's my mother. She says can she come to the office on Monday afternoon?"

"Great," replied Peter. "I'll be there. I'll let her know when we can see the family. Would a Sunday be best?"

"Yes, please."

"You know we are ready to help at any time," added his companion.

"Yes, thank you."

Bernard could see that she just wanted rid of them now. He followed them to the lane and waved goodbye. Why wasn't she looking happy and excited? He trusted these people to bring their daughter home and was glad he had time to get used to the idea. Would she be talking as well as walking? he wondered. Could he show her pictures and tell her some of the stories his mother told him? They needed to see her. They didn't know what size clothes she wore now.

He looked round for Katie but she wasn't downstairs. He guessed she was in the little bedroom and he was correct. She was sitting, pale faced, on the new bed, hugging herself as if it was cold.

"I'm scared, Ned," she said, "I'm so scared she won't like us any more."

He couldn't think of anything to say. He just sat beside her and pulled her towards him, rocking backwards and forwards as he cuddled her. He wished he had Rose's ability to sort things out.

Rose had problems of her own. Pat had heard from the brewery. They were not renewing her lease. She would have to be out by next Easter.

"They are going to open a themed restaurant," she wailed at Rose. "They say the place needs a complete change of image. They are furious that I didn't tell them straight away about the accident."

"Good grief – it was only two days ago."

"But it's bad publicity, Rose. What am I going to do? This is my home."

"Don't worry about that. Just get yourself together and give them the most profitable Christmas they have ever had. We'll show them. The customers will rally round."

"They'll have to go to the Dog and Duck in the village – but it's very small."

"Don't think that far ahead. We've got next Wednesday to organise. You'll be seeing George, don't forget."

"The motor-bike boys want to give Craig a proper send off."

"Well, they would. Have you spoken to Rachel?"

"His girl? Yes. She wants the wake in town – not at the pub."

"I see."

"But where am I going to live, Rose?"

"I've an idea about that – but I need to talk to the kids. You're needed in the bar now. We said we'd open tonight."

Rose knew she was pushing her sister-in-law but felt the customers would do her good. She waited until she was sure things were running smoothly and then rang Lane's End Cottage.

"How did it go?"

Bernard replied. "They were very nice. They said we had to meet with the foster family at a park. Katie will tell you."

Katie snatched the phone. "Oh, mum – it was awful. They said she may not remember us – her parents. Why didn't they let us keep in touch? I feel dreadful, mum. I don't know what to do."

"Bernard said they were going to arrange a meeting."

"Yes – on a Sunday – but we can't bring her home. You are seeing them, mum- you tell them we want her back now – before she gets more attached. Think what we've missed already. They told Ned she was walking. I missed it – I missed her first steps."

"Hold on, dear. You might have missed them anyway, being at work. It sounds like they know what they're doing. You have to be patient. Remember – it's Heather that matters – more than how any of us feel."

Katie was silent.

"When are you coming home, mum?"

"Sunday night – but if you want to come here for lunch we'd love to see you both."

"Thanks. We'll think about it. How's Pat?"

"Bearing up. The funeral's on Wednesday. We'll shut the pub that day, too. Katie – have you got anyone for the houseboat yet?"

"No. Why?"

"She may need somewhere to live – but not immediately. We'll discuss it on Sunday. I must go now." That would give her daughter something else to think about. She just hoped Bernard was coping better than Katie.

The bar was quiet. Three of the regulars had got Pat playing darts. Rose nodded at her and stood behind the bar. She hoped Pat hadn't told them about the changes next year. The longer they stayed ignorant the happier the place would be.

Bernard and Katie got to the park first. Katie had been very quiet on the way there.

Bernard took her arm as they left the car park. She felt cold and could not stop quivering as they walked to the children's playground and sat down on the bench.

Suddenly she grabbed his hand and squeezed it hard. A man and a woman were walking round the park, pushing a pushchair.

"That's them," Katie whispered.

The family entered the playground and the man reached into the pushchair and lifted out a little girl. Holding her over his shoulder he approached Katie and Bernard.

"Hallo," he said. "May we sit down?"

They moved along and he sat next to Bernard, turning Heather so she sat on his lap. His wife pushed the chair up next to them and held out her hand to Katie.

"I'm Susan," she said, "You must be Katie."

"Yes – and this is Ned – Bernard."

The man was jiggling Heather on his lap and Bernard was making clip-clopping noises.

Katie could not take her eyes off her daughter. She had changed so much! She looked so bold, so alert. A lump came in her throat.

"Shall we go on the swings?" asked the man. Heather waved and giggled at Bernard.

The three of them rose and went over to the baby swings and the women watched while the men took turns pushing the child and running in front of the swing, pretending to be afraid. Heather chuckled delightedly.

Susan sat down next to Katie, who was shaking with a mixture of emotions. "I just want to grab her, Susan," she stammered. "Grab her and hold her and never let her out of my sight again."

"I know. She's a lovely little girl. Just give her time."

"She's so big. I've missed so much." She began to cry.

Susan waited a while and then said. "I brought some bubbles. If I bring her over in a moment you could blow them for her. Just so she'd get use to your face."

"She doesn't remember me, does she?"

"Not yet – but I'm sure she'll settle down."

"Thanks for not bringing the children."

"I thought it might be a bit too much. David – that's enough! Show them how far she can walk."

David took Heather out of the swing and stood her up. Then he and Bernard took a hand and she toddled back to the bench.

"Mimi," she said as Susan picked her up.

"Look what we've got for you," she said as Katie blew a bubble into the air. Heather reached to catch it but it popped.

Katie blew some more and then gave the pot to Bernard. While their daughter watched the coloured orbs she put out her hand and very gently stroked her hair.

"We kept all the cards you sent, Katie. We would have told her about you when she was older."

"She'll miss you all," whispered Katie.

"And we'll miss her – especially Lucy. Heather has become quite attached to her. She calls her *see*."

Katie smiled sadly as Heather turned towards her. "*See*?" she said.

"*See* is at home. We'll be there soon," cooed Susan. Then, addressing Katie, "There's a lot to show you. Can you come to tea next Sunday?"

"I'll have to check with my mother. Thanks for everything." She looked for her husband. Bernard and David were standing some way away, deep in conversation. What can they be talking about? she thought as she felt a splatter of rain.

"David – we ought to get home soon," called Susan and she began tucking Heather into the pushchair.

"Bye bye Heather," waved Katie. Heather waved happily back. The rain was falling steadily now and Bernard took her hand and they ran back to the car.

Once inside, she shivered violently.

"Thank goodness," she said out loud.

"Are you OK, Katie?"

"Yes. At least she didn't take an instant dislike to me. What were you and David talking about?"

"I was telling him about the camp site. He was very interested. Their family go camping a lot."

"But it's only a few miles away from where they live."

"He said it doesn't matter. He was going home to tell the others that Heather was leaving and he thought telling them they could camp with us would be a good way of making it better."

"I see. They are both very thoughtful, aren't they?"

She put the car in gear and drove away, jealousy gnawing at her insides.

Rose was exhausted. They had found someone to help Pat behind the bar but when she wasn't serving she was finding it impossible to concentrate. They had told George about losing the lease and, although he was angry at first, he soon cheered up when the opportunity to live at the houseboat was explained to him.

"We've a bit saved, Patsy," he had told his wife. "No need to fret. Treat it like early retirement."

But Pat did not want to retire and Rose promised she would enquire about part time work near the harbour. Meanwhile she was visiting Tim at the prison every Saturday. At first she had not want to talk to him about events at home but he noticed her new hairstyle so she found herself telling him about the pub.

"George had all our money there," said Tim, suddenly alert. "Half of it belongs to me."

Rose was frightened. Should she tell anyone? She tried to change the subject, "You needn't have worried about your grandchildren, you know. Heather is quite advanced for her age."

Tim didn't appear to be listening. He was staring into the distance.

"It doesn't really matter," he said, eventually. "It will all come to him in the end."

"Why are you talking about that, now?" she chided.

He glared at her, his eyes seeming to burn into her face. "You have everything," he said, bitterly. "You have my home, my land, even my dog. I'll leave the child something when I go. She could turn out better than her mother – but when there's no boy to carry on it makes everything seem a waste of time."

It was a longer speech than she had heard for years and Rose was shocked by the sincerity of it. Her husband was suffering more than anyone had realised. He seemed to have given up on life.

She had her eyes closed when Bernard and Katie returned from Stenton. Leaving their steaming clothes in the porch they burst into the kitchen, exclaiming at the warmth.

She didn't feel like getting out of her chair. Her back and eyes ached – so she waited until Katie entered the lounge."Did you see her? How was she?"

"Fine. She's grown so much, mum. She didn't remember us but she didn't cry either."

"Why should she?"

"Oh, I don't know. I just thought she might."

"You silly thing. What happens next?"

"They want us to go to tea – but I don't want to. I think you should go instead."

"Me? Why?"

"You are the one she is going to be with all day. Susan can tell you what she likes to eat and what her routine is."

"Don't you want to see their place?"

"No. And I don't want to see the children either. I feel bad enough about taking her away from them. Please, mum. I just don't want to go."

Rose was puzzled. She could see the logic in what Katie was saying but couldn't imagine feeling the same.

"All right. I suppose it does make sense. I'll take Bernard."

"He was great. He didn't seem upset at all. He just acted naturally."

"He's good for you. Don't take him for granted. He's got that site almost ready for the builders. If he was insured he could have had the old stables knocked down by now."

"Are the plans approved?"

"They should be next month – as long as we can start work by March we might even be up and running by July."

"And then what?"

"And then, my pet – we could have a little farm shop down there and if my plans work I know the ideal person to run it."

"Pat?"

"Exactly."

"Oh, mum. I do hope so."

Rose smiled. Although she tried to sound optimistic for her daughter she knew so much could still go wrong – and she feared that one thing, at least, would never be right. Tim would never again be the man he had been and the pity she felt for him diluted he excitement she felt at the idea of having her granddaughter home.

Bernard had told the college he would not be returning after Christmas. He was miserable at having to leave but he wanted to be with Heather. The director said he would have him back any time he felt able to return.

There was also the problem of money. Bernard had enjoyed being a wage earner. The smallholding only just broke even and although Rose took no payment for their board it gave him no income. He needed to discuss this with someone and the obvious person was Zak.

"You've done the right thing, planning to have a couple of units for rent," said his friend when he phoned him, "They should give you a regular income. The Government is keen on start-up businesses. I'll look into the possibilities and get back to you. Meantime, don't forget you are a qualified gardener. Surely you could fit in some maintenance work, locally?"

Bernard wasn't certain. He felt restricted by not being able to drive. How could he transport tools – even to the village? He was more confident about the units and ready to tell Rose he had spoken to Zak.

"He's right, Bernard," said Rose when he told her. "The architect said the same thing. He's adding some more parking spaces. We'll look at the plans tomorrow and see a solicitor to make you a partner in the business."

Bernard thought he was already a partner. They had planned everything together and shared the work. He grew the produce and she sold it. She'd even sold the geese. They had kept the grass down but were too fierce to be around Heather. The last one was in the freezer – for Christmas.

Katie was sitting alone at home the following Sunday afternoon. She had tried watching television, listening to the radio and reading the paper but she couldn't settle. There was a strong wind blowing outside but she needed to get out. She decided to take Jenny for a walk.

The social worker had suggested that, as Heather was used to being with other children it would be a good idea to join a mother-and-baby club. Katie knew there was one in the village but not when it met. The Parish notice board would tell her.

If she took on more night shifts she could arrange to go with Heather. Her daughter would be happier and being with other mums would boost her own confidence.

She hadn't been able to explain why she was afraid to go with them today. She did not want to know what she was taking Heather away from. She wanted to forget the months they had been apart and carry on as if they had never happened. Once she could hold her daughter, feed her, talk to her, bathe her, cuddle her – everything would have to come right. She would show them all she could be a better mother than any rich dentist's wife.

While Lucy and Patrick showed Bernard round their house Susan showed Rose how they had been caring for Heather. "She's learning a new word every day," she said proudly. "And she uses the potty. She eats almost the same as us and just has a bottle at bedtime."

"She's changed so much," answered Rose, "No wonder Katie was surprised."

"I expect you remember what it was like with your daughter."

"It's a long time ago, now – and Heather looks so much bigger and stronger. She takes after her dad."

"He's a natural, isn't he?"

"Yes. He's very good with children."

"I'm glad she's coming back to you. David says we may visit in the summer."

"If everything is finished. That will be lovely."

They returned to the living room where everyone was sitting on the floor – throwing soft balls at some rather unsteady plastic skittles. Every time one fell over Heather laughed. It was such a happy scene Rose immediately understood why Katie had not wanted to come.

Bernard was thoroughly enjoying himself. The family had made him so welcome. No one had asked him to read or write. They were taking turns in a game that was fun for them all and no one was arguing or getting upset. This was the kind of life he wanted for Heather – where everyone encouraged and supported each other. If only he could get Katie to stop being so afraid and to see the future as he saw it. He was certain, now, that he could be a provider for his family, a husband to Katie and a father for Heather.

He knew, too, that he could never have reached this point without Rose. It was Lane's End itself that had been the treasure he was meant to find.

"Can Heather's dad come and play with us again?" asked Patrick when the time came for them to leave.

"Of course," replied his mother. "He is welcome at any time."

"And you can come to our camp site when it is ready," said Rose. "You can test it out for us and tell us what else is needed."

"You've got a perfect position," said David. "We are looking forward to it."

"We are going to have a party for Heather," said Lucy, "before you take her away."

Her face looked so sad Bernard didn't know how to respond. He looked at Rose for help.

"You'll always be her first best friends," she said. "In fact, she hasn't got any cousins. You can be cousin Lucy and Bernard can be your Uncle Bernard. All right Bernard?"

Bernard grinned. He felt he had gained so much in one day. Could you be too full with love?

"Thanks," he said, "I'd like that."

A silver BMW parked by the wall of Lane's End cottage. David opened his door and went round to the passenger side. Susan climbed out and then turned to Heather. Putting her down on the ground between them they held her hands and let her toddle towards the gate.

A black and white dog came running up towards them, wagging its tail, and then ran round them in circles as they approached the cottage.

Rose opened the inner door, a broad smile on her face.

"Come in, come in," she welcomed. Inside Bernard and Katie waited. The adults had had time to get used to the idea of the transfer but none of them knew how Heather would react.

Katie pressed herself into Bernard's side as they sat on the sofa. She was sure she could feel her heart pounding in her chest. Had they done enough or would her daughter resent them for ever? They had a playpen full of toys in the corner of the room. The blue bedroom had been painted pink with a big rainbow across one wall. Everything was ready.

The adults let go of Heather's hands and Bernard held out his arms to her.

"Dada," she said as he lifted her onto his knee.